Justice For Max

Scott Daniel

Sentinel Media of Michigan, LLC

Contents

For Cora

Chapter 1

TUESDAY, AUGUST 11

"What kind of relationship are you looking for?" she asked, brushing long red bangs away from her face. She picked up her martini, took a small sip and smiled.

"You're direct," he said. "I like that."

"I'm on the other side of thirty," she said, leaning in and looking him square in the eyes. "I've already wasted too much time on relationships that were doomed from the start."

"Fair enough, and I think I get how you feel. I've spent the last five years of my life building a career, or at least trying to. I've ignored the rest of my life. So, I'm looking for someone to go with me to concerts, a ball game here and there, maybe a late evening dinner on a whim."

"That's cool," she said, pulling away. She drained the martini before speaking again. "You're looking to live a little, have some fun and create balance."

He smacked the bar with his hands and pointed at her. "Exactly. That's what I'm looking for."

She smiled. "You're, what—"

"Twenty-seven."

"The thing is, I've already got that balance," she said, "and am ready for more. You're a handsome guy with that square jaw and wavy, dark brown hair. But, hon, we're in far different spots on the game board."

He smiled, not knowing what to say. She sat her martini glass down, got up from the bar and kissed him on the cheek. "Good luck to you."

She walked away without another word.

"Need this?"

Ray Harper turned and took an ice-cold Corona with lime from a bartender. "Thanks."

"Rough first date?" asked the bartender, a tall, thin man with a dark beard who vaguely reminded Harper of Abraham Lincoln.

"Dating apps aren't what they used to be."

"That brew is on the house, pal."

He tipped the Corona toward the bartender and drank a quarter of it in a swallow. Harper glanced at a television above the bar and saw the Detroit Tigers were getting pummeled yet again. His stomach growled. As much as he wanted to fill it with a Sheehan's half-pound cheeseburger, duty called. He took a final pull from the beer, dropped a few dollar bills on the bar as a tip to Mr. Lincoln and left.

He walked to his car, which was parked in front of the sports bar. Traffic on Ann Arbor Road hummed louder the closer he got to his ancient Honda Civic, as if he were walking toward a beehive. The mid-August Michigan sun was still hot at half past six, the air sticky, and he felt beads of sweat popping up on his forehead.

Harper fished in his pocket for the key, but a pair of boys running first by and then away from him grabbed his attention. He looked up and saw them in full sprint in the intersection, young teenagers with short black hair, laughing and jawing at each other as they ran. Harper smiled, returned his attention to his car and put the key in the door lock.

He glanced back up at the boys before stepping to get in. The younger of the two had made it across, while the other was still in the roadway.

"Look out!" the teen on the side of Ann Arbor Road screamed. "Max!"

A fraction of a second later, the older boy was sent flying. Harper, frozen in place as if caught in a spider's web, got a split-second glance at the vehicle that must have hit the boy. It hadn't slowed down, let alone stopped to render aid. Harper's glance wasn't enough to distinguish its make or model.

"Max" had landed about forty feet away from the intersection in the westbound lanes of Ann Arbor Road. Car tires screeched to avoid hitting him. Harper shoved his car keys in his pocket and then ran to the teen, who lay facedown in the road, his arms and legs splayed at unnatural angles.

He knelt beside the boy, who appeared to be about sixteen, and then rolled him gently onto his back, cupping his head as best he could to try to protect his neck from further damage. Gravel was embedded in his face, a large patch of skin was missing from his forehead and blood oozed from both ears. Harper could see slight movement from his chest, which caved inward on the right side, appearing to have taken the brunt of the collision with the vehicle. The teen's breathing was shallow.

"I'll call 911," a woman shouted, running toward Harper and the boy from a nearby Rite Aid parking lot. Other motorists who had exited their vehicles gathered around. Harper moved into a sitting position and supported the boy's upper torso, placing his head in his lap.

The other boy pushed through the small crowd, wailing. "I'm sorry, Max. I'm so sorry."

"Is this your brother?" Harper asked.

The boy nodded. "It's my fault. Oh god, Max, it's my fault."

Harper felt Max move as he held him. He was trying to speak. Harper put his ear next to the teen's lips but the sounds came out as unintelligible gurgles.

Harper motioned for the brother to come near. He felt Max stiffen and gulp for air.

"What's happening? Max, what's happening?" his brother said. "You're going to be okay, Max. You're going to be okay."

The boy touched Max's face, wiping away a few of the bits of gravel from his cheek. Max went limp and stopped breathing after a few weak convulsions.

"Does anyone know CPR?" Harper screamed, looking around at the bystanders.

A heavyset woman with short red hair stepped forward and a man in cargo shorts said he could do chest compressions. Harper laid Max's head carefully on the pavement and the duo went to work, the woman inflating the teen's lungs with massive breaths and the man pumping his chest.

Harper heard sirens coming toward them and got to his feet. Seconds later, a pair of Plymouth police cruisers pulled up and blocked off the intersection where Ann Arbor Road met Main Street. Paramedics arrived, got the boy onto a backboard and then a stretcher. One of the paramedics picked up CPR duties and got into the back of the ambulance with Max.

"Where are you taking him?" Harper asked.

"Saint Joe's," said the second medic, who slammed the ambulance doors closed. He headed toward the front of the ambulance. "You family?"

"No," Harper said, following him.

"Then I will need you to step back, sir."

Harper complied and watched as the ambulance sped away. He looked at his once white shirt. It was streaked with blood. He glanced at his watch and it read 6:50 p.m. He had a decision to make: follow the ambulance to Ann Arbor, talk to eyewitnesses at the hit-and-run scene or attend a Plymouth city commission meeting.

As editor of the local newspaper, the *Independent*, he knew each option had value. Judging by the teen's condition, the hit-and-run would likely wind up as a fatality. Going to the hospital might allow him to gather facts no other news outlet would get. He could also snag a picture of Max being rushed into the hospital, a dramatic shot not often found in small a community newspaper.

Staying at the scene could also provide investigative detail that he wouldn't have a second chance at. He could canvass businesses in the immediate area to see if one might have inadvertently captured the hit-and-run on video, too.

Harper ran through the city commission's meeting agenda in his mind. There was nothing he couldn't follow up on later. He scratched that option off his list.

"Decided to become part of the story instead of just reporting on it, I see," one of the Plymouth cops said as he approached Harper.

"Didn't exactly plan it that way, detective," Harper said. "Is the kid going to make it?"

"We on the record?"

Harper felt anger flush his face. "No, I mean, I just want to know if he's going to live. Jesus Christ, Adams."

"Step into my office and we'll talk," he said, and motioned to an unmarked police car.

Adams opened the passenger-side front door and Harper wobbled in, feeling the aftereffects of spiked adrenaline on his body. Adams, a cop Harper had frequently dealt with in his five years at the *Independent*, killed the screen on a mobile computer and then pulled a small notebook from a shirt pocket.

"Since you're the main eyewitness," Adams said, "I'm going to ask the questions for a change. Walk me through it, step-by-step."

Harper filled him in, including the boy's unintelligible attempt at speaking.

"How many beers did you have at Sheehan's?" Adams asked.

"What does that have to do with anything?"

Adams looked up from his notepad. "I've seen Good Samaritans sued, even criminally charged. Believe me, that kid's family and their lawyer are going to look at your actions with a fine-tooth comb. It's possible you made things worse, ya know?"

Harper shook his head and ran a hand through his hair. "I do the right thing and I have to worry about getting sued?"

Adams shrugged. "How many beers, Harper?"

"Two. A couple of Coronas."

"One of our officers will give you a breath test," Adams said. "You should come in under the limit, which will help you if the family—"

"Decides to be assholes?" Harper asked sarcastically.

"Do you know who that kid is?"

"Not a clue."

"This stays off the record. You get confirmation on the kid's identity from another source," Adams said.

The statement irritated Harper. He'd thought he had earned Adams's trust over the years. Apparently not.

"Okay," he said, trying not to sound terse. "Who is he?"

"Max Bell. The best quarterback prospect in the state. Started for the Wildcats last season as a freshman and made second team all-state."

"Did you talk to the brother? What's his name?"

"Sammy," Adams said. "Going to be an eighth grader at East. Fast-as-hell running back that'll tear up the middle school league."

"Wait a minute," Harper said. "Are those boys Jake Bell's kids?"

Adams nodded. Bell was a prominent developer in southeast Michigan, primarily known as "Mr. Bigfoot" in Plymouth. His company specialized in purchasing old homes near the community's quaint downtown, then razing and replacing them with leviathans on postage-sized lots.

"You sure you didn't get a better look at the car?"

Harper fidgeted in his seat, reached for the air conditioner and turned it down a couple of notches. Goose bumps had formed on his skin from the cold air. "I'm not even sure if it was a car. I don't know how fast it was going when it hit the kid, but it seemed to pick up speed afterward. I only saw the back end for a split second."

"Do you remember anything about that back end?"

Harper closed his eyes, squeezing them tight as if to wring out a memory. "The bumper was black," he said, and then paused for a long moment before speaking again. "I think the rear window was rectangular."

"Good, that's something we can work with, Ray," Adams said. He pointed to the ceiling with his right index finger. "The cameras above the intersection probably got more detail, too."

"Hope so," Harper said. "Are we done?"

"For now. Like I said, you're the main witness. I'll need you to stick around until we get you tested. I'll have the office take a statement from you, too."

"I have to repeat all this?"

"Standard procedure," Adams said.

Harper got out of the squad car. He wondered if Jake Bell had heard about his son. Then he remembered seeing the other boy, Sammy, on his phone. Neither parent was on the scene when Harper went into the patrol car to talk to Adams.

He scanned the area and saw police directing traffic. Ann Arbor Road was blocked off in both directions from Main Street heading west to Harvey Street, about a quarter mile away. Police officers were interviewing witnesses, who had been herded into the pharmacy parking lot. There was no sign of Sammy Bell, meaning he had probably been taken to the police station for questioning and to contact his parents.

Harper's conversation with Adams eliminated the idea of driving to Saint Joseph's hospital. He hurried to his Honda and grabbed a steno pad from the backseat as well as a fresh pen.

Harper checked the battery life on his iPhone, seeing if it had enough juice remaining to record interviews. It read 13 percent. He preferred relying on his handwritten interview notes but liked the recordings to get exact quotes.

As he walked toward the police and witnesses, Harper replayed the hit-and-run over and over, hoping his mind's eye would remember some detail that would help with his investigation, Adams's or both. But there were only a few scant milliseconds to process.

He thought the vehicle's bumper was black, but wasn't every bumper black? He also didn't think the rear window had a wiper, which, if accurate, would eliminate most SUVs and minivans.

Perhaps one of the witnesses had gotten a better look. Harper was about to find out.

Chapter 2

TUESDAY, AUGUST 11

Sadie Rodgers's phone beeped as she drove west on Ann Arbor Road. She picked it up and looked at a text. "Can we count on you tonight?" She hit reply and typed, splitting her attention between the road and her iPhone. "Do you really need to ask? You're so paranoid."

She looked up as she approached Main Street. Sadie saw the light was red but cars on Main were slowing to a stop. Her lane was clear, and she pressed the accelerator, knowing the light was about to change to green. Her attention returned to her phone and Jake Bell's follow-up message read, "Just checking," and ended with a smiley-face emoji. She rolled her eyes and then tossed the cell phone on the passenger seat.

Sadie looked up as her car zoomed into the intersection. A figure appeared to her left and before she could react, she struck whoever it was.

The figure went flying away from the intersection. Sadie's entire political career flashed before her eyes. Time seemed to stop. She saw a banner headline on the front of the *Detroit Free Press*: "Plymouth Mayor Arrested After Killing Pedestrian." She saw hordes of reporters jabbing microphones in her face as she did the perp walk from a police car into a packed courtroom. She saw and heard a jail door closing behind her and the lights going out.

Sadie's right foot twitched between the accelerator and brake as the figure landed, bounced and came to rest on the pavement. She veered to the right to avoid the body and then punched the accelerator. Thankfully, the airbag hadn't deployed.

Sadie reached for the phone, picked it up and dialed Plymouth Police Chief Neil Flaherty. He answered on the second ring.

"I just hit somebody!" she screamed. "I hit somebody and left them in the middle of Ann Arbor Road!"

"Calm down," Flaherty said. "Are you sure?"

"Yes, I'm sure. I'm going to go to jail. You're the cop. Do the math."

"Where'd it happen?"

"The intersection of Ann Arbor Road and Main Street," Sadie said. "Whoever it was has got to be dead. I was doing at least fifty."

"Keep driving, sweetheart," Flaherty said, sitting in his office at Plymouth city hall. "Which car are you in?"

"The Taurus."

"Take it to Keystone. I'll have somebody get you."

"I'll be there in less than ten," Sadie said. "Make sure you've got somebody there when I arrive. I can't be late for the city commission meeting. Make this shit go away, Neil."

"I will," Flaherty said. "I love you, Sadie."

"Love you, too," she said.

FLAHERTY DISCONNECTED the call and placed the cell phone on his desk, taking care to make sure it was perfectly parallel to the memos and reports that awaited his signature. He picked up his desk phone and dialed Detective Adams.

"I've got something I need you to take care of immediately," Flaherty said. "Get over to Ann Arbor Road and Main Street."

"What's going on?"

"Hit-and-run. I want the investigation buttoned down and you report directly to me. Any blowback, you send it to me. All angles need to be covered here, Mike. Know what I mean?"

"Yeah. I'll handle it. I'm in the area. My ETA is less than two minutes."

Flaherty hung up. In his early fifties with light red hair graying at the edges and a taut six-foot frame, he sprung from his chair, grabbed his charcoal-gray suit jacket and headed for the dispatch room.

Flaherty's office sat on the other side of city hall, away from the rest of the police department. He walked through the lobby and ignored a greeting from an officer assigned to the front desk. Flaherty swiped his identification card to open a side door that led down a hallway to dispatch.

The room, a thirty-by-thirty box, housed four dispatchers and a shift lieutenant. It wasn't uncommon for Flaherty to pop in to see what was going on in his city of about thirty-five thousand residents. He was known as a hands-on police chief.

"I hear we've got a hit-and-run," Flaherty said to the lieutenant on duty. "Fill me in."

"We received multiple calls in the last fifteen minutes," said Rob Snyder. "Got three squads on-scene and Detective Russell is interviewing witnesses."

"Adams will arrive momentarily," Flaherty said. "Have Russell coordinate with him. The sergeant takes lead as incident commander."

"Sir?" Snyder said. "Captain Chamberlain is in route to take command—"

"Send him home. Adams has handled plenty of these."

A flash of puzzlement crossed Snyder's face as he spoke again. "The victim is a male, sixteen."

"Plymouth kid?"

"No identification yet," Snyder said. "But it doesn't look good."

Flaherty put his hands on his hips. "What are the witnesses saying?"

"Russell hasn't reported back yet," Snyder said. "Some callers said a silver sedan hit the boy. Others thought it was an Outback station wagon."

"Any ID on the driver?"

"Nothing definite, Chief. Could be a man or woman at this point. Nobody seems to have gotten a good look."

"I want to see the video," Flaherty said. "How many feeds do we have at the intersection?"

"Both ways on Ann Arbor Road. Nothing on Main Street," Snyder said.

"Why the hell not?"

"Ran out of grant money," Snyder said. "Those cameras are going up next spring when the next round of federal dollars rolls in."

Flaherty thought his job of "making this shit go away" had just gotten a little easier. He moved into the lieutenant's office, took the chair and faced the computer screen. He pushed the chair away from the desk, and Snyder leaned over to the keyboard. In seconds, he had a replay of the traffic camera video going on a split screen.

One feed showed eastbound Ann Arbor Road, the other westbound. The cameras were perched above the intersection on long green arms that also held "Main Street" signs.

A car on the outside lane of westbound Ann Arbor Road came to a stop as the light went from yellow to red. Video showed the driver and a passenger looking down at something, possibly cell phones, after the car stopped.

The cameras were stationary and set to record only the width of the road. The camera facing west caught the boys running, heading north. The smaller of the teens pulled ahead before they reached the middle of the road.

The camera facing east showed a fast-moving vehicle approaching the intersection in the inside lane without slowing. Frame by frame, Flaherty and Snyder watched the feeds side by side. The smaller teen ran out of camera view as he reached the other side of the road. Meanwhile, the larger teen ran past a stopped car.

The next eastbound frame showed the inside-lane car driving through the intersection.

"That's no damn Subaru," Snyder said. "Looks like a Buick or maybe a Ford."

Flaherty and Snyder's attention then turned to the westbound feed. The vehicle's driver-side quarter panel grazed the teen and spun him around like a top. The driver's side-view mirror smacked him in the chest as he fell.

"Replay that," Flaherty said. "Focus your attention on the driver."

Snyder complied. Bright sunshine obscured most of the driver's face. Some of the person's hair was visible on the right side, but the black and white video made it impossible to tell the driver's hair color. It could've been pure blond, strawberry blond or some other color.

"Can't tell if it's a man or woman," Snyder said.

"Short hair," Flaherty said. "But that doesn't mean anything these days. Can you enlarge the images in the video?"

"The state police lab in Northville might be able to do something with it," Snyder said. "But we don't have those kinds of capabilities."

"Let's hang on to it," Flaherty said. He stood, straightened his tie. "Package the video up and send it to Detective Adams and myself ASAP. We're going to solve this in-house."

"In-house, sir?" Snyder said. "As you're well aware, the state police are the ones with the accident reconstructionist on staff. I've got a call in to—"

"Are you questioning my judgment, Lieutenant?" Flaherty snapped.

Both men stood. "No, sir," Snyder said. "I'm just confused about why we're not following protocol."

"I'm not going to debate this with you. And I want the intersection reopened in two hours or less. We can't keep our business corridor down all night."

"I do not care how busy the road is," Snyder shot back, his face flushed red. "We get one shot at the scene—once the roadway is open, that is it. Once cars start driving through it, any trace evidence we missed is gone."

"Follow the order, Lieutenant," Flaherty said.

Snyder hesitated but finally gave the chief a slight nod. Flaherty left dispatch and let out a long sigh in the hallway. The east-facing camera feed didn't identify the love of his life, Sadie Rodgers. The west-facing camera wouldn't likely produce a license plate number.

Television cop shows made pulling plate numbers appear easy, when in fact the odds were always slim. Either way, Neil Flaherty would make sure the video from both cameras would never reach the state crime lab or be seen by another set of eyes.

Chapter 3

TUESDAY, AUGUST 11

Harper counted a dozen people in the pharmacy parking lot either talking to police or waiting to be interviewed. Adams, a second detective and uniformed officers were conducting the interviews, jotting notes on pads small enough to fit in a shirt pocket. He walked toward the woman who had helped perform CPR on Max Bell.

"You may have saved that boy's life," Harper said as he reached her.

"I dunno about that, I just wanted to help," she said, holding her hand up to shield her face from the sun. "It was good you got to him as quick as you did."

"Thanks. My name is Ray Harper."

"I'm Ashley."

"Ashley, I'm the editor of the local newspaper. Can I ask you a few questions about—"

"Editor?"

"Yes. I write for the *Independent* here in Plymouth."

"Oh, sure," Ashley said, her face slightly blushing. "I live in town. I've seen the paper."

Harper opened his steno pad with his left hand and grabbed his iPhone with his right. "Mind if I record?"

She shook her head. "I saw almost the whole thing. It was like everything happened in slow motion."

"Where were you?"

"In the car with my boyfriend. I was driving and he was in the passenger seat."

"Were you on Main Street or Ann Arbor Road?"

"Ann Arbor Road."

"When you say you saw 'almost the whole thing,' what do you mean?"

Ashley dropped her hand to her side and turned to face Harper, her back to the sun. "We were stopped at the red light. I was looking at my phone, scanning my Facebook feed. A few seconds later, Brandon told me the light turned green—"

"Were you guys going east or west?" Harper asked.

"We were going west," Ashley said. "We were in the right lane. When I looked up, I pushed the accelerator and started to go. That's when I saw the car fly by me on the left and then hit that boy. It was so horrible."

"Was it a car or some other kind of vehicle that hit the boy?"

"It was a car for sure," Ashley said. "Silver."

"Any idea what kind of car?"

"No, it was going too fast, and my eyes stayed on the boy. He looked like a rag doll flying through the air."

"Did you see anyone else in the silver car besides the driver?"

"No."

"So, you saw the boy get hit, fly through the air and land. What did you and Brandon do next?"

"Everyone stopped when they saw what happened," Ashley said. "Brandon and me, we were pretty shook up and didn't move right away. That's when I saw you run to him. I got out of our car a few moments later and then heard you call for help."

Harper was disappointed she hadn't gotten a better look at the car or the driver. "Ashley, can I have your last name?"

"Jones."

"Mind if I snap a picture of you?"

"Do you have to? I really don't like having my picture taken."

It was a refrain Harper heard more times than not. Head shots couldn't be counted among the most exciting pieces of "art" to add to a story, not like an action shot of a wide receiver catching a touchdown pass, but something was better than nothing. Readers' eyes tended to gravitate to stories with pictures, and engagement metrics showed they stayed with those stories longer than they did those without.

"My boss will yell at me if I don't," Harper said. "It would be a big help."

"Oh, all right then," Ashley said. "Go ahead."

Harper took the picture and then interviewed two additional witnesses, neither of whom had gotten a definitive look at the driver. One thought it was a woman and the other couldn't be sure whether it was a man or a woman.

As he worked the parking lot, he made eye contact with Adams, who scowled at him. The detective grabbed a uniformed officer, said something to him and then nodded at Harper. The uniformed cop made a beeline to Harper.

"Sir, this is an active investigation, I'm going to have to ask you to stop interviewing witnesses," the cop said.

"Just trying to do my job," Harper said, "probably asking the same questions you guys are."

The cop shrugged. "I get it. But the sergeant has advised me to arrest you for obstruction if you don't put your notepad away. He says you're a witness and he doesn't want you swapping stories."

"I guess he hasn't heard about freedom of the press?" Harper said. "That little thing guaranteed in the Constitution?"

"Sir—"

"All right, all right. But the sergeant's boss is going to hear about this bullshit."

The officer escorted Harper away from other witnesses and told him to wait to be interviewed. Despite Adams's heavy-handed tactics, he was determined to continue gathering information.

Harper opened the steno pad and leafed past his interview notes to a fresh sheet of paper. He drew a map of the intersection. Looking east on Ann Arbor Road, he jotted down the name of every business and then repeated the process in the other three directions.

When the cops finally released him, he would visit each of the businesses on the map to interview workers and obtain video. Odds seemed to favor one or more of the businesses' outside cameras capturing the silver car. With any luck, Harper would get not only the make and model of the vehicle but a description of the driver.

Chapter 4

TUESDAY, AUGUST 11

An hour after Harper was separated from the other witnesses, a uniformed officer took his statement. Harper had plenty of time to think about why the police needed to interview him a second time.

It could have been just as Adams had said, standard procedure. Then again, the cops might have been checking to see if his story remained consistent. It was a common technique used to catch suspects in lies. He obviously wasn't a suspect, so what was the endgame?

Harper's breath test came back at half Michigan's legal limit of .08. He hadn't expected to "flunk" the test but was relieved anyway. Adams's statement about the Bells potentially coming after him was unsettling.

Perhaps Adams was looking for some kind of leverage against him? The thought struck Harper as odd considering their working relationship had been solid over the years.

He shook it off, walked to his Honda and pulled out from Sheehan's parking lot onto Main Street. With the intersection completely closed, Harper was forced to drive a half mile south, then a mile east before heading north back to Ann Arbor Road.

The Plymouth cops could keep him away from the crime scene but not from doing his own version of canvassing. Harper drove back nearly to the intersection before pulling into a BP gas station that sat kitty-corner from Sheehan's.

He exited the Honda, walked to the back of the store and took a Coke from a cooler. He went to the counter to a clerk standing at the cash register.

"Hot one today, isn't it?" Harper asked.

"A buck ninety-nine," the clerk said, not answering Harper's question.

Harper handed him a pair of singles, and then tossed the penny change into a "take one, leave one" cup.

"I'm the editor from the *Independent* newspaper. Would you mind if I ask you a few questions?"

"About that accident?"

Harper nodded. "Did you—"

"Man, I didn't see nothin'," the clerk said.

Harper noticed a name tag that read "Derek."

"Were you standing here at the register when it happened?"

"Man, I already told this shit to the cops."

"Two minutes. That's all I need, Derek."

The clerk scowled. "Whatever. Ask your damn questions."

"Were you at the register?"

"Naw." He pointed in the direction of a row of salty snacks. Derek, who appeared to be in his early twenties, sported two days of dark stubble on his face. His straight, long hair was brushed back and traveled well past his ears. "Stocking chips, pretzels, Doritos. Rush-hour folks picked us clean. First chance I had to get stuff back on the racks."

Windows ran along the small brick building's south wall facing Ann Arbor Road, and also along the east and west walls leading up to glass doors on either side. There were no windows on the north side of the building, where Derek worked the register.

If he had been paying attention, Harper realized Derek could've seen the silver car coming through the intersection, hitting Max Bell and then continuing west. But if he was stocking the shelf, he was likely facing away from the intersection.

"So, you didn't see the car hit the boy?"

"Naw, already said that. I heard a bunch of cars slamming on their brakes to stop and turned around."

"What did you see when you turned around?"

"People getting out of their cars. I started to walk out of the shop to see what was going on, but a customer came in and I went back to the register."

"When you first turned around, do you remember seeing any cars heading that way?" Harper pointed to westbound Ann Arbor Road.

"Naw, man. My eyes were on the intersection."

"I noticed you have quite a few cameras on top of the building. Do you have video of the accident?"

"Cops already took it."

Harper pulled a business card out of his wallet. "Thanks a lot, Derek. You've been a big help. Can I get your last name?"

"Wallace. This going into the paper? You gonna make me all famous and shit?"

"It might, but you're not going to be famous. Trust me."

Harper got back in the Honda and snaked his way through a neighborhood to Harvey Street. He saw a number of bigfoot homes that were probably some of Jake Bell's handiwork. Harvey took him back to Ann Arbor Road, where the only option was to go west.

Harper made stops at a pair of restaurants and a fitness equipment store. He talked to patrons and employees. Nobody had seen the suspect's vehicle. Video recorded shortly after the hit-and-run had either been gathered by the cops or didn't exist.

Harper was astonished by the speed at which the cops had vacuumed up the video. Realizing he was spinning his wheels, he stopped the search and pulled into a donut shop parking lot to regroup. He looked over his notes and sifted through comments, which amounted to little more than speculation.

Despite his better judgment, he decided to give his video scavenger hunt one last shot. Harper left the Honda at the donut shop and walked back toward the intersection behind various businesses so as to not be seen by the cops.

He found a back door to the Cap N Cork party store, noticed a mounted camera and decided to walk in. If they had one covering the back lot, they'd have one in front, too, he thought. Perhaps it caught the silver sedan as it zoomed by.

"Afternoon," Harper said to a young woman at the cash register. "Are you the manager?"

"That'd be my pop," she said. "Who are you?"

He introduced himself and the young woman disappeared into a back room. A minute later, a man, presumably her "pop," emerged with his daughter close behind. His appearance seemed off to Harper. He looked more like an accountant. His short gray hair was parted immaculately on the left, and he wore black glasses that looked circa 1975, black dress pants, a long-sleeve shirt and a sweater vest, despite the August heat.

"David Casey," he said, extending his hand. "What can I do for the *Independent*?"

"I'm investigating the accident from earlier this evening," Harper said. "Did either you or your daughter see anything?"

"Not directly. My daughter just got here. She was registering for classes at Eastern Michigan—she's studying to become a teacher. I was the only one working and I had customers lined up."

"What about your outside cameras?"

"Just had those installed a week ago," Casey said. "Blink XT2, the best you can get on a budget. Records in HD 1080p during the day. I haven't figured out how to customize the motion detection function, so it's recording all the time right now. To answer your question, yes, the camera recorded traffic on Ann Arbor Road at the time of the accident."

Harper's heart went from calm to thumping in his chest. "Do you still have the video or did the police take it as evidence?"

"I gave them a flash drive that showed twenty minutes leading up to the accident and ten minutes after it happened. They told me not to give it to the media if any showed up."

"Figures," Harper said. He rolled his eyes. "Why shouldn't—"

"Relax," Casey said. "I advertise in the *Independent* every week. And besides that, your boss Henry Reston and I go back all the way to grade school. He's a good guy and a heck of a newspaperman. I'm happy to burn a flash drive for you, too."

Newspaperman? Harper hadn't heard that term since his early days at Central Michigan University, and even then, it was in a media history course.

"What about the police?"

"If they were doing their jobs, I wouldn't have needed to buy the security cameras," Casey said. "We've been broken into three times in the last year. To hell with them. Give me a couple minutes and I'll have it for you."

Harper thanked him and then turned to his daughter. "Have you watched the video that your dad is copying for me?"

"No," she said. "I mean, I'm sorry someone got hurt and all. Are they going to make it?"

"It's too early to tell. I didn't get your name?"

"Sophia. Maybe you can help catch the person that did it."

"I hope so," Harper said. He searched for something else to say. "How long has your dad had this place?"

Sophia Casey was no more than twenty, he guessed. Her rich dark brown hair had natural curl and hung to the top of her shoulders. Her eyes were the deepest shade of green Harper had ever seen. He found her looks more than appealing.

"Since he was my age," she said. "My grandpa started the store but retired early. Pop has run it ever since."

Harper suddenly wished Pop would take a little longer with the flash drive. He handed a business card to Sophia and wrote his cell phone number on the back. "If either of you remember anything—"

"Oh, sure, yeah. We'll call you right away."

David Casey returned and handed Harper a black and white flash drive. "I hope you find what you're looking for, Mr. Harper. Someone said it was a boy that got hit."

"Yes, a teenager."

"Is he going to make it?"

"I was there with him before the ambulance took him to the hospital. He's in rough shape," Harper said, holding the flash drive up. "Thank you for this."

"You got it," David Casey said. "Let me know if there's anything else I can do."

Chapter 5

TUESDAY, AUGUST 11

At eight thirty Harper arrived at the *Independent*'s Main Street office, a converted single-family home. He walked through what had been the kitchen, then past a bathroom and finally into the newsroom. He tossed a pair of steno pads on his desk, then sat his iPhone and the flash drive from Cap N Cork near his laptop.

With the print edition of the newspaper having gone to press hours earlier, Harper's hit-and-run story would be limited to the *Independent*'s web page. That was if publisher Henry Reston would allow it. "Doc" wasn't fond of cannibalizing the print edition with breaking news on the website.

Harper heard the floorboards creak and groan as if they would give way at any moment as Reston walked toward him. The place had a certain charm he liked. The *Free Press* didn't have a functional bathtub on any of its floors, he thought. The *Detroit News*' conference room hadn't been someone's bedroom at any point in its history.

"You smell like a distillery," Reston said.

"I had a couple of beers before tonight's fireworks, Doc," he said. "No big deal."

Reston leaned against Harper's desk, his bony backside hanging over a corner. In his late fifties, Doc was fit, perhaps even a little too thin. His face looked gaunt when he was tired, his eyes sunken. He sported a salt-and-pepper goatee, and his thinning hair was jet black, flecked with gray.

Harper had called Doc while canvassing Ann Arbor Road businesses for video. Reston had said he would assign the hit-and-run to Emily Jackson, the *Independent*'s newest reporter. Harper had chosen not to make an issue of it over the phone, deciding instead to confront Doc face-to-face.

"Jackson doesn't need to do the story," Harper said, swiveling in his chair to face Reston. "It's my beat and I was there. Just because—"

"You're too close to it, Ray," he said.

"Too close? I did what anyone would've done in the situation. That doesn't make me emotionally involved, and it's not like I'm related to the Bells."

"Maybe not," Reston said. "And maybe you've got your act together enough to do the story, although judging by the work you've done lately—"

Harper saw red. "I'm sorry if covering Art in the Park and the Fall Festival doesn't get the juices flowing for me anymore. But this story matters. Am I invested? Damn straight. Tell me why that's a bad thing."

Reston unfolded his arms from across his chest and put both hands on the desk. "The appearance of objectivity is just as important as actually being objective in your reporting. Having that kid nearly die in your arms would rattle anyone, make anyone with a heartbeat care whether he makes it or not. There's no way you can be objective on this one."

Jackson, who had graduated from Michigan State a few months earlier and taken over the school beat from Reston, came from the other side of the office to join the conversation. Her hands were tucked in the back pockets of her jeans.

"Nothing personal," Harper said, glancing at her.

"For what it's worth, I agree with Ray," Jackson said. "I'm still new in town and I don't have the sources that Ray does. From what I've seen, he's a real pro. I think he can handle this, Doc."

Reston stroked his goatee and then exhaled loud enough for them to hear. "That's pretty gracious of you, Jackson. I'm not sure I like your willingness to give up a story so easily."

"I call them like I see them," she said. "Would it be a good byline for me? Sure. But we're a team here—at least that's what you've preached since I started. I'm happy to pitch in where I can, help run down leads. But this needs to stay with Ray."

Reston shook his head and turned his attention back to Harper. "I'm not convinced. Final argument?"

"Let's make a deal," Harper said. "If you detect even a whiff of subjectivity, a slanted sentence or even so much as a comma out of place, you can give the story to Jackson and I won't complain."

Reston looked at Harper with eyes that suggested skepticism. His lips puckered as if he had just bitten into an overripe lemon. "I'm going to hate myself in the morning," he said. "I—"

"Thank you," Harper said. "You won't—"

Reston raised his hands and stopped Harper midsentence. "Don't say it, because I probably will."

Doc returned to his office. Harper held his fist out and Jackson bumped it.

"Thank you," he said.

"I made some calls while you were out talking to people," Jackson said. "Checked a few towing services to see if any silver sedans had come in."

"Anything?"

"No. Whoever it was probably figured it would be the first place the cops would check, too. Called the Plymouth cops and talked to Chief Flaherty. He said a lot but didn't give up any new information. I was kind of surprised my call was sent straight to him. Don't lower-level officers usually handle these kinds of incidents?"

"Not with Flaherty. He's way too much of a control freak. Anything above a retail fraud, and you've got to deal with him."

"That stinks," Jackson said. "Does he allow the officers in the department to speak to you much?"

"I have access to them, yes," Harper said. "But they all pretty much toe the company line. I usually have to go off the record to get them to open up."

Jackson nodded. "I've heard stories it wasn't always like that."

Harper shrugged. "Maybe in other towns. Flaherty has always had his department buttoned down. I don't mean to cut this short, but I better get to it."

"I'll send you what I've got."

"Thanks again."

He yelled in the direction of Reston's office. "Am I doing the story now, or do you want me to wait until tomorrow?"

"I'm not sitting here at nine o'clock for the fun of it," Reston said. "Chop-chop."

Harper got up and walked over to Doc's office. "One other thing."

Reston looked up from his computer screen. He gestured with his hands as if to ask, *What now?*

"I was able to get video from the time of the accident from a party store on Ann Arbor Road."

"Cap N Cork?" Reston asked.

Harper nodded. "I haven't watched it yet. The owner says there's about thirty minutes of footage from before and after the hit-and-run. You want me to look at it before I write the story?"

Reston stroked his goatee before replying. "No, let's get what we have out there. I don't want to get scooped. Save the video for a follow-up story tomorrow."

"Will do."

Harper already had the lead paragraph written in his head and started typing before Reston finished answering. Thirty minutes later, he sent the story to Doc for editing. Even after five years, it wasn't uncommon for Reston to call Harper into his office to go through Ray's latest story line by line. It was like having a tooth pulled, only twice as excruciating.

Harper couldn't deny that he had learned a lot from the old scribe. Still, he was happy this wouldn't be one of those teachable moments. Jackson was the new protégé; let her have all the fun.

He pulled her email up and sifted through her notes. She had written two paragraphs based on the calls she had placed to the towing services. There were also quotes from a few neighbors of the Bells. Harper was impressed. Jackson had moxie and drive, attributes that would get her out of the *Independent* and to a real newspaper sooner rather than later.

Reston would try to sell her on staying at the *Independent*. He'd pump her full of praise and give her frequent small raises. Harper hoped she would be smarter. Doc had already started his campaign.

Yes, he would do everything he could to prepare her for bigger and better. But what daily paper of any size was stable? Gannett and Digital First Media owned almost all the larger papers in Michigan, and they in turn were owned by giant hedge funds. Profits ruled the day. Every holiday season brought a new round of bloodletting among editorial staffs around the state, Reston said. Death by a thousand cuts.

The *Independent*'s financials were rock-solid by comparison. Unlike most suburban newspapers, the *Independent* still had a healthy foundation of local advertising. The business community preferred to see their ads in print, not on Facebook, Google or even the *Independent*'s website. It was as if Plymouth were lodged in some of kind of 1980s time vortex, immune to the newspaper industry's twenty-first-century realities.

Harper had fallen for Doc's sales job and had come to accept his fate as a small-time reporter. He would do what he could to keep Jackson from avoiding the same fate.

He pushed those thoughts aside and grabbed a tuna sub from a Jimmy John's bag on his desk. Harper didn't work well on an empty stomach. A few cashews at the bar had long since worn off. He tore into the sandwich and started typing.

A 16-year-old Plymouth boy is in critical condition after a hit-and-run accident on Ann Arbor Road Tuesday evening. Plymouth Police Chief Neil Flaherty said police are currently following up on multiple leads.

"Our sympathy goes out to this young man and his family," Flaherty said. "No stone is being left unturned in our investigation. And that's why I'm asking for the public's help. This incident occurred at about 6:30 p.m. We're asking anyone that was in the area of the Ann Arbor Road and Main Street intersection at that time to call. Every bit of information is helpful."

Harper stopped writing for a moment. He was already thinking about how he was going to follow up on the story in the morning. Trying to find out the status of Max Bell was job one. But then it was time to start digging for the identity of the driver. He couldn't rely on the police alone for information.

Flaherty was using the *Independent* as a platform to seek help for his investigation. Harper could do the same via social media. He double-clicked a social media managing app from his laptop dashboard and simultaneously sent a message out to Facebook, Twitter, Instagram and Snapchat asking both his and the *Independent*'s followers for tips.

He then did a deeper dive on Facebook. Harper belonged to three Plymouth-focused pages, "Plymouth Uncensored," "All Things Plymouth" and "I Grew Up In Plymouth, Michigan." In the old days, people had left anonymous notes in the newspaper's mailbox or picked up the phone and chewed the local reporter's ear off. In the digital age, monitoring a town's social media feeds was a must, a new paradigm of Reporting 101.

Harper finished off the sandwich and then the story. He kept it brief and to the point. "Sending it your way, Doc," he yelled across the newsroom.

"Got it," Reston called back. "Don't go anywhere. I might have questions."

Harper started packing his gear up. He took a final swig of the Coke he had purchased to wash down the sandwich and tossed it in the trash can under his desk. He looked up and Jackson was standing next to him.

"You didn't have to put my name on the byline," she said.

"Yeah, I did. I copied and pasted your stuff right into the story."

"We're a team, right?"

Boy, did she have a lot to learn. He regarded her for a moment in less than a professional way. She was short and curvy with blond hair she wore down past her shoulders. She smiled easily, and something about her blue eyes was electric. Doc had warned him not to pull his Rico Suave moves on her, and he had heeded the warning.

Until now.

"Yeah, absolutely, a team," he lied. "But you've got to take credit where you can get it in this business, you know?"

Harper stood and took a step toward Reston's office.

"Are we good?" he asked.

"I punched up the lead a bit," Reston said. "But it was fine otherwise. Good night."

He turned his attention back to Jackson. "Want to grab a beer?"

Chapter 6

TUESDAY, AUGUST 11–Wednesday, August 12

After an uneventful Plymouth city commission meeting and a quick stop in the police department's dispatch office, Neil Flaherty headed straight to Sadie Rodgers's office. He found her in her leather chair, one hand holding a tumbler filled with scotch and the other a cigarette. Her suit jacket was flung on the floor halfway across the office, and he could see she had also kicked her shoes off underneath the desk.

"The Taurus is being taken care of," Flaherty said, turning her chair to face him. "There will be no evidence left behind. Our guy at Keystone Auto Service is very good, very discreet."

"Isn't there anything he can do to save it? You know how much that car means to me."

The car was a gift from Sadie's father. Despite having logged more than two hundred thousand miles, the Taurus had been in pristine condition prior to the evening's earlier events. She'd won her first campaign in the Taurus as well as re-election. Now the old girl, whom she often referred to as "Lulu," was back in action, helping her in a bid for a third term as Plymouth's mayor.

Flaherty sat on the desk near her, took the tumbler from her hand and finished the drink. He wiped his mouth with the back of his hand and then gently caressed Sadie's cheek. "I'm afraid not. It's evidence, a risk that we can't afford to carry."

Sadie, whose short blond hair drifted in bangs across her forehead, stamped out the cigarette and exhaled the last bit of smoke. She stared blankly straight ahead. "What a shitshow. There's probably going to be enough evidence to point to me even without Lulu, isn't there? I'm so screwed. One more term in this town and then it was supposed to be on to Lansing or DC."

Flaherty walked away from the desk and picked her navy blue jacket up from the floor. He wondered whether he figured at all into Sadie's political equations, or whether he was just a useful tool for the moment. Their relationship had already ended his marriage and strained his relationships with his children, perhaps beyond repair. He brushed the jacket with his free hand as if to knock off dirt or grime, which couldn't possibly exist in Sadie's immaculate office.

"Stand up," Flaherty said. "Nothing is over. I told you I would handle it and I am."

She slipped the jacket on with his help. "I wish I could be as sure as you, Neil. If you're wrong, it's not just my political career that's over. I'll go to jail and so will you."

He spun her around and pointed toward her door. "Enough. You can't go out there and project guilt. Do you understand? You can't do one thing out of the ordinary. You must carry on as if this never happened, you must *believe* that this never happened."

"And how do I do that?"

"You get in your Explorer, you grab a Starbucks to get the booze off your breath and then you go home, collect your husband and get over to the hospital as fast as you can."

"What? Are you nuts?"

Flaherty smacked Sadie's desk with both fists. A picture of Sadie's lone child, Sara, toppled over face-first. "Jake Bell is your neighbor, right? Cindy Bell is one of your best friends, right? If you don't go, what does that tell the world? At times like this, what do friends do?"

"She's not a real friend," Sadie said, her light blue eyes radiating unchecked rage. "She's a business acquaintance. The only reason she has anything to do with me is because Jake told her to. If I wasn't the mayor, do you really think that bitch would give me the time of day?"

"The reality of your 'friendship' doesn't matter," Flaherty said. "It's the appearance that counts right now. The public believes the two of you are tight."

"Oh, screw the public," Sadie said. "Ninety-five percent of these morons don't know where city hall is, don't know who the hell I am or who you are."

"Don't underestimate them," Flaherty said. "Those five percent are the ones that will keep you in office."

Sadie slipped her shoes back on, moved in front of him, grabbed his suit lapels and pulled him close. She kissed Neil Flaherty hard and then moved her hands around his waist.

Flaherty felt himself loosen up. The warmth she radiated was unlike anything he had ever experienced as if her smile were pure sunshine that could penetrate the darkest, deepest woods.

SADIE RODGERS convinced her husband he and Sara should remain at home while she supported the Bell family at the hospital. With school set to start in a few weeks, would it really be wise to keep their daughter out who knows how late? Eighth grade was a pivotal academic year that would set the tone for high school and beyond. Never mind that Sara and Sam Bell were friends. Never mind that Sara had once had a crush on Max Bell. It wasn't important.

She pulled out of her subdivision on Plymouth's far west side driving a black Ford Explorer, a vehicle she received a stipend for every month from the city. A nice perk that took some of the sting out of her dismal $120,000 annual salary.

She aimed the Explorer south on Beck Road and then drove west on Ann Arbor Road. With the sun fully set in the summer sky, Sadie would be at Saint Joseph Mercy hospital in twenty minutes or less.

What would she say once she got there? "Sorry, didn't mean to turn your son into hamburger." "No worries, his face isn't too messed up." "Why didn't you fuckers teach your boys to cross the road properly?"

Sadie passed Washtenaw Community College and then turned left into the hospital, a place that held terrible memories for her. Her father had died there a few years earlier, wires, an IV drip and a ventilator hooked up to him before he slipped away. Two miscarriages lying helpless on her back. Only Sara had made it out of the place alive.

Tim had been there with her for each event. Cried every time. Husbands were supposed to be strong, a rock to lean on. Not Tim. After this crisis was over and her re-election won, she planned to file for divorce.

Sadie popped a piece of gum in her mouth and then punched the key fob to lock the Explorer. A quick stop at the information desk revealed the boy was in the intensive care unit. As she left the elevator at the seventh-floor ICU, she spotted Plymouth city clerk Don Easton standing in the hall. He stood just outside a room she knew was designated for family and friends of patients.

"Family in there?" Sadie asked the middle-aged tub of lard, who was trying to steal her job. As if someone who handed out dog licenses and begged senior citizens to work polling stations at city elections could do her job. It was a joke.

"Don't go in there," Easton said. "Leave 'em alone."

"Cindy and Jake are my neighbors," Sadie said. "I am here for them. They need to know that."

"You're here for yourself," he said, rolling his eyes. "You don't do anything that isn't designed to help yourself."

"You want to challenge me politically, fine. But do not question my loyalty to a friend. Now move out of the way."

Easton scowled at Rodgers before relenting.

She knocked on the door twice and stepped inside. Despite what Flaherty had said, Rodgers wondered if she was playing it right, coming to the hospital. Would her appearance—sneakers, jeans and a long-sleeved white blouse—make her relatable? Could she pull off the right emotional responses to seem supportive?

Cindy Bell stood from a chair, stepped forward and hugged Sadie. "Thank you for coming," she said. "Max is too weak for surgery. His lung is collapsed, his ribs—"

Her words turned into sobs. Rodgers continued the embrace and rubbed her back.

"This is my fault," Sam Bell wailed. "It's my fault, Mom. I challenged Max to beat me across the street."

"It's not your fault," Jake Bell said, taking the boy in his arms. "That car ran a red light. It's not your fault, Sam."

The moment of impact between Lulu and the boy replayed over and over in Sadie's head. She released Cindy and tears came to her eyes. The image of the Taurus's being crumpled into a cube of metal and sold for scrap pushed thoughts of Max Bell out of her mind. She felt heat behind the tears.

Sadie sat on a small couch next to Sam. The boy leaned against her and she clasped her arms around his shoulders. She kissed him on top of the head.

"Are there any leads on the coward that hit my boy?" Jake asked.

"I've been in constant contact with Chief Flaherty," she said. "Everything that can be done is being done. Our best detectives are on it. We will get whoever is responsible. You can take that to the bank."

"I can't believe someone would just leave Max in the middle of the road to die," Cindy said, "like some kind of animal."

"I'm going to strangle the son of a bitch to death," Jake said.

Sadie reached, grabbed one of Jake's hands and squeezed. "I'll help you."

As the minutes passed, she wondered what would be the right length for her visit. Thirty minutes? An hour?

Much to her dismay, her acting had gone over a little too well. The family seemed to draw comfort from her presence. As the clock hit midnight, all three were dozing. Thirty minutes later, Sadie drifted off, too.

A knock on the door woke everyone shortly before two in the morning. A doctor stepped inside the room. The dour look on his face sent Cindy into tears and Jake springing to his feet.

"What's going on?" he said. "Can we see Max?"

"You should come right now," the doctor said, his hands stuffed into a white lab coat. He led the family out of the room.

As Sadie stepped out, she noticed Easton was gone, thank god. She was unsure if she should follow, but Sam Bell held her hand and pulled her along. None of the nurses or other hospital workers paid attention as they moved down the corridor.

"His vitals are deteriorating," said Dr. Khalil Beydoun, a man of Middle Eastern heritage with thick, black hair and a day's stubble on his face. "There's not much else we can do at this point. His injuries are catastrophic."

"No, no, no," Cindy Bell said, her words muffled by the hand over her mouth. She sprinted the remaining fifty feet to her son. Jake raced after her and Sam followed suit.

The family surrounded the bed. Cindy held one of Max's hands, Jake the other. Sam placed both his hands on his brother's fractured leg.

"Don't give up, buddy," Jake said, tears flooding his eyes. "You can beat this. You can, son. You can beat this and I'm going to be so proud when you step back on that football field."

"We can put Max on a vent—" Beydoun said.

"No," Jake said. "He's going to beat this on his own, just like everything else that's come his way. You'll see."

"Would a ventilator buy enough time for his vitals to improve?" Cindy asked. "Maybe it would give him a better chance, Jake."

Beydoun folded his arms across his chest. Before he could answer, Max's heart monitor flatlined. A pair of nurses rushed into the room seconds later, one motioning for the family to step outside while the other placed a mask over Max's face. She pumped oxygen while Beydoun charged a defibrillator.

"Clear," he said, placing the paddles on the teen's chest. The jolt of current had no effect. "Increasing to three hundred joules."

Max's body jerked. The flat line on the monitor spiked for a split second before falling back to nil. Beydoun upped the voltage to its maximum setting. Max's heart didn't respond. He was gone.

Chapter 7

WEDNESDAY, AUGUST 12

Harper sat alone at Sean O'Callaghan's nursing a Guinness a few minutes before two a.m. Jackson had politely declined his invitation for a pint at the Irish pub, which sat at street level a story below Doc Reston's Penniman Street loft. By the time he finished the amber nectar and left the bar, he realized she'd done him a favor.

A light fog had formed. It didn't stop him from finding the Honda, parked a few doors down on the one-way street. Harper poured his six-foot-one-inch, hundred-and-eighty-pound frame into the vehicle, cranked the engine to life and then turned from Penniman onto Main Street.

Harper's apartment in Plymouth's Old Village was less than two miles away. He'd rented half of a duplex a couple of years earlier from a young couple with a toddler who was always set to extra loud.

As he drove along Main, the fog thickened and enveloped the historical museum, a law office and Bode's, Plymouth's corn beef and fish and chips emporium. Moments later, Harper pulled into the duplex's gravel driveway from Starkweather Street. His phone rang before he could exit the Honda.

"The Bell kid died a few minutes ago," the voice said. "Thought you'd wanna know."

"Who is this?"

"Lieutenant Snyder, Plymouth PD. I can't give you any more details than that right now. I'm sure the chief will have a press conference at some point this morning."

"Is there something else? You said you couldn't give me more details right—"

"I'm off at seven a.m. and am going to grab a few hours of sleep," Snyder said. "You know Sandy's by the Beech?"

"No, I'm not familiar with it."

"Five Mile Road near Redford Township hall. Meet me there at two p.m."

"Why? What's going on?"

"Just be there," Snyder said, and disconnected the call.

Chapter 8

WEDNESDAY, August 12

As he rolled up on Plymouth city hall, Harper wasn't surprised to see trucks from several local television stations parked outside. Police Chief Neil Flaherty had called a news conference for ten a.m., just as Snyder had predicted.

Deaths resulting from hit-and-runs weren't uncommon stories for metropolitan Detroit news outlets. Local papers did the in-depth work on them, while television stations relegated most to a few seconds of airtime.

But Max Bell's death had a few hooks demanding additional attention from the big fish. Jake Bell's status as a businessman and philanthropist thrust him into the news cycle several times each year. Max's own status as a football phenom had drawn the interest of sports writers and big-time college coaches from the University of Michigan and Alabama, among others.

Harper decided to play it cool at the press conference and let other reporters ask questions. He'd see how much, if anything, they knew.

He was suspicious of Snyder's motives for calling him. While the lieutenant hadn't spilled any details, the fact that he wanted to meet was telling. It suggested something was amiss, at least in his mind, about the department's handling of the hit-and-run.

In Harper's eyes, Plymouth's police department was about as rock-solid as they came. In his daily perusal of newspapers around the state, stories of police misconduct and brutality popped up from time to time. But not in Plymouth. Flaherty ran a tight ship. A few months back, he'd fired a twenty-year veteran who was discovered to have lied on his résumé. He'd demoted a captain for a sexist remark aimed at a female dispatcher in Harper's first year with the *Independent*.

Whatever Snyder told him would require additional digging on Harper's part. Doc Reston wouldn't publish unsubstantiated conspiracy theories, even from a respected cop.

Harper pushed thoughts of the upcoming interview with Snyder aside to focus on the press conference. The commission chambers had been rearranged for the event with the dais normally used by residents to ask questions and gripe about city services moved from the side of the room to front and center.

Three rows of chairs were placed in front of the dais for reporters. Television camera operators set up shop a few feet behind the chairs and exchanged beefs about the heat, their reporter sidekicks du jour and other upcoming assignments.

Harper spotted a reporter from the *Detroit News* he'd crossed paths with, walked up and shook his hand. He noted a few other scribes milling about, including a rat named Ivan from the *Plymouth Chronicle*, the *Independent*'s chief competitor for local news.

Flaherty walked into the room at ten a.m. on the dot. He was dressed in his usual dark suit, white shirt and red tie. Harper thought he looked like a guy straight from central casting for a television police procedural. Reporters took their seats, and cameramen adjusted their lenses as Flaherty placed what appeared to be notes on the dais.

A uniformed officer came in behind the chief with an easel and placed an enlarged photo on it. He then took a position behind Flaherty. Adams led a gaggle of Plymouth officers into the room, and they formed a shoulder-to-shoulder wall behind Flaherty. It was a common, not-so-subtle show of force and cohesiveness law enforcement agencies liked to put on display at news conferences.

Harper examined the photo. The grainy black and white close-up depicted someone with shorter, dark hair. The photo, as big as it was, didn't reveal whether the alleged suspect was a man or woman. The person was holding a cell phone, which obscured a portion of the face. The photo was tight on the driver's face. It showed only an outline of the car window. It could've been the silver sedan or almost any other vehicle.

"Good afternoon," Flaherty said. "I'm going to make a short statement and then I'll take your questions."

He went through the basic facts of the case methodically in much the same way Harper had seen assistant Wayne County prosecutors do at the Frank Murphy Hall of Justice. Harper averaged a couple of cases at the Detroit circuit court each year. The goal for prosecutors and for Flaherty was to build each sentence on the last as if laying a foundation.

"That brings us to the matter of the photo you see to my right," Flaherty said. "While it is early in the investigation, we believe this is a person of interest."

"Can't really tell much from that photo, Chief," said Ivan, who was known for his spicy writing style, which wasn't always constrained by the truth. "Never let the facts stand in the way of a good story," he'd say to anybody who would listen.

Flaherty nodded at an officer. The officer stepped to the easel and flipped the photo around. A second photo depicted a wide-angle, clearer image. Harper thought the car had been less than a hundred yards away from the video camera when the image was captured.

"From eyewitness accounts and video surveillance taken from around the intersection of Ann Arbor Road and Main Street," Flaherty said, "we believe this is the vehicle involved in the hit-and-run. I'll take your questions."

"Do you have a make and model of the vehicle?" a television reporter asked.

"Not definitively at this point. It's obviously a sedan but we're not far enough along to say if it's a Honda, Ford or GM of some variety. This is one of the reasons we invited you all here today. We're trying to cast as wide a net as possible. If anyone watching this report has seen the person in the photo, we ask that you call the Plymouth Police Department immediately."

"Is it a man or woman driving the car, Chief?" one of the television reporters shouted.

"We haven't made that determination."

"When exactly did the hit-and-run happen?" a cameraman asked. A Fox 2 reporter shot him a scowl as if to say, *I ask the questions*.

"You can't see it in either of these enlarged photos," Flaherty said, "but they were time-stamped at 6:41 p.m."

"What store did these photos come from?"

"A gas station that sits on the northeast corner of the intersection."

"So, this would've been a few seconds before impact?" Harper asked, breaking his own rule.

Flaherty looked at him and gave him a slight nod. "That's correct, Ray."

A man pushed through the media throng and walked directly toward the dais. Harper recognized him immediately.

"Can I say a few words?" Jake Bell asked. A pair of officers stepped forward to stop him from reaching the dais.

Flaherty appeared caught off guard but shook his officers off. He smiled awkwardly at Bell. "Everyone, this is Jake Bell, the father of the victim in this tragic incident. He would like to address you."

"Thank you, Neil," said Bell. He turned his head from side to side, looking at the reporters and finally into the television cameras. His chin quivered and tears rolled down his cheeks. "Right after school let out this summer, we took a family trip to Tahquamenon Falls in the UP. Max and I walked off the trail to get closer to the falls. I'm a photography nut and I wasn't going to be happy until I could get just the right angle. I climbed up on an outcropping of rocks and squatted to get my shots.

"I snapped a couple photos and then shifted my weight. That's when the rocks gave way and I started to fall forward. But a pair of strong hands grabbed me from behind and pulled me back. The risk of helping me didn't matter to Max. All he knew was his dad was in trouble and he was going to do something about it. That was how my son lived. When he did something, it was one hundred percent. No regrets. No looking back."

The room had gone stone quiet. Harper breathed hard and was about to stand up from his chair and ask a question when Bell spoke again.

"Someone ran over my son and left him to die last night. What kind of coldhearted coward would leave the scene like he just ran over a squirrel or stray cat? This was a human life, my son's life. I'm here as a father asking for your help."

Bell stepped away from the microphone and said something to Flaherty, who nodded. The police chief went back to the dais.

"The Bell family is working with Crime Stoppers to help find justice for Max. There will be a one-hundred-thousand-dollar reward for information leading to the arrest of the individual responsible for Max Bell's death."

Flaherty's statement ended the press conference. Harper bolted for the door and in a little more than five minutes was in the *Independent*'s parking lot gathering his notepads, his pens, a digital camera and his cell phone.

Once inside, he took the flash drive given to him by David Casey and inserted it into his MacBook Air's USB port. Harper was so intent on writing the follow-up to the hit-and-run story, he hadn't bothered to even say good morning to Doc Reston or Emily Jackson.

The video came up on-screen after he double-clicked the flash drive's lone file. Despite its being a solid thirty minutes past rush hour, Harper noticed heavy traffic on Ann Arbor Road prior to the hit-and-run. The gorgeous summer weather could've had something to do with it, or perhaps he just didn't drive the road frequently enough at that time of evening to make a judgment call about traffic volume.

The video was time-stamped. Harper wrote notes on a steno pad, marking what was happening when. At 6:42 p.m. Tuesday, a silver sedan changed from the inside to the outside lane of Ann Arbor Road a split second after passing the Rite Aid drugstore. The quick, swerving move nearly caused an accident with a pickup truck. Its driver managed to hit the brakes fast enough to avoid being clipped by the sedan.

Undaunted, the sedan driver accelerated and changed lanes again just before leaving the Cap N Cork video camera's field of vision. Amid thirty minutes of video, the vehicle appeared on-screen for less than three seconds, Harper noted. He replayed the precious few ticks of the clock a dozen times.

The lane change was the only clear view of the car in the clip. Vehicles heading west on Ann Arbor Road provided the sedan with cover. A glance at its rear was all that Harper saw of the second lane change. It was enough time, however, for him to discover a clue. The silver sedan had an oval rear window, not a rectangle as he had told Adams on the scene.

He did a Google search for "vehicles with oval rear windows." Numerous pictures of the iconic VW Beetle popped up. Near the middle of the page, Harper spotted a 1996 Ford Taurus. It had the oval rear window but not the black bumper he'd thought he saw. He closed his eyes and concentrated on his memory of the hit-and-run from the night before. He still saw black.

Harper kept scanning the search results and finally came to a picture of another Taurus, but it was a 1999 model. It had the oval window and the bumper was still the same color as the body of the sedan. But the taillights were arrayed in a black bar above the bumper, just below the top of the trunk. Bingo.

He put the detail near the top of his story, just after the long quote from Jake Bell about his son's bravery at Tahquamenon Falls. Doc edited out Harper's supposition about the sedan's being a 1999 Ford Taurus. The story was posted to the *Independent*'s website a few minutes after one p.m. and included the still photos from the press conference as well as ten seconds of the Cap N Cork video.

Harper blasted the story onto social media and was excited to see page views take off almost instantaneously. If the video had only captured the driver's face, the story would have been a slam dunk for him and a solved case for the Plymouth Police Department. But the video camera was simply too far away, despite the crystal-clear images it produced.

"Damn good story, Ray," Reston said. "Now get on outta here. I want you fresh tomorrow morning. We've got to keep pounding on this story."

"Thanks," Harper said. "I've got to get something in my gut. Haven't eaten since breakfast."

Doc pulled a money clip from the front pocket of his pants, peeled off a couple of bills and stretched out his hand for Harper to take them. "On me. But don't tell Jackson. I don't want her thinking I'm made out of money."

"Oh, I don't think there's any danger of that happening," Harper said. "Combine our salaries and it might be half of what a first-year lawyer earns."

Reston returned the clip to his pants pocket and let out a long sigh. Then he started playing an air violin. "If you're worried about money, you're in the wrong business, kid."

Harper laughed. Doc's sarcasm didn't come close to touching the high he felt from nailing the story. "See you tomorrow."

Chapter 9

WEDNESDAY, August 12

Harper arrived at Sandy's on the Beech about ten minutes early for his meeting with Plymouth Police Lieutenant Rob Snyder. The bar and grill's name was a play on words, a nod to nearby Beech Daly Road, the closest thing Redford Township had to a Main Street.

Sandy's reflected the blue-collar town it served. It was built of sturdy, dark brown brick, while inside a liberal amount of wood paneling covered the walls. The sizzling of hamburger on the grill mixed with the smell of deep-frying French fries and onion rings. The aromas were intoxicating to Harper's growling stomach.

He scanned the bar but didn't see Snyder. He asked a waitress and she pointed him in the direction of a covered patio. He found Snyder sitting at a high-top table with a glass of iced tea in front of him.

"Great day, hot already," Harper said, extending his hand.

"Didn't ask you here to talk about the weather," Snyder said, shaking the reporter's hand with a firm grip.

"I'm all ears. Is this going to be on the record?"

"No. What I have to tell you is for your background, so you actually have a clue for once."

"Hey, thanks, Rob. I always enjoy starting off an interview by being insulted."

A waitress came by and took their orders. Snyder smiled at the waitress, a frazzled-looking woman in her early thirties, her black hair pulled back, her Sandy's T-shirt a little too tight and tattoos covering her skinny arms.

"The investigation on that hit-and-run from last night ain't being done right," Snyder said.

"How's that?" Harper asked.

"For starters, the intersection should have been shut down all evening. You sure as hell can't process a scene like that in less than two hours."

"You were on patrol for what, a dozen years?"

Snyder took a sip of the tea and crunched a couple of ice cubes. "More than that. Listen, it takes many hours to process a scene. The first thing we do is look at and gather all the physical evidence on the roadway. Take photos of their position in the road. Our crime scene techs weren't done when they were told to clear."

"By whom?"

"Adams. He was the highest-ranking officer on-scene."

"Why weren't you out there? I mean, wouldn't you normally go out on an incident like that?"

"No, my job is to manage the shift globally. I notified Captain Chamberlain, and he was on the way when the chief advised that Adams would handle the scene. I was also tied up at the time with the chief."

"Flaherty?"

Snyder nodded. "He wanted to see the video."

"Did he know it was Jake Bell's kid that had gotten hit?"

"He did, but it wasn't me that told him. Not sure how he found out."

"What you're telling me doesn't make a lot of sense," Harper said. "Flaherty knows it's a high-profile member of the community but then decides you showing him video is more important than having you help process the scene correctly?"

"They don't necessarily need me out there to do their jobs," Snyder said. "But I did think the timing was odd. And besides that, the chief didn't want the state police working with us."

"Is that unusual?" Harper asked.

"Very much so," Snyder said. "The state cops have accident reconstructionists on staff. We don't."

"That seems kind of odd. I mean, that Plymouth PD doesn't have anyone trained in accident reconstruction."

"We're a small department. Sure, we've got a couple of guys who have a bit of training in the area. But nobody I'd trust to do the whole job."

"So that set off a red flag for you?"

"Big-time," Snyder said. "It just pisses me off. We got very little evidence from the scene. There was some transfer of paint from the vehicle to the kid's body. A few bits of glass and plastic from the car on the grounds. That's it."

"Doesn't seem like much to go on."

"No, no it ain't."

"Have you talked to Adams about why he cleared the scene so quickly?"

The tattooed waitress brought their food, a cheeseburger for Harper, a club sandwich for Snyder. She sat a bottle of ketchup on the table and asked if they needed anything else. Snyder shook her off.

"No. And that's the other thing," he said, taking a bite of the triple-decker. "The first two or three days after a hit-and-run are critical to solving the case. You've got to bring in multiple detectives and really blitz the hell out of it. And even then, most of these cases are only solved when the driver turns themselves in."

"So, is that what you guys have been doing this morning, blitzing the hell out of it?"

"I'm off today. But I've talked to a number of guys at the department. Jack-shit is being done. I mean nothing. Adams is handling everything himself and nobody seems to know where he is."

Harper sat his burger down in a red serving basket that also held a mound of fries. He grabbed a couple, dabbed them in ketchup and popped them in his mouth. He considered what Snyder had told him, then remembered a fragment of conversation with Doc Reston from a few years earlier.

"Can I play devil's advocate?"

Snyder nodded.

"Didn't you go for the police chief's position along with Flaherty?" Harper asked.

"What does that have to do with anything?"

"I heard that there was some bad blood between you two about it. Is that accurate?"

"I wasn't happy about it," Snyder said. "I'm Plymouth born and raised. Came up through the ranks. He was an outsider."

"But the commission went with him. Now you seem like you're casting aspersions on him about how this investigation is being handled. You may think I'm wet behind the ears, and maybe I am. But I know Adams reports directly to Flaherty. Are you implying the two of them are trying to brush the investigation under the rug?"

Snyder reached across the table and grabbed a handful of Harper's shirt. He pulled him toward the center of the table and leaned within a fraction of an inch of the reporter's face.

"I'm telling you what I see, you jagoff. I'm not implying anything."

Harper slapped his hand away and pushed the older man backward. "Get off me. You are implying something, don't be a pussy about it."

"Everything okay here, gentlemen?" the waitress asked, stepping between them. Harper guessed she had seen a barroom fight or two and knew how to handle herself.

He straightened his shirt. "We're fine. Can I get a beer, a Corona?"

She looked at Snyder. "Just the check."

"I appreciate you sharing your thoughts, Rob," Harper said. "But I really don't know you, don't know if you have an axe to grind. Maybe this is payback, or maybe you just want things done by the book. I don't know. Asking questions is what I do, and sometimes that means trying to figure out what people's motivations are for telling me stuff."

Snyder drank the rest of the tea and crunched away the remaining ice cubes as if it would help him cool off. He waited a beat before responding. "I shouldn't have grabbed you. Sorry. I'm not a fan of the chief. He's a politician, not a cop."

"And that makes you suspicious?"

"Yeah, it does."

"You don't think Adams had his own reasons for not following procedures?"

"No. His nose is so far up Flaherty's ass that when the chief farts it comes out of Adams's mouth."

"So, what you're really saying is that Flaherty ordered that scene cleared prematurely. Why? Jake Bell's lawyers will be looking at this from every angle. Isn't Flaherty exposing the city to potential litigation for negligence or malfeasance?"

"What does that tell you?" Snyder asked.

Harper thought for a moment. "At the very least, Flaherty has some sort of motivation to wrap the hit-and-run investigation up as soon as possible. By not involving the state police and having Adams keep a tight lid on the investigation, he's limiting exposure. One thing that troubles me here, Rob."

"What's that?"

"A number of your officers were on the scene," Harper said. "You can't be the only one that's second-guessing how the investigation is being handled."

"I'm not," Snyder said. "But let me say this and then I've got to go. The Neil Flaherty the public sees, that you see, isn't the one we see."

"Meaning?"

"Patrol officers aren't going to say anything to anyone, and neither will most of the command staff. You remember Smith's firing earlier this year?"

"The guy that lied on his résumé?"

"That was a bullshit story fed to the public," Snyder said. "Smith dared to call Flaherty out on his political maneuverings. He was gone less than a month later."

Chapter 10

WEDNESDAY, AUGUST 12

Most Wednesday evenings were a time for Henry Reston to relax and regroup. The print newspaper was on the street, and the process of producing next week's *Independent* would kick off in the morning. But the damn internet version always needed fresh content.

So, at nine p.m., Doc sat at his desk editing one of Jackson's stories. Then there would be business briefs to write. Using the *Independent*'s WordPress website, he'd close out the night by setting both to publish prior to Thursday morning's rush hour.

It wasn't a pace he liked. Before the digital transformation, he'd close up shop on Wednesday afternoons and play nine holes of golf. Having no deadlines for almost another week afforded a more genteel pace. Those days were long gone, even with the steady stream of advertising income from local merchants. They might have been happy with their once-a-week print ads, but readers demanded regularly updated websites. The news cycle was now twenty-four/seven.

At nine fifteen p.m., he heard a knock at the front door. Doc left his office and saw the figure of what appeared to be a man through the sheer curtains covering the wood and glass door. He opened it a crack, keeping the safety chain on.

"Henry, it's Lieutenant Snyder. Can we talk?"

Doc unhooked the chain and opened the door. "Of course, come in."

Snyder was dressed in jeans and a blue button-up, short-sleeved shirt. He followed Reston up a set of creaky wooden steps to the *Independent*'s conference room on the second floor. They took chairs facing each other on either side of a small oblong table. Snyder rested his arms on the table for a moment and then began rubbing his temples.

"Your story is bullshit," he said.

"Which story?" Doc asked.

"The one you just published on the hit-and-run."

"What do you mean 'bullshit'? My reporter—"

"Only got it partially right. Listen, Flaherty is lying about the driver of the silver sedan, okay?"

Doc shifted in his chair and nodded at Snyder to continue.

"The driver doesn't have dark hair like the photo at the press conference showed," Snyder said. "I saw the video, played it for Flaherty myself."

"Video from where? The gas station?"

"No, traffic cameras above the intersection. I didn't get a good look at her face, but the hair was definitely blond or a lighter color, not dark."

"You said 'her.' How do you know the driver is a 'her'?"

"It was hard to tell with a cell phone up to her face and sun reflecting off the windshield. But the more I watched the video, the more I saw it. The cut of the hair, the shape of the face. It was feminine."

"Why didn't Flaherty say that at the press conference? Has he studied the video as much as you?"

"Probably more," Snyder said. "He had me bundle all the traffic camera video and send it to him and Detective Adams. He didn't want anyone else looking at it."

"What about you?"

"Chain of command. Once I sent the video, that was supposed to be the end of it for me. That's the way it works."

"Sounds like you didn't follow the chain of command."

"I sent them their package. Kept a copy for myself. I told your reporter the investigation was mishandled right from the start. The chief tried to keep a tight lid on it and keep the state police from helping us work the investigation. It ain't right."

Doc stroked his goatee. "Do you still have your copy?"

"In my pocket."

"I want to see it, hang on."

Doc flew downstairs, grabbed his MacBook Air off his office desk and rejoined Snyder in less than a minute. He faced the computer toward the lieutenant, picked up a silver flash drive from the table and stuck it into a USB port. The video popped up on the screen and he hit play.

The first thing that struck Doc about the video was the amount of sun glare on the windshield. The traffic camera was aimed east, capturing the silver sedan as it moved west on Ann Arbor Road. The glare was blinding but lessened just enough for Doc to see what Snyder was talking about a fraction of a second before the car struck the teenager.

Doc rewound the clip, this time playing it frame by frame. The shape of the driver's face looked familiar to him, the hairstyle, too, yet he couldn't quite put it together.

Snyder pulled the laptop toward himself, pushed pause on the video and then opened a second file from the flash drive. It showed video from the camera capturing traffic traveling west. Faces of drivers going east could be seen, while the rear of vehicles heading west could also be viewed.

Again, the video advanced frame by frame as the silver sedan went through the intersection and struck Max Bell. Glare from the sun wasn't nearly as intense despite the cameras facing it directly. Doc agreed with Snyder's initial assessment of the driver's hair being blond. The answer that had been on the tip of his tongue a moment ago became clear.

"It's Sadie Rodgers in that car," Doc asked, "isn't it?"

Snyder nodded and then folded his arms across his chest. "I believe it is. She and Flaherty have been an item for a while now."

"How the hell do you know that?"

"Oh, they've done their best to keep it discreet," Snyder said. "But city hall is a small place."

"How long has it—"

"More than a year," Snyder said. "Flaherty's wife put all his shit on the front porch when she found out. He ended up buying a condo at Daisy Square. Rodgers's city-issued vehicle has been seen there on numerous occasions by patrol officers and me."

"So, you think Flaherty is covering it up because his girlfriend hit Max Bell?"

"I do."

"Have any proof?"

"Not yet," Snyder said.

"That means you're working on it. How?"

"I'm not prepared to get into that right now," Snyder said. "After my meeting with your reporter today—"

"Goddamn it," Doc said. "Harper didn't tell me he was going to interview you."

Snyder shrugged. "A few things came together after I talked to him. I'm not all the way there yet on my line of investigation."

"Anybody else at the department know you're looking at your own chief?"

"Captain Chamberlain. That's it. Dan is a short-timer at the department. Flaherty can't touch him. He's the only one I could trust."

Doc stood up from the table, turned and looked out into the black night through a window in the conference room. A few cars passed by on Main Street, which was otherwise dead. "I thought I knew this town."

"Not all of it," Snyder said as he stood. "It's probably better that way."

"Why are you telling me, then?"

"Like I said, this ain't right. None of it. I'm gonna put a stop to it."

Chapter 11

WEDNESDAY, August 12–Thursday, August 13

Turner pulled a chrome-plated, Swiss Army–looking object from his pocket. Kneeling at the back door of the *Plymouth Independent*, he extended a pair of tools from the H & H, paused for a moment and then looked up.

"Hook pick or DeForest pick?" he asked his partner.

"Where did you get that gaudy-looking thing?" Alexander said.

"On the web," Turner said. "LockPickWorld. It was a steal at nineteen ninety-nine, don't you think?"

"Let me see it."

Alexander held it close to his face and extended the remaining four tools from the pocket lock pick set multitool. He studied it intently.

"It's James Bond meets Ethan Hunt, don't you think?" Turner said, the excitement in his voice palpable.

"I don't like it," Alexander said, his thick gray mustache angled down on both sides. "Too goddamn shiny, you feel me? Reflects light like a motherfucker. The fancy chrome could chip off, too. You think about that?"

"Oh, don't be such a Debbie Downer," Turner said, taking back the H & H. "Use the same tools all the time and this job becomes a total bore. Now, answer the question. Hook or DeForest pick?"

Alexander, still broad shouldered with a V-shaped torso from decades of weight lifting, never rushed a decision no matter the situation. Turner liked to rib him about his "deliberate" style.

"You're the elder statesman of Detroit hitters," he'd say. "The Gray Ghost."

"You're just as goddamn gray as I am," Alexander would fire back. "I mean, what kind of honorable hit man wears short, tight little dreadlocks? You should be teaching African-American literature somewhere."

"Well," said Turner. "Sometime today?"

"Hook and the tension tool. Ain't it obvious?"

Turner pushed the other four tools inside the H & H. A moment later, the back door's lock twisted open. The Dynamic Duo stepped inside, and Alexander turned the lights in the kitchenette off while Turner killed them in an office and then what looked to be a newsroom. The entire first floor was dark.

Alexander slunk his six-foot-two-inch frame into a chair behind a desk in the office's front room. Turner pulled a chair from another desk and rolled it a few feet from his partner.

"Journalists are apparently slobs," he said in a whisper. "Notepads, pop bottles, old issues of the paper all over the place. How on earth can they write intelligent articles?"

Alexander rolled his eyes. "Perhaps you should tidy up?"

Turner pulled a Sig Sauer SRD45 silencer from his back pocket, secured it to his weapon and then rested it on his thigh. While he wasn't as broad as his partner, Turner carried considerable muscle on his five-foot-ten-inch frame. He contained his bulk neatly in an athletic warm-up suit when working. It reminded him of his track days at Detroit's Cass Technical High School and also allowed freedom of movement, which could be important if an assignment went sideways and he had to get up close and personal.

Thus far, the evening had gone better than a pair of old killers could've hoped for. Getting the drop on a police officer was never easy. But when the target went for an evening ride and wound up at a place of considerable angst for their client, well, it was a two-for-the-price-of-one waiting to happen.

Sitting in a Honda Odyssey at a car repair shop across the street, it was hard to tell who or how many people were inside the newspaper. Variables were never good on a job. You did all you could to minimize them, but you also had to improvise in their line of work. A little collateral damage couldn't always be avoided.

It was an aspect Turner didn't like. He figured his targets deserved to be recipients of his services in some way, shape or form, but the others? Hard to justify. It wasn't a thorn his partner wrestled with, "as long as the money was green." Alexander, otherwise a pretty decent fellow with his charming seventies gray mop-top, could be cold that way.

A few minutes after ten p.m., Turner heard footsteps from above.

"What the hell?" he heard someone say. "How'd these lights get turned off?"

A staircase was illuminated a second later. Turner and Alexander were still sitting in the dark, their guns drawn and aimed toward the top of the stairs. The target was trailing behind a man not much older than themselves. The publisher of the paper, no doubt. Who else would be there after ten on a Wednesday night?

Alexander pointed his gun at the man's head as he reached the bottom of the steps and squeezed the trigger, and a flash later brains and blood were dripping down a wall finished with high-gloss white paint. The target was halfway down the steps when the publisher's head exploded.

The man pivoted and made it up one step before Turner put a forty-five-caliber round from the Sig Sauer in his knee. He fell backward and tumbled down the steps, coming to a stop after crashing into the publisher's corpse. The target reached for a weapon of his own. His hand had just made it to the pistol when Alexander and Turner fired rounds into his chest.

After seeing there was no movement from the target, Alexander lowered his gun and went back to the desk he had been sitting at moments ago. He opened a small black duffel, reached in a pulled out two Tapco road flares.

"Never leave home without 'em," Alexander said.

"That's my partner," Turner said. "Always prepared, just like a cute little Boy Scout."

"You notice that morgue when we walked through the kitchen?"

"Morgue? What are you talking about? The only morgue I know is the one the target is going to along with his unfortunate friend."

Alexander pulled two more flares from the bag. "Well, I am disturbed. Here I thought you were an educated man and you don't even know what a newspaper morgue is?"

"Show me!"

The killers walked back to the kitchen. Across from the sink in what had once been a closet, sets of large black books stood on three rows of shelves. Each book had gold lettering on its spine that read *Plymouth Independent* and gave the publication dates. The books went in chronological order, starting from the upper corner of the top shelf and then going left to right. There were ten years' worth of back issues.

"The reporters and editors use these as reference tools," Alexander said. "Christ, didn't you ever see *Citizen Kane* or *All the President's Men*?"

Turner flushed and put his hands on his hips. "Ashamed to say I haven't. One question."

"Yeah, shoot."

"Why would they need these bound volumes when they have computers? Wouldn't you assume they have computer archives?"

"That's a fair point, I guess," Alexander said. "Don't matter much at this point, I reckon."

He set two of the flares on the lower shelves of the newspaper morgue. Turner held the other two flares up and shrugged his shoulders as if to say, *What do we do with these?*

Alexander strode through the newsroom back to the target and the other dude. He took latex gloves from the duffel, put them on and positioned the dead men with their backs to the wall. He opened the publisher's mouth, while the target's mouth was already drooping wide open.

A bolt of recognition flashed across Turner's face. "You, sir, have a sick sense of humor."

Alexander lit the flares and then shoved them in the dead men's mouths. "Don't everyone deserve a last smoke?"

He grabbed the duffel from the desk as the flares charred and burned the faces of the assignment and the publisher. The Dynamic Duo then raced through the office, lit the second pair of flares and made sure the morgue was burning before they fled.

THE PHONE ON HARPER'S NIGHTSTAND RANG AT 2:40 Thursday morning. He had long since fallen into a deep sleep and the "Old Telephone" ringtone didn't rouse him on the first try. When it went off again, he opened his eyes and grabbed the phone. It was Emily Jackson.

"Jackson, what the hell?"

"The *Independent* is gone!" she screamed.

"What? Gone? What are you talking about?"

Her voice was just short of hysterical.

"Burned to the ground, and Doc was inside. Doc was inside the office. They pulled his body and somebody else's a few minutes ago."

He tossed on pants and a T-shirt. "Where are you at?"

"Across the street. The place is still smoldering. I can't believe it. I can't believe Doc is gone and the paper—"

"Stay put. I'm on the way."

He disconnected the call, shoved the phone in a back pocket and picked up his wallet and car keys from the nightstand. He was in the Honda seconds later, his heart thumping and the adrenaline flowing. He did seventy miles per hour flying across Main Street. He saw smoke as he approached the edge of downtown.

Police had closed off Main at Wing Street, about a quarter mile from the *Independent*'s office. Harper flashed his press credentials at a cop and was told to park on Forest Avenue a block away. The cop would let him through but only on foot. He followed the instruction and then ran from his car to the office.

Harper counted fire trucks from three municipalities and more than a dozen firefighters on-scene. Even as dread crept up his spine and spilled into his gut, he couldn't help gathering facts. It didn't occur to him he didn't have a newspaper to report those facts. Not anymore.

Jackson sat on a curb and Harper could see the tears on her face as he approached. He sat beside her and put his arm around her shoulders. She leaned in and cried harder.

He looked up and saw what was left of the office. Stone steps that led to a porch and the front door. A brick chimney that shot up from the basement past what had been the second floor. Harper saw Doc's classic Ford Mustang in the rear parking lot. It was covered in debris and an ember burned on its hood.

Then memories started cascading through his mind. His first interview with Doc for the reporting job. When he bombed Doc's on-the-spot spelling test, he thought he'd blown it. After he'd been offered the gig and accepted, Doc said he wouldn't hire a reporter who could ace his spelling test. They both laughed.

Harper smiled at the thought of his first professional byline. His father had taken a picture of him holding the tabloid paper and pointing at the headline, "Plymouth Flips Switch on New 911 System." When he thought about going through his stories line by line with Doc in those early days, he hugged Jackson tighter and he cried, too.

Chapter 12

THURSDAY, AUGUST 13

From outward appearances, Henry Reston was a frugal man. He dressed modestly, ate at the same local dives as everyone else, and drove a nondescript sedan most of the year. In summer, Doc tooled around town in a classic 1967 Ford Mustang. It was the lone indulgence Harper had ever witnessed.

Sitting in the man's downtown Plymouth loft, Harper realized appearances could be deceiving. The walls were filled with high-quality reproductions of Renoir and Monet impressionist paintings. Doc Reston also had an appetite for ultramodern furniture with clean lines and hand-blown glass chandeliers. The flooring was black slate arranged in large rectangles. It gave the loft a masculine, warm tone that accentuated its artwork. Harper thought the living space was tony enough to be featured on an HGTV design show.

In all the years he'd worked for Doc, Harper had never been invited to his inner sanctum. He drew a hard line between work and leisure, and while he was personable, Doc was difficult to know. Harper wanted to ask Victoria Reston-Coble, a late-thirties woman with features bronzed and hardened by the Arizona sun, if that was what had led her to build a life far away from her father.

He fought the urge. Harper sat across from Victoria at a dining table made of steel and glass, while Emily Jackson was to his right. On a typical Thursday afternoon, they would have been formulating story ideas, setting up interviews, and visiting cop shops to pick through the latest police reports. Not today. Shit, maybe never.

"I am so sorry for your loss," Jackson said. "I didn't get to work for your dad long, but he taught me—"

"And me," Harper interrupted, "a ton about reporting."

Victoria stared at her empty wineglass, reached for a bottle of chardonnay, and poured. She didn't offer a glass to either Harper or Jackson. She remained silent long enough for a bad moment to turn awkward. A church bell chimed twice and she smiled.

"I grew up with those bells," Victoria said.

"In the loft?" Harper asked.

"No. A block from here on Harding Street. A tiny place, really, fewer square feet than this place."

"Next to Fairground Park," Jackson said. "Doc talked about taking you and your mother there for picnics."

"I was more interested in the monkey bars than the picnics," Victoria said. "I was something of a tomboy. I'd climb those monkey bars, then refuse to get down. Mom was scared of heights. Dad was tall enough to pull me down, but he never did. I think he liked waiting me out just so he could chase me around. If I made it to the metal slide without his touching me, I was safe. I loved that slide, even if it did burn my legs on a day like today."

She nodded in the direction of a nearby window. It was one in a row of five-foot-tall windows on the loft's northeast wall. Light poured through and caught the corner of the table. Harper ran his hand over the illuminated glass and then down one of the table's steel legs, feeling the heat as Victoria must have all those summers ago.

He glanced up and saw her rubbing her eyes. Victoria had taken an early morning flight into Detroit Metro Airport from Phoenix after getting a call from the police in the middle of the night.

"What is it, ten thirty?" Victoria asked rhetorically. "I shouldn't be drinking this early. Guess I'm not up on proper protocol for this kind of situation."

Harper didn't know much about Victoria's relationship with Doc. He had seen her at the office only once in his time at the newspaper, a few days before Christmas two years ago. Doc, it seemed, only talked to Jackson about his daughter. The one thing he did know: Victoria had just inherited the *Independent.*

"We're not here to judge," Harper said. "If a glass of wine helps—"

"Thanks. It doesn't. I'm just numb at this point. I need answers."

"I'd like some, too," Jackson said.

"That's going to take time," Harper said. "I stopped at the office before coming here. The fire marshal and his investigator were on-site. It'll be a while before they know how the fire started. The county will be doing an autopsy on your father and the other person tomorrow morning."

"Any idea of who the other person was?" asked Victoria.

"A second car was in the parking lot," Harper said. "The cops are trying to track down the owner now."

Victoria pushed her wineglass aside. "Is it possible the fire was deliberate?"

"I'd find that hard to believe. Your dad was well-liked in the community," Harper said. "It always amazed me how he could rip the Plymouth city commission or the school board a new asshole in an editorial and then shake hands with them a few days later at a Chamber of Commerce luncheon or town festival."

"My father always commanded respect," Victoria said. "He was tough but played it straight down the middle."

"Weren't you his first reporter at the *Independent*?" Jackson asked.

"I was, yes. But only for six months right after college. I had no desire to be in journalism for the long haul. Still don't."

Harper sighed. "Does that mean you're going to shut the *Independent* down?"

"My life is in Arizona," Victoria said. "I knew I would inherit the paper at some point. I just didn't think it'd be this soon. I'm not prepared for any of this."

She broke down, her sobs silent and compressed inward. Her face reddened and her hands balled into tight fists. She slammed them into the table, knocking over both her glass and the chardonnay bottle. Jackson righted the bottle a moment later and then hurried to the kitchen for towels.

Harper stood and offered Victoria a shoulder. She took it, turning to face him and then embracing him. He felt her considerable strength and wondered if her tomboy streak had continued into adulthood; perhaps she'd traded monkey bars for mountains and weight training.

Victoria regained her composure a minute later. She looked about the loft, her eyes scanning as if she was trying to make sense of it all. Tears trickled down her face intermittently.

"Any idea how long the paper's advertising contracts run?" she asked, looking first at Harper and then Jackson.

"He kept most of them on a monthly auto-renewing basis," Harper said. "The standard contract says both parties have to give thirty days' notice."

"What about the Plymouth Fall Festival advertisers? He used to give them free months if they bought display ads for the Fall Fest issue."

Harper shook his head. "He stopped that a few years back. He said it was giving money away. We lost some advertisers, but Doc didn't care. Called them freeloaders."

"He liked that term," Victoria said. "Dad was pretty conservative, as I'm sure you both know. He idolized Ronald Reagan and about disowned me when I voted for Al Gore."

"He was just as excited about me voting for Hillary Clinton in 2016," Harper said.

Victoria got up from the table and stepped into the kitchen. She grabbed three bottled waters from the fridge and returned. She pulled out her iPhone and studied it for a moment before looking at Harper and Jackson.

"I want the two of you to get notice out to the *Independent*'s advertisers today," Victoria said. "Our last issue will be Wednesday, September 30. Ray, I'm naming you publisher. You know the lay of the land better than me or Emily. If you need to hire a freelancer to help write stories, do it. Go out and buy whatever you need to get the paper out."

"I'll need to replace my laptop," Harper said. "What about you, Emily?"

"I took mine with me last night, so I'm good," Jackson said. "We will need some office supplies. I'm assuming we're going to work from home these last few weeks?"

"No," Victoria said. "You can work here in the loft. I think Dad would've wanted it that way. I'll have keys made today. What about software for your laptops? Will you need to buy the newspaper design program?"

"Everything is cloud-based these days," Harper said. "That won't be an issue."

Victoria took his hand and reached for Jackson's. "I'm sorry it has to be this way. Dad wanted me to carry on when he was gone, I know deep down he did. It's just not in me. I can't—"

"It's okay," Jackson said. "We understand. This whole thing is devastating, to lose your father that way, I can't imagine. Please don't worry about us. We're journalists. We're used to adapting and overcoming."

"I don't want either of you leaving before the last issue," Victoria said. "I will give you both six months' severance if you stick around."

"That's very generous of you," Harper said. "It's not necessary. I owe it to your dad to see this through to the end."

"Absolutely right," Jackson said. "I'm not leaving."

Victoria squeezed their hands. "Thank you. But you're going to get that money. I don't want to hear another word about it."

Chapter 13

THURSDAY, August 13

Harper had a new MacBook Pro up and running before dinner. Unlike most news organizations, the *Independent* didn't allow readers to comment at the end of articles on its website. Years earlier, Harper had gone off on a rant about metrics, besieging Doc about engagement time, reader retention and how commenting enhanced click-through rates, telling him it was stuff he could and should pitch to advertisers.

"We're leaving dollars on the table," Harper advised.

The old man wasn't having it. "You want to keep readers and engage them? Write better stories. We're not wading into that cesspool."

Now, as publisher, Harper could do just about anything he wanted. Victoria was working on arrangements for her father and then would be heading back to Phoenix until the funeral. The police had promised to keep her in the loop on any developments in the case. As for the paper, Harper was to take the editorial ball and run. She'd handle the financial tasks from Arizona.

The woman was direct and to the point, a trait she'd inherited from Doc, Harper thought. He was just glad she wouldn't be looking over his shoulder and tossing "that's not the way Daddy did it" grenades at him.

He pulled up the *Independent*'s website and was pleased to see it was unaffected by the past twenty-four hours' events. A silly thought, really, as if the flames could reach into cyberspace and burn down a digital newspaper. He wasn't surprised to see hundreds of new emails in the paper's inbox.

Neither he nor Jackson had written about the fire or Doc's death. Other news outlets had. Harper acted as the spokesperson for the *Independent*, doing phone interviews with radio stations, the *Detroit News* and *Free Press*, and even Ivan from the *Chronicle*. He took special care to give Ivan as little as possible.

Most emails expressed heartfelt condolences and came from every corner of Plymouth, from business owners to local politicians, residents and readers, members of the clergy, teachers and high school sports coaches. A few were not so thoughtful or kind.

"It was nothing but a bunch of fake news anyway," an anonymous note read. "Good riddance."

Others called the *Independent* a "liberal rag," a "right-wing propaganda machine," a "dinosaur," and dismissed Doc and his reporters as "losers" who might now be forced to get real jobs. After seventy emails, Harper gave up reading them. Doc had been right not to allow commenting on the paper's articles.

Harper's apartment had two bedrooms, one he had converted into an office after moving in three years ago. Sitting at a small, black desk in the middle of the room, he closed his eyes and leaned back in his chair. He ran through every story he needed to jump on in the morning.

The impending closure of the newspaper would be a sidebar to Jackson's story on the fire and Doc's death. The hit-and-run case that had so dominated his thoughts seemed a million miles away. Still, another follow-up needed to be written. It was lot to juggle along with taking over mentoring duties with Jackson.

She was good for a cub reporter. Had a way of cutting through bullshit and developing sources in a New York minute. But even prodigies needed editors. While Harper hadn't been around as many blocks as Henry Reston, he knew what pitfalls to avoid and which hills not to die on.

Since he'd been a cub not so long ago, his memories of rookie mistakes were still fresh. And despite Victoria's hands-off approach, Harper couldn't afford any major mistakes. Not if he wanted to continue reporting after the *Independent* closed.

Going on just a couple of hours of sleep, Harper was physically exhausted. He closed the MacBook, got up from the desk and left the office.

Harper walked into the kitchen, immediately hearing the wailing of little Astrid below, a toddler whose meltdowns were epic, the daughter of Dave and Elizabeth, the duplex's owners. It did nothing to settle his nerves. Perhaps a beer would help. He scanned the contents of the fridge and found a Bass ale hiding in the back. Drinking a cold one at ten thirty at night was becoming a habit, and not a good one considering his waistline had ballooned two inches in the past year.

He stood at the kitchen sink taking long pulls from the beer. Harper couldn't shake the image of the burned-to-the-ground *Independent*. Poor Doc. What a way to go. For all the sorrow he felt, guilt was coursing through his veins, too.

While it was officially the Plymouth Police Department's job to bring Jake Bell's hit-and-run driver to justice and find Henry Reston's killer, Harper could make a name for himself by the way he handled the stories. It wouldn't be easy. Reporters were on the outside looking in on criminal investigations.

Despite their own efforts at getting the word out via social media, police departments still relied on newspapers and television stations to help glean tips from the public. All too often, it was the only follow-up story reporters got until cases were solved.

Harper didn't have the luxury of waiting out the investigations with the *Independent*'s closing in six weeks, nor was he going to be satisfied with whatever scraps the police decided to feed him. He would continue to push the envelope with his own sleuthing on the hit-and-run and now Doc's death.

That's where the guilt came in. Trying to capitalize on his mentor's demise. It felt ghoulish to Harper. But he couldn't deny the sense of excitement he felt at the opportunity to score big with stories that could lead to a job with one of the daily papers downtown or someplace else.

Harper took the last swig of beer and set the bottle on the counter.

Chapter 14

FRIDAY, August 14

Adams sat in front of Neil Flaherty's desk sipping coffee and shaking his head. "We're trying to keep a lid on this, and you invite the media in on the autopsy? Tell me, in what universe does that make any sense?"

Flaherty straightened his tie and pulled his suit jacket down as a flash of annoyance crossed his face. "We're walking a very fine line," Flaherty said. "We have to give every appearance to the public we're doing all we can to solve this case."

"That's fine and dandy, Neil," Adams said. "You're the public relations expert, I'll give you that. But this doesn't make sense from any angle. Number one, this is an ongoing investigation, which means we don't have to give the media squat. Secondly, no police agency I can think of ever invites reporters to an autopsy. I think you're throwing up a red flag where there doesn't need to be one."

"I didn't invite the entire Detroit media," Flaherty said, "just the kid from the *Independent*. I understand the risks involved here, sergeant, and they are significant. But there is a saying I've always lived by professionally and it has served me well: 'Keep your friends close and your enemies closer.'"

"Really? You're going to quote *The Godfather*?" Adams said. "Man, you've been in this ivory tower too long. I guess you're going to do this no matter what I say. So, how do you want me to play it?"

Flaherty opened a bottle of water and took a sip. "Let the medical examiner take the lead. Linda Morris will perform the autopsies. She's an old friend. She knows how to handle the media."

"What about Snyder?"

"Give it to him," Flaherty said. "Tell him we identified the body."

Adams exhaled and then laughed sarcastically. "Well, shit. Why don't we just tell them we hired the hitmen, too?"

"Watch your tone," Flaherty said, coming around the desk and getting in Adams's face. "I'm calling the shots here. I know what I'm—"

"Like hell you do," Adams said, standing to meet Flaherty's challenge. "You're thinking with the wrong head. It's going to get us all a one-way ticket to prison."

"Keep your fuckin' voice down," Flaherty said, towering over the five-foot-seven-inch detective.

They stood inches apart before being interrupted by Flaherty's administrative assistant. She knocked on his closed office door and then stuck her head in.

"Chief, the reporter from the newspaper is here."

Flaherty turned his white-hot gaze from Adams to his assistant. "Detective Adams will be with him in just a moment. Thank you.

"I'm going to tell you this once, Mike," Flaherty said after she closed the door. "You're gonna follow my orders. You will not speak of this matter in my office, around city hall or with any member of this department again. If you do, I will know. Understand this: My debt to you is paid in full. If you become a liability in any way, shape or form, you will be dealt with. Am I clear?"

"Saving your brother's ass only goes so far, I guess," Adams said. He grabbed his own suit jacket and headed for the door

"Detective," Flaherty said.

Adams looked back.

"Don't fuck this up."

Adams closed the door behind him.

DESPITE THE RECENT DROP IN HOMICIDES IN DETROIT, business at the Wayne County medical examiner's office remained steady. While the number of murders had dipped below three hundred per year starting in 2017, Detroit remained behind only Saint Louis and Baltimore for the highest murder rate in the United States.

Plymouth, a western Detroit suburb that sat near the Wayne and Washtenaw county border, averaged less than one homicide per year. Harper thought about the crime statistics story he did every year and wondered how Plymouth residents would react to a potential 200 percent increase in murders.

For now, he was thankful he was allowed to tag along on the autopsies for Doc and the other victim. Reporters were rarely granted such access. Adams laid out strict ground rules on the drive into Detroit: No photographs, and no questions for the medical examiner during the examination. Quotes, in fact, would be limited to what the detective decided to give them.

"The only reason you're here is because of what your boss did for me," Adams lied. "The former police chief threw me under the bus for a botched prostitution bust. He went riding into the Red Roof Inn with two television news crews following along and they found exactly nothing. The pimps had been tipped off, and that, somehow, was my fault. But your boss knew better and reported it. Saved my ass."

They arrived at the East Warren Avenue medical examiner's office in thirty minutes. A clerk offered Vicks VapoRub to Harper before he entered the examination room. A dab smeared under the nose helped those unaccustomed to the sights and smells of the place keep the contents of their stomachs inside their bodies. He refused.

It wasn't Harper's first visit to the medical examiner's office. He'd written a story about a pair of Plymouth police detectives learning the finer points of evidence recognition and collection at murder scenes a few years back. The course "final" was held at the county morgue. A few things from that visit had stuck with Harper, including the sight of a dead infant lying on its dead mother's belly.

Adams led the way into the examination room. All of the county's dozen autopsy tables were full, including ones that held the remains of Henry Reston and the other victim pulled from the *Independent*'s ashes.

Despite his earlier experience, Harper wasn't prepared when the evidence sheet covering Doc's body was pulled back. Harper had expected charred remains. He hadn't expected the top quarter of Doc's skeleton to be gone.

"We almost never see bodies that have been exposed to temperatures above eleven hundred degrees Celsius from a house fire," examiner Linda Morris said. "The burns Mr. Reston suffered were above fourteen hundred Celsius. Just to give you an idea of how extreme those temperatures are, bodies are normally cremated between about seven hundred and nine hundred degrees Celsius."

"Were those temperatures consistent over the entire body?" Adams asked.

"Not at all," Morris said. "Since the skull and the top of the upper torso are missing, it's logical to assume the extreme heat was confined to those areas. That was for both victims, who, as you know, were in close proximity to each other. The fire was coldest at their feet, about six hundred Celsius."

"How can you be sure of the temperatures near the skull when it's missing?" Adams asked. "You just said bodies are cremated at nine hundred—"

"Fire doesn't burn evenly," Morris said. "I base those temperatures off of damage done to surrounding tissues and bone."

"How do you explain the difference in temperatures from the head to the feet?"

Morris turned to the detective. "We can't at this point."

"Do you have a theory?"

"Very few materials burn that hot," she said. "Pyrotechnics are one."

Adams shot her a skeptical glance. "No reports of fireworks going off Wednesday night."

"You asked for a theory, detective. I'm not saying it's probable that pyrotechnics were used, I'm saying it's one substance that burns that hot. Remember, too, pyrotechnics aren't limited to fireworks."

"Examples?"

"I'm not an expert," Morris said. "But you can certainly count consumer distress flares, both highway and marine, and powder-actuated tools like nail guns. Technically, ammunition for firearms uses pyrotechnic materials."

Adams turned his attention to the other fire victim. "You've completed your examination of this person?"

"I have," Morris said. "The victim is male. As you can tell, he suffered similar burn damage in the upper torso. But the fire didn't kill this man."

"How's that?" Adams asked.

"His left knee and T1 thoracic vertebra were pierced by bullets. The T1 shot almost assuredly hit the pulmonary artery or jugular vein. The victim would have bled out before the burns were severe enough to kill him."

"So, this was a homicide?"

"Without question," Morris said.

"You didn't find any evidence of gunshot wounds to Reston?" Harper asked. Adams turned and gave him a scowl.

"No, we didn't," Morris said. "That doesn't mean it couldn't have happened. I'll be curious to find out if your team recovers any bullet rounds from the scene, detective."

"To be clear, these are both homicides?" Adams asked.

"Yes. Gunshot wounds killed the second male victim. If they hadn't, the unnatural burns would've. For now, until and if additional evidence is recovered, Mr. Reston's death was caused by severe burns of a suspicious nature."

Adams and Harper thanked Morris for her work. After leaving the examining room and returning to the detective's unmarked car, Adams stopped before climbing in.

"I know the ME didn't make a positive ID on the second victim," Adams said. "But we know who it is."

"You were able to track down ownership of their car?" Harper asked.

"Yeah. He was one of ours, unfortunately. Lieutenant Robert Snyder."

"Snyder?" Harper said. "How could that be?"

His mind immediately went back to his interview with the lieutenant from the day before. A wave of panic washed across him, a perhaps not-so-irrational fear about his own safety. Harper knew in an instant why Snyder had been with Doc when they both died. It couldn't be a coincidence.

"So, we, uh, we know Doc and Snyder were murdered," Harper said. "Do you believe they're connected, or was the lieutenant simply in the wrong place at the wrong time?"

Adams rubbed his chin. "Way too early to tell. We don't know why the lieutenant was there or why anyone would want to kill him or your boss."

"Why are you telling me this?" Harper said. "I mean, your investigation isn't even off the ground yet. Don't get me wrong. It's not that I'm not appreciative of everything you've shared. But it seems—"

Adams put a hand up as if to stop Harper from asking any further questions. "We don't give anyone this kind of access. But our organizations have a mutual goal here: to find the shitheads responsible as soon as possible. You don't kill a cop and get away with it. I know you feel the same way about Henry. Besides that, I know you, Harper. Ain't no fuckin' way you're going to leave this alone."

"So, the chief thinks we can help each other out?" Harper asked.

"To a degree," Adams said. "I'll give you what I can. Expect you'll do the same for me."

"I can live with that," Harper said.

The detective got in the car and started the engine. Harper climbed in the passenger seat. Neither he nor Adams said a word the entire ride back to Plymouth.

Chapter 15

FRIDAY, August 14–Saturday, August 15

Being the publisher had its advantages. Instead of waiting for the print edition, Harper wrote a lengthy story detailing the autopsies, including the identification of the second victim. In less than an hour after he published it, WWJ, Detroit's news radio station, picked the story up, and television stations followed by sending reporters to Plymouth city hall for their six p.m. newscasts.

It was nice to be first on a story for a change. That good feeling didn't last long. Friday evenings often came with a sense of dread for Harper. The workweek was over, and aside from a trip to the gym or catching a Tigers game at Comerica Park, he had little to fill his free time.

Truth be told, he was lonely. Harper's one and only serious relationship, a two-year romance with a fellow journalism student at Central Michigan University, was ancient history. He had since tried dating apps, the bar scene, and a couple of blind dates set up by friends. All his romantic efforts had flopped.

Since meeting her while investigating the Max Bell hit-and-run, Harper couldn't get Sophia Casey out of his head. Perhaps it was her quick, mesmerizing smile, her long, rich brown hair, or her face, which was beautiful and mischievous all at the same time, but he felt his heart beat in a way it hadn't in years. It was a brief encounter she likely hadn't given a second thought. Sophia probably had a boyfriend at Eastern Michigan.

Harper pushed negative thoughts aside. Having already scored one victory, he decided to go for a second and pay a visit to the party store where Sophia worked. He pulled into the Cap N Cork's parking lot ten minutes later, looked at himself in the rearview mirror and exited the Honda before he could lose his nerve.

David Casey, the shop owner and Sophia's "pop," stood with a clipboard in his hands in the middle of a long aisle of red and white bottles of wine. He appeared to be doing inventory, at least to Harper's untrained eye. Sophia was at the counter with a customer.

She was dressed in a pair of jeans and a close-fitting T-shirt. A white block "E" separated "Eastern Michigan" on a dark green background. Her hair was pulled back, though a few pieces of her bangs fell across her forehead. Sophia smiled as she handed change to an older man, who smiled back, picked a case of Guinness stout up from the counter and walked away.

Harper went to the back of the store and grabbed a Coke. His heart started thumping as he made his way to the counter. Sophia was staring down at her phone and didn't notice him until he was nearly at the cash register.

"Just the Coke, or did you need to speak with Pop again?" Sophia asked.

He took her recognition as a good sign and smiled.

"Actually, it was you I came to talk to."

The expression on Sophia's face changed from a half smile to puzzlement. "Me? I really don't know anything about the accident."

"That's not what I wanted to talk about," Harper said.

"Oh?" She smiled awkwardly.

"I was wondering if you might be free for dinner tomorrow night."

Sophia blushed. Harper was sure he had just made a fool out of himself. David Casey approached from behind.

"Mr. Harper," he said. "I hope you found the video useful."

"I did, yes. Thank you."

"Such a shame about the Bell boy. Is there something else I can help you with or were you just thirsty?"

"I've got this, Pop," Sophia said. "You better finish your inventory before we start getting busy."

"Ah, you're right, my darling, you are absolutely right. Good to see you again, Mr. Harper. I will leave you in the capable hands of my daughter."

Sophia's green eyes twinkled. She was still blushing ever so slightly. She waited to speak until her father was busy counting again.

"I'm sorry," Sophia said. She leaned forward, put both elbows on the counter and rested her face in her hands. "I've forgotten your first name."

"My name is Ray. Ray—"

"I know your last name."

"Of course, I—"

"Pick me up here at seven. We can go to Black Rock."

HARPER WISHED HE SPENT MORE TIME AT PLANET FITNESS AND LESS AT AREA WATERING HOLES. The mirrored closet door in his bedroom told no lies. He didn't like what he saw: skinny chest, undeveloped shoulders, flat ass and the start of a beer gut.

His arms and legs had some natural bulk. He couldn't do much to show off his quads in khakis, but a light blue polo shirt would reveal his biceps. Harper shook his head at his own stupidity for letting himself get so out of shape. There must have been something Sophia liked about him, he rationalized.

Harper arrived at the Cap N Cork a few minutes before seven. The evening was perfect, as late summer evenings often were in Michigan. A cloudless blue sky with almost no humidity, and warm enough to eat comfortably outside if they preferred. The door to the party store was propped open.

David Casey was behind the counter with his attention squarely on a television mounted on the ceiling about six feet away from the cash register. Harper glanced up and saw a University of Michigan football player racing for the end zone with the pigskin raised high above his head. The Wolverines were pounding Eastern Michigan, which seemed to delight Sophia's father.

"You're a sly devil, Mr. Harper," David said, "asking my daughter for a date. But I can't blame you, no sir. My Sophia is a beauty. And let me tell you, she's as smart as a whip. You better have your 'A' game going tonight, my friend."

Harper extended his hand and gave him a firm handshake. "I always do. You don't survive long in my business without being on your toes."

Sophia walked up behind her father from a back room. Her hair was swept to the right, where it fell well past her shoulders. Her left ear was pierced with a small diamond in the lobe and a gold ring near the top. She wore a yellow sundress that accentuated her considerable curves.

Harper's heart went into overdrive. "Ready?"

Sophia shot a look at her father as if to say, *Can you believe this guy?* She looked at Harper and said: "Are you?"

"Let's roll. We have a long journey ahead of us. The restaurant is at least two or three hundred... yards away."

David Casey laughed. "Glad to see you have a sense of humor, Mr. Harper."

"Come on, wise guy," Sophia said, "let's walk."

Five minutes later they were seated at the Black Rock Bar & Grill. All the outdoor tables were filled. A hostess gave them a choice of seats at the bar or at a window overlooking Ann Arbor Road. Harper deferred to Sophia, who selected the window seat. A family of five sat on one side of them and a table of guys in their thirties or early forties on the other.

The sound and smell of sizzling steak filled the room. Black Rock's claim to fame was allowing its patrons to cook their own dinners on stones heated to more than seven hundred degrees.

"I love this place," Sophia said. "Have you been here before?"

"Driven by it a million times," Harper said, "but no."

"No worries. I won't let you make any newbie mistakes."

A waitress dressed in a black button-up shirt with dark hair pulled back and held in place with a pink bandana asked them for their drink order. Sophia ordered a Blue Moon beer with a slice of orange, and Harper settled on a Corona with lime.

"How hungry are you?" Sophia asked.

"I can definitely eat. What's a good cut for a newbie?"

"Something with a little extra fat. I'm going to say a nine-ounce Manhattan."

"What about you?"

"Sirloin all the way. It's a little leaner. You have to know what you're doing."

"And you do, I take it?"

She shot him a knowing smile. "Without a doubt."

The waitress returned with their drinks. "Have you all decided?"

Sophia added a baked potato and a salad with ranch dressing to go with her six-ounce sirloin. Harper went with mixed vegetables and a salad with a vinaigrette.

"So, you're going to teach?"

"That's the plan," Sophia said. "I have classes this semester and start student-teaching in January."

"Do you have a grade in mind?"

"The best teacher I ever had was my fifth-grade teacher. I've always wanted to follow in his footsteps. To me, it's the perfect grade. The kids aren't babies anymore and they're hungry for knowledge."

"Do you know where you will be student-teaching?"

"Not yet. Probably won't until late in the fall. How do you like being a reporter?"

"I love it," Harper said. "I get to meet interesting new people all the time and learn about aspects of life I never would have otherwise."

"That's awesome," Sophia said. "It can't be all fun, though, like writing about that hit-and-run?"

"Those kinds of stories are hard. His family is devastated. It bothers me, seeing people hurt and torn apart. In a small way, I feel like I'm working for them, trying to get to the truth."

"That's pretty idealistic. Aren't you supposed to be objective?"

Harper leaned back. "That's what they teach you in journalism school. Maybe other reporters can keep all their emotions in check. I can't. But it doesn't stop me from doing my job and reporting the facts."

Sophia raised her hands in surrender. "Sorry, didn't mean to hit a nerve."

"Ah, don't mind me. I'm a little overly sensitive these days. With all the 'fake news' bull being tossed around and people so negative toward the media, I tend to get defensive pretty quick. I'm sorry if it came off that way."

Sophia shrugged as if to say, *No big deal.* Her attention turned to pink-bandana waitress, who rolled a cart up to their table. She set black stones in front of them, steaks already cooking on top. She unloaded side items from the cart and asked if they wanted another round of beers. Harper nodded while Sophia requested ice water.

"Strong willpower," Harper said. "I like that."

"One beer always tastes good," Sophia said. "I'm just not one to keep pounding them back."

"So, what am I doing here?"

"Get some of this garlic butter on your knife and spread it on your steak. Trust me, it gives it a great flavor. It's pretty simple, really. Only cut a piece of steak off at a time. If you cut it into a bunch of small pieces, they'll get overcooked by the time you eat them."

Harper followed her instructions and the steak was, indeed, delicious. He had hardly touched his salad or vegetables before pronouncing himself full. Sophia pushed a small portion of her steak off to the side and Harper shot her an inquisitive look.

"I always bring a little home for Bernie," she said.

"Bernie?"

"Our dog. He's the sweetest little man. We got him when I was seven."

"You live with your dad?"

"Yeah," Sophia said. "I lived on campus my freshman year and didn't like it much."

Harper decided to steer the conversation back to safer ground. "What kind of dog is Bernie?"

Sophia pulled her phone out and thumbed to pictures of the pooch. There were selfies with Bernie, Bernie with her dad, Bernie with her girlfriends. Harper expected to see her mother in one of the photos. But there were no older women in any of the shots.

"He's a shih tzu. Isn't he just adorable?"

"He is, definitely," Harper said. "I noticed there weren't any pictures of your dad and mom with Bernie. Are they divorced?"

"No, Mom passed away ten years ago," Sophia said. She clicked the phone off. "Breast cancer."

There it was. The date had been going so well. But sooner or later, Harper always stuck his foot in his mouth. He was surprised he hadn't contracted foot-in-mouth disease by now.

"I'm so sorry," he said in as sympathetic a tone as he could muster.

"It's okay," Sophia said. "It has been just me and Pop for a long time now. I guess we're used to it."

Pink bandana came back and inquired about dessert. They agreed to pass, and Harper handed the waitress his debit card. He signed the receipt a few minutes later and they left the restaurant.

"I know you're a one-beer kind of girl," Harper said. "But what about a mixed drink somewhere else?"

Sophia grabbed his right hand and squeezed. "Not on a first date. Let's walk back to the store."

The sun was setting in front of them as they walked. It felt so good to hold a woman's hand, Harper thought. It had been too long since he had. He let Sophia set the pace. It was decidedly slower than the walk to Black Rock.

They crossed Ann Arbor Road at the same intersection where Max Bell had lost his life. Had the teenager not been killed, Harper wouldn't have been snooping around for video of the incident and never would've met Sophia. The irony wasn't lost on him.

She stopped walking about a hundred yards from Cap N Cork. She took Harper's other hand and leaned in. He kissed her lightly at first and then more intensely when she didn't back away.

They exchanged phone numbers after completing the walk. Sophia kissed him on the cheek and disappeared into the store. Harper sat in the Honda, not believing what had just happened. He relived their first kiss and could feel the electricity pulsing from his toes up through his brain.

Chapter 16

MONDAY, AUGUST 17

Thoughts of his date with Sophia lingered as Harper set up shop for the first time in Henry Reston's loft. He took the glass-topped dinner table, set his MacBook in the middle and then dumped notebooks, file folders and old print editions of the *Independent* on either side. He'd discovered long ago that a tidy workspace was counterproductive, at least for him.

Doc had needled him mercilessly about how his desk attracted rodents. Jackson, on the other hand, had a touch of obsessive-compulsive disorder, in Harper's humble opinion. Not only did she keep a tidy desk, but more often than not it smelled of lemony disinfectant.

He glanced up from his computer and shook his head at Jackson's near manic effort to clean her new desk. Harper had helped her move a small writing desk from Doc's bedroom into the living space near the tall vertical windows. She liked the view of Penniman Avenue with its steady stream of people visiting shops, restaurants and bars.

After Jackson was finally satisfied with her new setup, Harper called her over to his pigpen for a brief meeting.

"We've got seven print editions remaining," he said. "I don't think we should let the ball drop on any of our beats."

"I agree," Jackson said. "School will be starting in a couple of weeks, so I'm starting to ramp up my coverage this week."

"There's never any shortage of back-to-school stories to do," Harper said. "I know that's going to keep you busy, but in all honesty, I need help. I'll be doing the design work for the print edition now, plus I'm sure I'll wind up doing some business stuff, too."

"I thought Victoria was handling the business end of the paper."

"She can only do much from Arizona. Any circulation issues or immediate problems with advertisers, I'll need to step in."

"So, what does that mean for me?" Jackson asked.

"I'd like you to take over all social media operations," Harper said. "You're tons better at it than I am anyway."

"What else?"

"I want you to do the city commission meetings, too. My reporting time is going to be pretty much monopolized by investigating Doc's death and the Bell hit-and-run case. I'll pick up some other stories here and there when I can."

Jackson jotted notes in a skinny reporter's notebook as Harper spoke. She looked up when he finished. "It might mean a few less school stories, but I can manage."

"I know you're starting to get calls and emails from principals about upcoming activities at their schools," Harper said. "Those are fun stories to do, but in this business, you've got to be able to say no. Keep up with the big stuff and let some of the cute stories and features slide."

"Got it," Jackson said. "What about freelancers? Didn't Victoria say we could use a couple if we got overwhelmed?"

"Easier said than done," Harper said. "I really don't have any candidates, do you?"

"I know a couple of people from J-school that are in the area. I'll reach out to them."

Harper's iPhone went off. He glanced at the screen and saw it was a call from the Plymouth Police Department. He turned his head back to Jackson.

"I've got to take this," Harper said. "I think we're pretty much done."

Jackson picked her notebook up and took a dozen steps back to her own desk. Harper returned his gaze to his phone and hit the green button to answer.

"This is Ray."

"Ray, Chief Flaherty. I want to express my condolences about Henry. I didn't always agree with him and we had our share of battles over the years. But he was a good man."

"Yes, he was. Thanks."

"The great news is, we took a suspect into custody late last night in the Bell case," Flaherty said. "We expect to arraign the individual this afternoon."

"Man or woman?"

"A forty-year-old white female out of Belleville."

"Name?"

"Will be given at the arraignment," Flaherty said. "All the details you need will come out in the arraignment at three in front of Judge Burke."

"What are you charging her with?" Harper asked.

"Manslaughter and leaving the scene of an accident. They're both felonies. We will be going for the maximum penalties."

"How did you get her?" Harper asked. "I didn't think you guys were even close."

"It came together quickly," Flaherty said. "As you know, Detective Adams is the lead investigator and has worked nearly around the clock. All the details will be made plain at the arraignment. That's all I can say for now, Ray."

DARWIN L. BURKE SR., CHIEF JUDGE OF THE THIRTY-FIFTH DISTRICT COURT, tapped his gavel at precisely three p.m. Attorneys for the prosecution, and defense introduced themselves and Burke read the charges against the defendant.

Lisa Ann Patton's hair was cropped short and its color was close to his own shade of dark brown, Harper noted. She was petite and seemed to swim in an orange one-piece jumper provided by the Plymouth Police Department. The woman's eyes were trained on Burke, and her hands rested on a yellow legal notepad. The expression on her face wasn't hard for Harper to read: anger.

"Lisa Ann Patton," Burke said, "do you understand the charges against you?"

"I do, Your Honor."

"How do you wish to plead?"

"I am not guilty, Your Honor. These charges are bull—"

"I'll advise you to hold your tongue," Burke said. "Your attorney will begin your defense at the pretrial examination."

Patton's attorney grabbed her arm. It didn't deter the woman.

"Your Honor, I am a whore and I don't mind admitting it," Patton said. "I do what I have to do to survive and I do not apologize for—"

"We're not here for testimony today," Burke said. "Bailiff, remove the defendant from the courtroom."

"Bullshit!" Patton screamed. "All of this is bullshit!"

Harper snapped a pair of pictures of Patton as a court officer handcuffed her and pulled her away from the defense table. Patton turned her head to face the judge as she was being led away.

"I wasn't anywhere near that intersection. I didn't run over no teenage boy. They're pinning this on me, Judge. They—"

Patton was pushed through a courtroom side door before she could finish. Burke set the preliminary exam date for Monday, August 24.

As the arresting officer, Adams was seated near the prosecutor's table. He rose after Burke ended the arraignment with a tap of his gavel and spoke with an assistant district attorney. Harper slid his digital camera into its case and then made his way to the detective. Adams acknowledged him, raising his left hand and holding up his index finger for Harper to wait a minute.

A shake of the hand and slap on the back later, Adams left the attorney and walked around the bar to Harper. Adams carried at least two hundred pounds on his late-forties frame, most of it muscle in his arms, legs and barrel of a chest. What there was of his hair was shaved to within a quarter inch of his scalp in patches of silver and black. A pair of expensive-looking sunglasses was perched on top of his head, and he wore beige dress pants with a light blue oxford shirt that was unbuttoned at the top to accommodate his oversized neck.

Harper knew better than to reach for a handshake. The first time he'd met the then road patrol sergeant, Adams had squeezed Harper's hand hard enough to buckle his knees. A nod of the head now sufficed for their standard greeting.

"How did you track her down?" Harper asked.

"We on the record?" Adams said. He grinned as if it were the first time he had yanked Harper's chain with the quip.

"No, I just wanted to get a whiff of your aftershave. Old Spice?"

"You can never go wrong with a classic, my friend."

"So, tell me, Mike, how did you track down Miss Patton?"

"Me? I didn't do shit."

"That's not what your boss says."

"Ah, he's just trying to make the department look good. To tell you the truth, her neighbor called us."

"No shit?"

"I shit you not. Patton lives down there in the Belleville Manor trailer park. The neighbor saw the hit-and-run story on the news, and then the next day notices front end damage to Patton's Buick LeSabre."

"Silver LeSabre?

"Yeah, yeah. Silver '99 LeSabre. We get a search warrant and go in there with the Van Buren PD. It's sittin' there with a tarp over it."

A red flag went up in Harper's head. He hadn't seen a Buick LeSabre in his Google search for vehicles with oval rear windows. Before asking his next question, he made a mental note to research the appearance of the LeSabre to see if it matched what he'd seen on the party store video.

"We done here, Ray?" Adams asked.

"No, sorry. Was Patton there when you all got there?"

"Yeah, she was there," Adams said. "Went ape shit when we told her what we were there for. Had to cuff her ass to a kitchen chair. After what we found, I can understand why."

"What did you find?"

"Side-view mirror is dangling on the driver's side. Our techs pulled blood samples off it that we believe will match Max Bell. I'll bet you my next paycheck paint from her LeSabre will also match paint chips we pulled off of the kid. It's going to be a slam dunk of a case."

Harper checked his iPhone to make sure it was recording the conversation. His paranoia about it shutting off in the middle of an interview never went away. When he was satisfied that it was continuing to function properly, he asked: "Why is Patton screaming about the charges being pinned on her?"

Adams shrugged. "She already admitted she's a prostitute. Let me tell you, this isn't the first time she has seen the inside of a courtroom."

"What kind of priors does she have?"

"Your usual assortment that goes along with her profession," Adams said. He adjusted his shirt collar before continuing. "Drugs, retail fraud—"

"And prostitution, I would assume?" Harper asked.

"Three times in three different jurisdictions. As you can imagine, telling the truth ain't one of her strong points."

Harper nodded. "I missed what the judge said about bail."

"A hundred thousand, no ten percent," Adams said. "I'm guessing she don't have that kinda cash."

"So, she'll be at county until the prelim?"

"Yup."

"Anybody living with her in that trailer?"

"Two kids, eight and twelve. Both girls. Protective services has them. Not sure if they've been placed yet."

"Unbelievable," Harper said.

"She's a piece of shit," Adams said. He stretched his massive arms over his head and yawned.

"Why didn't you say anything about Patton on Friday?" Harper asked. "Flaherty said everything came together quickly, but are you really going to tell me you weren't looking at her when we were in Detroit for the autopsies?"

"I said I'd give you what I can," said Adams. "But that doesn't mean everything the very moment we put it together."

"Does that go both ways? I mean, if you're going to hold back, shouldn't I?"

"I think you're getting a little spoiled, Harper," Adams said. "Perhaps the chief and I should rethink this arrangement."

Harper turned off the recording app on his phone. "I feel like I'm getting played."

A slight smirk flashed across Adams's mouth. He pulled the sunglasses off his head, put them on and then brushed past Harper and left the courtroom.

Chapter 17

MONDAY, AUGUST 17

A pine tree and a red maple stood like sentinels guarding Lisa Ann Patton's home in the Belleville Manor trailer park. Harper parked the Honda with its tires against the curb and noted well-manicured flower beds around both trees and along the trailer. Hostas, day lilies and annual flowers were carefully placed. Flowers also hung in baskets from a small porch that was enclosed by a railing resembling a white picket fence.

Harper gave himself a mental slap across the face for assuming the admitted prostitute's home would be a run-down hovel with cigarette butts and vodka bottles strewn about. The outside of the mobile home was more like a slice of Americana. The only thing missing was an ice-cream truck with a horde of children waiting to buy eclairs and Popsicles. And maybe they were missing only because it had threatened to rain all morning.

Patton's Buick LeSabre was missing from a parking spot in front of the home. Harper walked up to the door of one of Patton's neighbors. The landscaping around this mobile home wasn't nearly as elaborate as Patton's but the small yard was tidy. Looking around, Harper saw more of the same neatly groomed yards along a tree-lined street.

After a second knock, the door opened and a woman appearing to be about sixty years old emerged. Her blond hair was pulled back and she wore a red, loose-fitting blouse and jean shorts. Other than heavily applied bright red lipstick, she wore no makeup that Harper could detect.

"I don't know what you're selling, young man—"

"Ma'am, I'm not here to sell you anything," Harper said. "I'm Ray Harper, a reporter from the *Plymouth Independent* newspaper. I was hoping I could ask you a few questions."

"About Lisa Ann?"

"Yes. Did you know—"

"Course I knew her. She's been my neighbor for the last five years. She's a good mama to those kids, I can tell you that. They never wanted for nothin'. A real shame, a real damn shame the cops came and took 'em."

"Did it come as a surprise to you?"

"No," she said. "It had to be her car that hit the boy. Heard that story on the news and saw Lisa Ann's car late that evening. It was all beat up."

"The cops told me she tried to cover it up with a tarp or something?"

"Yeah. Just made it obvious to me, you know what I'm saying?"

Harper nodded. "I'm sorry, I didn't get your name?"

"Rita."

"Rita—"

"Judson. Rita Judson."

"Did you confront her, Miss Judson? Sounds like you know her pretty well."

"She pays me to watch her kids sometimes, you know, when she's out on 'business.'"

"So, you know she's a prostitute?" Harper asked.

A flash of anger shot across Judson's face. "I shouldn't be talking to you," she said. "What if one of the girls reads your article and sees my name in it? I don't want to be the one responsible for them knowing what their mama does to put food on the table."

"Ms. Judson, I just came from Lisa Ann's arraignment," Harper said. "She admitted in open court she works as a prostitute, so it's going to be in the story. She also said the police were pinning her with the hit-and-run, but that she didn't do it. I'm trying to find out if what she said is true. You might be able to help with that."

Judson opened her screen door and let Harper in. She pointed to a Shaker-style kitchen table that looked like it came straight from an Amish furniture shop.

"Get you somethin'?" she asked. "I got Diet Coke and Faygo Red Pop."

"I'm good, thanks."

She took a seat with her back to a white refrigerator after pouring Red Pop over ice for herself. "Suit yourself. I'm mighty thirsty. Doctor doesn't like me drinking this stuff. But what ya gonna do? Somethin's gonna kill me anyhow, might as well be something I enjoy."

Harper smiled. He imagined it would be easy to spend an hour with Rita Judson. But time was getting tight and he had several stories to write.

"Rita, did you talk to Lisa Ann after she put the tarp over her car?"

"No, sir. I called the police. Took me a few minutes to work up the courage 'cause Lisa Ann's got a temper and I didn't want it aimed at me. But I felt so bad for that boy and his family. I just had to do something. Know what I mean?"

"I do. Tell me something. Do you know how long Ms. Patton had that car?"

"Couple years, I'd say," Judson said.

"Did she take care of it?"

"What difference does that make?"

"I noticed how nice she kept her yard," Harper said. "I just had a hunch that her home and car were probably well maintained, too."

"They were," Judson said. "Lisa Ann kept a clean house. I never rode in the car, but it looked okay from the outside."

Harper wanted to phrase his next question carefully, so as to not lead Judson to the answer he was looking for. "Do you, by chance, remember the shape of the LeSabre's rear window?"

The question raised a puzzled look from Judson. "The shape? You mean like square or rectangle? Why do you want to know that?"

"It could be important," Harper said.

Judson closed her eyes for a moment as if trying to picture the car in her mind. She shook her head. "No, I don't know what shape it was. Never paid it no mind."

Harper decided not to press and changed gears. "Were you awake when the police came?"

"Not at first. They didn't come in here with flashing lights and them horns going off. But I heard Lisa Ann screamin' at 'em. Woke me up."

"Do you remember what she was saying?"

Rita finished her Red Pop and licked her lips. "I heard a whole bunch of the F-word," she said. "She kept screamin', 'Why you doin' this? Who put you up to it?' Stuff like that. She went ape shit."

Harper's heart skipped a beat. "Ape shit" was exactly the term Adams had used to describe Lisa Ann Patton's behavior at her arrest. He stopped taking notes in his steno pad and looked up at Rita Judson. She smiled. He made a production out of looking at his watch as he stood up.

"Thank you so much for your time," Harper said. "You've been very helpful. I'm running—"

Rita grabbed his hands. "Now, you hold on a minute. I was nice enough to answer your questions. Least you can do is hear the end of my story."

Harper sat back down. "Fair enough. I'm listening."

"It was something I heard Lisa Ann say before they put her in that police car. Screamed that someone had messed up her car the day before. She didn't hit no boy. 'You settin' me up, you settin' me up'?"

"Do you think she was telling the truth?"

"I don't know. I've caught her in a few white lies over the years."

"About what?"

"Makin' up stuff to the girls 'bout where she'd been, stuff like that. I didn't think much of it at the time. Nobody wants their kids to know they're hookin' for a livin'."

"I suppose not," Harper said. "Did she lie about other things?"

"No, and that's what's buggin' me," Rita said.

"If someone had messed up her car, some random person, why would Lisa Ann feel the need to cover it up?" Harper asked.

"Been tryin' to figure that out. She always kept up on the news. Maybe she saw the same report I saw about that Bell boy and got scared. She goes into Plymouth a lot on business, you know what I'm sayin'?"

"Anything else, Rita?"

"No. You know what happened to her girls?"

"The cops told me child protective services took them. They'll probably go into a foster home from there if no family member steps forward."

Rita shook her head. "Damn, Mr. Harper, Lisa Ann ain't got any family 'round here. All her kin is down in Alabama. I'd take those girls and keep 'em until Lisa Ann gets home. Can you tell 'em that?"

"I will," Harper lied. He didn't have time to play social worker. He got up from the table and shook her hand. "One last question. Have you heard from Jake Bell or Crime Stoppers? They were offering a hundred thousand dollars for information—"

"They called and offered me the money," Rita said. "I ain't takin' it, no, sir. I saw what I saw, but that's it. I don't know if Lisa Ann did what they say, and I ain't 'bout to be obligated to them folks."

"Thanks, again, for your time."

The rain had finally come, in big drops. Harper took off in a sprint to his car. He managed to get in before being completely soaked. He swept his rain-matted hair off his forehead and then set his steno pad and pens on the passenger seat.

He replayed the interview with Judson in his mind as he started the Honda and pulled away. He glanced one last time at Lisa Ann Patton's home and shook his head. With her sordid history and illegal occupation, Patton's leaving Max Bell for dead in the middle of Ann Arbor Road made twisted sense. She couldn't afford further contact with the police, not if she wanted to keep her children and life intact. Yet, her forthright statement in court about being a prostitute seemed to contradict that notion. The details about her character from Judson also pointed to the possibility she was telling the truth.

For now, Harper would write simply what he'd observed in the courtroom and sprinkle in a few quotes from Judson. But nothing about Max Bell's case seemed settled. The upcoming preliminary examination would shed additional light on the police case against Patton. Not all their cards would be laid on the table, just enough to prove probable cause and get it bound over to Wayne County Circuit Court.

Harper would keep digging until the hearing. While there were currently no leads on the killer or killers of Doc Reston and Lieutenant Snyder, he thought about the commonalities between the hit-and-run and the double murder.

The Plymouth Police Department. Detective Adams. Lieutenant Snyder. An alleged cover-up and an alleged frame job. As Harper took the exit from I-275 north to Ann Arbor Road, a shiver ran down his spine. What if the ties between the cases went beyond perceived commonalities and had a direct cause-and-effect relationship?

Chapter 18

TUESDAY, AUGUST 18

Under different circumstances, Harper would've written Patton's arraignment story when he returned to the office from his interview with Rita Judson. He'd have turned his attention to other stories and spent his Tuesday cranking out additional copy to help fill the *Independent*'s pages. It wasn't uncommon for him to write eight to ten articles per edition.

But everything had changed. Harper couldn't concern himself with quantity at this point; he had to get the hit-and-run story, and eventually, Doc's murder story, right. He had to be thorough and cover every angle.

Jackson's increase in story output would help. But he'd cut pages out of the *Independent* if he had to. The paper's only real obligation was to print enough pages to contain all the paid advertisements. Still, like his mentor, Harper preferred balanced newspaper pages where news stories held more prominence than advertisements. It meant the paper's last few editions might vary a bit in length, a thought he decided he could live with.

Harper was becoming less and less married to Doc's unwritten rules of newspaper publishing. That included doing some work from home instead of the office, something he knew Doc didn't do. He'd scrambled three jumbo eggs and was on a second cup of coffee when he sat down at his computer in his apartment's office.

The shape of the Buick LeSabre's window had bugged him the night before. He had tried to put it out of his mind as he had a casual dinner with Sophia at Leo's Coney Island. Even a make-out session with her hadn't pushed it completely away. Instead of doing research when he got home, when he was physically drained, he had decided to sleep on it. A fresh mind was less likely to make mistakes, he reasoned.

Harper finished the last bite of eggs as he typed "1999 Buick LeSabre" into Google and hit the return key. A link to Kelley Blue Book came back as the top result of the search. But he wasn't trying to determine the car's value.

He clicked on the images tab and a variety of pictures of the vehicle came up. Most showed the LeSabre's front end on an angle. Harper scrolled through the results and finally found a picture of its rear end.

The taillights were not arrayed with any kind of black stripe, as he had remembered from his brief glance at the car that hit Max Bell. More important, the rear window of the LeSabre was a rectangle, not an oval, as Harper had seen in the video from David Casey.

He right-clicked on the photo and downloaded it to his desktop. He'd pull a still shot from the party store video showing the oval window of what he still believed was a 1999 Ford Taurus and post it in his story next to the picture of the LeSabre's rear window.

It would be a bold move, essentially telling the world the Plymouth Police Department had fingered the wrong suspect. The evidence certainly seemed to point in that direction. Harper tried to think it through. He decided to play devil's advocate with his own suppositions.

The idea the cops had screwed up relied on his own memory of the hit-and-run. The taillights of the sedan that hit Max Bell were arrayed in a black bar above the bumper to the top of the trunk.

What if his memory was faulty? He had written enough police stories to know that witnesses' memories were often wrong because of the traumatic situations they were involved in. How was he any different? Could hubris be clouding his judgment?

Even the video from the Cap N Cork wasn't conclusive. It only picked up the silver sedan after it was through the intersection of Main Street and Arbor Road. So what if it had an oval rear window? It wasn't direct proof the vehicle had hit Max Bell.

The eggs Harper had downed seemed as if they might come back up. He pushed away from the desk, leaned back in his office chair and stared up at the ceiling. He closed his eyes and concentrated on his next move.

A minute of deep breathing later, Harper opened his eyes and reached for his phone on the desk. He dialed Neil Flaherty's office and asked if Connie, the chief's administrative assistant, could squeeze him in for a quick interview. She penciled him in for eleven thirty.

Harper showered, shaved and even tossed on a necktie for the occasion. It wasn't something he wore frequently, but he wanted to give the impression of being serious and professional. Some townies, including a fair number of those filling city hall offices, liked to refer to the *Independent* as the "local rag."

Whatever. They might think differently when he nailed the story.

NEIL FLAHERTY ROSE AND SHOOK HARPER'S HAND AT PRECISELY ELEVEN THIRTY. He then sat straight up in his leather chair, placed his elbows on its armrests and steepled his fingers together. It was a somber look even for the chief, whose usual demeanor was formal with a dash of stiff.

Harper decided to record the conversation and take notes. Paranoia deluxe. "This has to be a difficult time, Neil."

Flaherty waited a beat as if searching for just the right words. "Without question, Ray. Lieutenant Snyder was one of our very best officers. His presence will be sorely missed. Connie is working on a short bio right now that you're welcome to."

"Yes, thank you. As I'm sure you're aware, the medical examiner has ruled Rob's death a homicide. Can you comment on that finding?"

"It's just"—Flaherty paused—"it's just unbelievable. First that he's gone and secondly that foul play was involved."

"Any leads on your end?"

"I can't comment on what leads, if any, we may have," Flaherty said. "This is a very sensitive investigation."

"Have you asked the state police for help in the investigation?"

"We're handling this in-house."

"Isn't that going against your own procedures?"

Flaherty's facial expression showed a tinge of displeasure with the question. "Believe me when I tell you, no other agency is more motivated to solve this case than the Plymouth Police Department. To answer your question directly, we do often partner with the state police on internal investigations. But this isn't a disciplinary or misconduct matter. This is a homicide investigation of one of our own. While I'm not opposed to utilizing resources of other agencies if the need arises, we're going to be the lead on this investigation, one hundred percent."

Flaherty's forceful response might be a tell, Harper thought. If he was flustered at a routine question, Harper might be able to crack his Teflon veneer enough to see if there was anything to the conspiracy Snyder had floated. His heart kicked up a notch and he could feel his tongue thicken.

"I'd like to change gears," Harper said. "I met with Lieutenant Snyder last week. He had some serious misgivings about how the hit-and-run investigation of Max Bell was being conducted. One thing he mentioned was how quickly the accident scene was cleared. What is your response to that?"

"He was rather vocal with me about it, too," Flaherty said. "As you know, Detective Adams was on-scene. He has extensive experience with these kinds of cases, and he made a judgment call—the right call, in my opinion."

"What was to be gained by clearing the scene so quickly?"

Flaherty's hands dropped to his lap. "There simply wasn't a lot of physical evidence. We have limited resources and we felt they were better deployed elsewhere."

"Trying to locate the driver?"

"Yes. And it paid dividends."

"Patton's neighbor called her in. I don't see—"

"I don't mind telling you we were well on her trail and would've apprehended her without that phone call," Flaherty said. "You'll hear more about it at her preliminary examination."

Harper shifted in his chair, calibrating his next few questions. For his part, Flaherty looked somber and in control. The momentary flash of anger at his earlier question was gone. If he was lying about the hit-and-run investigation, he was doing a hell of a sell job.

"In my interview with him," Harper said, leaning forward and raising his voice, "Snyder went on to imply that you and Adams were covering something up, perhaps the identity of the driver."

Flaherty starred at Harper. He swiveled the leather chair to his right and reached over to a Sony stereo system. He clicked a button and jazz started playing softly.

"That's nonsense. You'd best think twice about printing something like that, Ray."

The not-so-veiled threat told Harper that he'd hit a nerve. He decided to pursue it further with additional questions.

"You know me better than that," Harper said. "I'm not going to print speculation, even if it was from one of your guys. Henry wouldn't have and I'm not going to, either. But you've got to admit, the optics of this don't look very good. Snyder was murdered along with my boss—"

"I don't give a damn about the optics," Flaherty said, matching's Harper's elevated voice. "Do you have any other questions?"

Harper straightened up and threw his shoulders back. "As a matter of fact, yes. You saw the video of the silver sedan we published last week, right?"

Flaherty gave a slight nod.

"You might have also noticed that that vehicle had an oval-shaped rear window," Harper said. "The vehicle owned by Lisa Ann Patton is a Buick LeSabre. It has a rectangular rear window. How do you account for that?"

Flaherty stood, his face flushed crimson. "If you think your half-assed sleuthing is better than our professional investigation, I can't stop you from printing it. But I'm not going to dignify that line of questioning. We're done here. I've got to tell you, this pisses me off. I've always been straight with you, and I've always gone out of my way to make sure you get the scoop first."

"And I've reciprocated," Harper said, "by reporting fairly and accurately. That's all I'm supposed to do. I'm not here to be your public relations flack. My duty is to the people of this community. If that pisses you off, well, I can't help that. That's your problem. I've got to tell you, Chief, it sure feels like you're deflecting here."

"Out of my office," Flaherty barked. "Now."

Chapter 19

TUESDAY, August 18

Sunshine momentarily blinded Harper as he walked away from the police station. He felt the warmth on his face and stretched as if he were a flower aiming itself at the sun. Rather than move the Honda, he decided to take the five-minute walk to the Penniman Deli, which sat across the street from Doc's loft.

His stride was slow despite hunger pangs that gnawed at his stomach. He walked between the Gathering, a covered portion of the lot that doubled as a farmer's market on weekends, and the Penn Theatre, a single-screen relic that celebrated movies from bygone eras, with murals of *Gone with the Wind*, *The Wizard of Oz* and *Star Wars* on a side wall.

Harper glanced across from the Penn to Kellogg Park, a village green that hosted everything from a fall festival to an ice-carving spectacular each January. It was alive with a lunchtime Music in the Park concert, aimed at pleasing people sitting in lawn chairs and moms with baby strollers.

He crossed Main Street, passed a fudge shop on the corner and was at the deli a few moments later. When he opened its old time screen door, his senses were immediately attacked with the smell of pastrami, corned beef, fresh baked bread, chicken soup and spicy chili. Black and white pictures showed the deli from decades ago, with men in white paper hats and aprons slicing lunch meat, working behind the counter and taking time out to mug for the camera with suit-wearing patrons.

Harper grabbed a red tray from the stack and made his way to the self-serve soup bar. He found white bean chicken chili and heaped it into a large bowl. He then got in line at the counter, where the owner was taking sandwich orders.

"What are you having today, Ray?" asked Russ, the deli's owner for the past twenty years. "Just pulled some fresh Italian bread from the oven if you're leaning that way."

"I'm going to go with something a little lighter," Harper said. "You make a mean veggie pita, Russ."

"One veggie pita. Anything else? You gonna buy something for young Scoop Jackson over there?"

"She can fend for herself."

"Now, what kind of boss is that?" Russ said with a smirk on his bearded face. "You're a real cheapskate."

"Trying to guilt your customer into a larger order, I get it."

Russ smiled and called the order back to a teenage sandwich slinger. The pita was completed and wrapped by the time Harper made it to the cash register. He took his tray and headed to an outside seating area. He parked at a two-seat table, a pair of businesswomen sitting behind him and two middle-aged men in front of him.

Harper took two enormous bites of the veggie pita and then dove into the chili. The rest of the world disappeared for a few minutes as he satiated his hunger. He broke the spell with a long drink of icy cold water. He sat the glass down and one of the middle-aged men, an African-American with short gray dreadlocks, nodded at him.

Harper returned the nod and tried to figure out whether he knew the man from somewhere. Gray dreadlocks' lunch partner, a broad-shouldered man with a mop-top and a mustache bushy enough to hide small children in, turned and smiled.

"Hell of a nice day, wouldn't you say?"

"Yeah, sure is," Harper said. "I'm sorry, do I know you gentlemen?"

Bushy mustache glanced back at gray dreadlocks and shrugged his overdeveloped shoulders. "Wait a minute, wait a minute," gray dreadlocks said. "I've seen you on Plymouth cable TV. You're that reporter from the newspaper. Hunter, Hartman—"

"Harper. Ray Harper from the *Plymouth Independent*."

The African-American man stood and took a step toward Harper. He extended his hand.

"That's right, I remember now," he said. "Well, it's not every day you get to meet a local celebrity."

He nudged bushy mustache's arm. "This is my hubby, Barney, and I'm Patrick. We read your stories every week, Mr. Harper. I'm a big fan. We were so sorry to hear about the tragic passing of your publisher, Mr. Reston. Isn't that right, honey?"

"Oh, it sure is," Barney said. "That man had a real set of balls, I tell you. Never seen anyone fight city hall the way old Henry did. Am I right?"

Harper's appetite suddenly vanished. He had never encountered newspaper groupies and wasn't quite sure how to act.

"Nice to meet you, fellas," he said. "And yes, my boss was a great journalist. I've got big shoes to fill—well, at least for a few weeks."

"A few weeks?" Patrick asked.

"Unfortunately, the newspaper will be shutting down at the end of September."

"Well, shit," Barney said, tossing a white cloth napkin down on the table. "Where are we going to get our local news?"

Patrick put his hands over his mouth and his eyes opened wide as if he had just heard his mother died. "No, no, no. There has got to be something we can do to stop this. Barney, pull out your checkbook. Is money the problem, Mr. Harper?"

"No, it's not the reason we're closing," Harper said.

"What then?" Patrick asked.

"Mr. Reston's daughter inherited the paper," Harper said. "She lives out of state and doesn't want to keep the paper going. Journalism isn't her thing."

"That right there is a damn shame," Barney said. "You just don't find quality local journalism like back in the day. Am I right?"

"Unfortunately, yes, you are right," Harper said. "Too many small papers were bought by giant hedge funds that don't care about anything but profit."

"I've heard that many states have 'news deserts,' towns that get little or no coverage at all," Barney said. "That true?"

Harper nodded. "Listen, gentlemen, it was nice to meet you both," he said. "But I really should be getting back to work."

Patrick shook Harper's hand for a second time. He extended the gesture by placing his other hand over Harper's.

"We're real damn sorry to hear this," Barney said, and slapped him on the shoulder. "You're a good reporter, son. You'll land on your feet somewhere. You have a real flair for writing."

Chapter 20

WEDNESDAY, August 19

The old neighborhood was changing. Like Plymouth, Harper's hometown of Royal Oak was transforming from its blue-collar roots to an upscale community filled with oversized homes, underutilized by small families.

His parents had lived at the end of Houstonia Avenue their entire twenty-nine-year marriage. The ranch-style home was substantially less than two thousand square feet, a mark being doubled by a two-story giant under construction next door. Both homes had a nice view of the Red Run Golf Club, but that's where the similarities ended.

Still, even with all the changes, the neighborhood was a sight for Harper's sore eyes. So much had happened in the two weeks since he had last visited his parents.

After making the thirty-minute drive from Plymouth east across I-696, Harper was ready to stretch his legs. He parked in front of the house under a maple tree he had climbed too many times to count as a kid. The interior door was open and the screen door unlocked. Harper announced himself before stepping inside.

NBC's Lester Holt belted out the latest breaking news from his father's television. John Harper was transfixed to the point of not even acknowledging his son's presence.

Stepping quickly past the television, Ray made his way to the kitchen and was hit by the smell of a beef roast. His mother stood at the stove, whipping mashed potatoes.

"Your timing is perfect as usual," Ruth Harper said. An apron covered her white blouse and extended past her waist. "Dinner will be ready in a couple of minutes."

Ray put his hand up to his ear. "What's that, Ma? I can't hear you."

She slapped him on the shoulder. "You know your father's hearing isn't what it used to be. Now, hush with that nonsense and give me a smooch."

He complied and then gave her a firm hug, too. Also as instructed, he set the dinner table with plates, utensils, napkins, and water and wine glasses. Five minutes later, Ruth turned the news off and the three of them sat down to eat.

"I've got to tell you, I'm more than a little concerned about your safety," John said, passing a bowl of peas to Ray. "Henry and that cop being murdered at your office? I read your latest story this morning. You honestly think the police chief is lying about the car in that hit-and-run?"

Ray savored a piece of roast before answering. "That's where the facts seem to be leading. He tossed me out of his office yesterday for even suggesting it."

"Do you think it's wise to keep pursuing this?" Ruth asked. "No story is worth risking your life."

"I'm a big boy," Ray said, "and 'risking my life' is probably a stretch."

"Wasn't a stretch for Henry," John said.

"This story is exactly why I went into journalism. The people paying Neil Flaherty's salary deserve the truth, especially if he's trying to cover something up."

"Well, what are the police doing to solve the murders?" Ruth asked.

"I haven't really learned anything new since going to Detroit for the autopsies. They stopped being cooperative even before my dustup with the chief."

"That's got to make you even more suspicious, doesn't it?" John said. "I mean, you've had a good working relationship with the cops up until now, right?"

"Yeah, pretty straightforward. I generally get what I ask for, even with ongoing investigations. They trusted my discretion—"

"Until it didn't suit their purposes," Ruth interrupted.

Ray set his fork down. "Exactly right. Good observation."

"So, how are you going to get to the bottom of this?" John asked. "I don't mind admitting I'm biased. But I think you're a damn good reporter. Better than some of those pretty faces I see on the local news."

Ruth glared at her husband. "Language."

"Oh, lighten up, Ma," Ray said. "It's not like I haven't heard or said worse. As for you, sir, are you saying my mug ain't pretty? I look just like you—well, twenty-seven years ago."

"Poor bastard," John said.

Ruth tried hard not to smile but then broke into laughter. The two Harper men followed suit.

Still smiling, Ray finished his roast and then pushed his plate away. "I dunno how I'm going to get to the bottom of it, to answer your question. But I'm not backing down. I can't.

"I've got to admit, I never saw myself sticking around a tiny paper like the *Independent* this long. When Henry hired me, I thought a year, maybe eighteen months, tops. Then it would be off to a daily somewhere. I had hoped to be working at the *Free Press* or *Detroit News* by now."

"I never understood why the *Tribune* wouldn't hire you," John said.

"As much as I love you guys, if I'm honest, I wanted to get away from Royal Oak. I never applied there."

"Why?" Ruth said.

"A man needs to spread his wings," John said.

"It's a cliché, but it's true," Ray said. "I also didn't want any blowback from one of my stories to fall on you guys."

Ruth poured herself a second glass of red wine. "I wish you would have told us that five years ago. First of all, your father and I can take care of ourselves. We don't give a shit—pardon my French—about what people say. Secondly, I think you'd be farther ahead in your career if you had started off at the *Tribune*. Daily papers like to hire reporters from other dailies, isn't that what you always said in college?"

Ray nodded and stared down at his hands resting on the white tablecloth. "I did. Nothing I can do about it now."

"Well, there's something you can do right now, and that's come back and stay with us until this whole thing blows over," John said. "I mean it. I don't like you in that tiny apartment by yourself. You're a sitting duck."

Ruth buttressed his argument without even saying a word. Ray knew the look. It was the same one he'd seen periodically growing up, the old don't-argue-with-me-because-I-brought-you-into-the-world-and-I-can-take-you-out-whenver-I-want look.

"No way," Ray said. "Why would you even ask me that? As the two of you have pointed out, the people I'm writing about are dangerous."

John raised his right hand and made a "stop" gesture like a school crossing guard. "Follow me."

He led his son down a hallway leading to the master bedroom. Once inside, John walked around a king-sized bed to his nightstand and stuck his index finger on the left side of a black box that read "SentrySafe" in bold block lettering on top.

An instant later, the lid of the box opened, and he pulled out a handgun. Ray recognized it as a Glock nine-millimeter.

"For any unwanted guests," John said. "And I'm a damn good shot. Ask anyone over at Target Sports."

"Since when do you own a gun, let alone know how to use one?" Ray asked.

"Since all these houses started getting torn down and rebuilt. You should see some of the men working on these crews. They look like hoodlums. We didn't feel safe, so I did something about it."

"The answer is still no, Dad. I'm not moving home."

His father returned the gun to the safe and then brushed by him. Looking over his shoulder, he said, "I thought I raised you better than to be a damn fool."

Ray's face flushed. Funny how a few words could ruin a nice evening. He helped his mother clear the dinner dishes. When they finished, he gave her a final hug.

"I gotta go, Ma, busy day tomorrow."

"You think about what we said, Raymond."

She was the only person on the planet he allowed to use his full name without protest. He nodded, but they both knew it wouldn't happen.

"See ya, Dad."

John Harper, who had returned to his favorite end of the couch to watch more television, said nothing.

Chapter 21

THURSDAY, AUGUST 20

The ornate furnishings of the Stafford Funeral Home pissed Harper off. It started with the marble fireplace behind the reception desk and the red and gold wallpaper draping the lobby and ended with the vases of fresh, bright flowers that sat on pedestals near the entrance of all four funeral parlors. It was like visiting the mansion of a Hallmark movie billionaire.

Everything was strictly for show, a lame attempt at consoling the grieving. His anger wasn't aimed directly at the Stafford family. It was just the nature of the business that didn't sit well with Harper. The feelings, he knew, traced back to his grandfather's passing when he was ten.

Everyone had been wearing their best suits and dresses, milling around a place just like Stafford. All he'd wanted to do was scream at them. How could they smile? How could they tell stories about Grandpa and laugh? The man who had taught him how to catch a baseball, the man who had read stories to him at nap time, the man who had made the best sausage biscuits for breakfast, was gone and there was nothing he could do about it.

Henry Reston was in parlor three, according to the receptionist. Harper exited the lobby and walked through a wood-paneled hallway to the back of the funeral home. He signed the guest registry and then stood at the doorway to the parlor.

He spotted Victoria Reston-Coble standing near Doc's closed casket as he walked in. She was talking with three women who appeared to be close to her age. He was surprised to see her smiling.

Perhaps the week since her father's murder had given her a trace of perspective or somehow enough time to accept it. Then again, she could just have been putting on a brave face. Despite the numerous funerals he had attended since his grandpa's passing all those years ago, he'd never developed one.

Sadie Rodgers and Neil Flaherty were talking up dignitaries from Wayne County on the opposite side of the room from Victoria. The parlor was nearly full. Harper estimated more than a hundred people were in the room.

"Are you going to mingle or just stand there?" Emily Jackson asked, coming up from behind.

"Yeah, I just hate funerals."

"Why is that?"

"What do you mean 'why'? You like 'em?"

"You're just looking at it the wrong way."

"How's that?"

"Funerals aren't for the dead," Jackson said. "They're for the living. This is a celebration of Henry's life."

"Yeah, I've heard that before," Harper said. "It's trite bullshit. Funerals are endings. I'll never be able to talk to Doc again. I'm never going to hear another war story about his days as a reporter. There's no upside to this. None."

"Sorry you feel that way."

"How can you not? We don't even know who killed him or why, at least not for sure," Harper said. He pointed in the direction of Flaherty. "He had something to do with it. I know he—"

"You're in a bad place right now, I get it," Jackson said. "But I'm not listening to this, not today."

She left him standing there, went to Victoria and hugged her. A funeral parlor employee announced that the service would begin in five minutes. The first two rows of seats were reserved for Doc's family and closest friends. Harper chose a seat at the end of the second row nearest the door. He wanted a quick escape route if his emotions started getting the better of him.

At Victoria's request, there were no flowers around Doc's casket. She had asked for donations to Gift of Life Michigan, an organ and tissue donation nonprofit. Harper's eyes settled on a blown-up picture of Doc. It depicted a much younger Henry Reston, a notepad in his left hand and a pen in his right. He was gesturing with the pen, almost like a maestro conducting an orchestra. With a host of other reporters around him, it looked to be a press conference, with Doc no doubt firing a question at some official standing at a podium.

From the hairstyles and dress, Harper guessed the shot was from the early to mid-1980s. Doc's hair was long, and he sported a thick mustache. The goatee he wore as an older man hadn't made its appearance. He wasn't sure why Victoria had chosen the shot to enlarge but was glad she had. It was pure Henry.

The service started. Doc hadn't been a regular churchgoer. Still, he was well-known and liked by the local clergy. The lead pastor of a large Plymouth nondenominational church began the eulogy by reading the twenty-third psalm. After a thirty-minute talk that tied Doc's personal and professional accomplishments together with scripture, the rows of mourners were ushered to his casket to pay their final respects.

Harper couldn't bring himself to join the line. Tears welled in his eyes. He silently vowed to double down on his efforts to get at the truth of Doc's death. It didn't matter what roadblocks were thrown in his way or how many threats he received. He would keep pushing until the job was done.

Chapter 22

THURSDAY, AUGUST 20–Friday, August 21

After years in the news business, the human side of crime stories rarely entered Harper's thoughts. Get the details of the incident, at least as much as the cops would give you; get the upcoming court dates for the suspect(s) and their criminal history; churn a story out and move on. If he bothered to follow up and attend a court hearing, he'd quote the victim's friends and family and might feel a twinge of empathy. But that's about as far as his involvement in the story extended.

If he'd written, "John Smith showed no emotion at the hearing," once, he'd written it at least fifty times. The hit-and-run death of Max Bell wasn't just another story. Yes, he realized it could help his career. But unlike with all those other crime stories, he cared about justice being done.

And he thought about the Bell family. How were they coping with their son's death? Was it even possible for them to move on at this point? After Doc's funeral, Harper sat at the Kellogg Park fountain for the better part of an hour thinking about his mentor and about the Bell family. While honoring Doc's memory by keeping the *Independent* alive for at least a few more weeks, he wanted to do something for the Bells, too, to somehow ease their pain.

Telling their story might be a start. Harper stepped away from the fountain and walked a few feet to an oak tree. Leaning his back against its trunk, he pulled his cell phone from his rear pocket and dialed Jake Bell's number. It went straight to voicemail and Harper left a message.

"Mr. Bell, this is Ray Harper calling from the *Independent* newspaper," he said, trying not to sound nervous. He wiped cold sweat from his free hand on his suit pants and continued. "I'm sorry to bother you, sir. But I wondered if I might be able to interview you and your wife about where the investigation in Max's death is, and also find out how you all are doing."

He ended the call by leaving his contact information, even though he knew Bell's cell phone would show his phone number. Old habits. Much to his surprise, Bell called back in less than five minutes.

"Actually, I've been meaning to call you," Bell said. "Cindy and I want to keep Max's story alive. We thought someone might see the story and remember something that could help the police."

"I know talking about it is going to be difficult," Harper said. "But I think it's an excellent idea. I want to do everything I can to help."

At ten a.m. Friday, Harper pulled into the Bells' driveway. Mr. Bigfoot's home didn't disappoint. While the lot it sat on couldn't rightly be called postage stamp sized, more than half of it was covered by a brown brick fortress. Its roof had multiple peaks with dormers for what were likely cavernous bedrooms.

To the Bells' credit, the home's exterior wasn't landscaped to excess. Hydrangea bushes dominated a large bean-shaped bed in the front. It sat adjacent to a stone walkway that led to steps and the front door. Harper, with notepads, camera and a fully charged phone in hand, rang the doorbell.

Jake Bell answered the door about thirty seconds later. He appeared to be in his midforties; his hair was fashionably gray, his skin a light shade of olive, and he sported salt-and-pepper stubble. He led Harper to a seating area in an open-concept main floor.

Cindy Bell sat on a leather sofa with a glass of lemonade at her side. Her dark brown hair was pulled away from a face that was taut and angular. Harper noted she was in extraordinary physical condition.

"Can I get you something cold to drink, Mr. Harper?" Cindy Bell said.

"Bottled water would be great, thank you."

Jake Bell sat in the middle of the sofa next to his wife's spot. Harper wondered if Sammy Bell was around and would take part in the interview but wasn't going to ask. He was a kid who'd witnessed his brother's death. He didn't need any more trauma.

Harper took an oversized, matching leather chair next to the sofa. He sat erect and pulled a set of questions away from the steno pad he'd flipped open. Harper didn't often write out questions in advance as he had done routinely out of journalism school. His brain was always working on the next question as his subject was answering the previous one. Cindy Bell sat the bottled water on a small, circular drink table that was placed between the chair and couch.

"Thank you both for agreeing to be interviewed," Harper said. "I can't imagine the pain you're going through."

The Bells nodded in unison. "Where would you like to start?" Cindy asked, leaning forward with her arms tucked tightly across her chest. Despite the warmth of the August day, she wore a long-sleeved, navy blue cotton sweater. Likewise, Jake Bell sported a long-sleeved light blue T-shirt that looked like late spring boating attire.

"As you know, we've written pretty extensively about the incident itself," Harper said. "I'd like to focus more on what your day-to-day lives are like right now, how you're coping with the loss of Max and where you all go from here. I also want the readers to get a sense of who Max was beyond the budding football star. Jake, at the press conference, you said Max was always one hundred percent all in no matter what he was doing. Was he like that as a little boy?"

It didn't take him long to formulate an answer. "Oh, yes, absolutely. When he turned six, we bought him a Lego *Star Wars* kit," Jake Bell said, his right arm resting on the cushion behind his wife. He smiled at the memory. "It took him a few days, but he built an X-wing fighter all by himself. He'd just look at the pictures in the instruction book and do it. It was amazing."

"Max fell in love with everything Lego," Cindy added. "In six months, he had several bins filled with nothing but Lego pieces. He'd hunt through those bins all day to find the right pieces. He made ships, cars, houses, and cartoon characters, all from his imagination. It was the darnedest thing you've ever seen."

Harper's posture loosened and he took a sip of water before his next question. "What interests did Max have beyond Legos?"

"He was never much for video games, thank goodness," Cindy said. "When he got a few years older, he'd have some of his friends from the neighborhood over and they would play Avengers."

"Which hero was Max?"

"He took turns being all of them," Jake said. "I think Iron Man was his favorite. He thought Tony Stark was cool with all of his tech gadgets."

"What about sports?" Harper asked. "When did that start?"

"Relatively late," Jake said. "He really didn't become interested until he turned ten. That's when we signed him up for the Steelers."

Modeled after the black-and-gold-clad professional team from Pittsburgh, the Plymouth-Canton Steelers played in the area youth football travel league.

"Did Max start off playing quarterback?"

"No," Jake said. "He was big for his age, so they had him on both lines. I believe he was in seventh grade before he started playing QB."

"So, he progressed really rapidly?"

"Max had a great arm," Cindy said, "and the position just came naturally to him, yes."

Harper checked his iPhone on the coffee table in front of the Bells to see if it was still recording. Reassured by the recording app's detection of sound waves, he pressed on. "It's obvious you both were very involved in Max's life. Does any of this seem real? I mean, that it's even possible he could be gone?"

The light went out of Jake Bell's eyes as he rubbed the stubble on both sides of his face. Cindy Bell reached for her lemonade, took a sip and then shook her head no.

"He wasn't like most teenagers," she said. "Sure, he could do dumb things and be moody at times. But our son was wise beyond his years. He knew football was just a tool that could help get where he wanted to go."

"Which was where?" Harper asked.

"He wanted to be a physical therapist," Jake said. "Max loved older people, to listen to their stories of how things used to be. It bothered him to see them in physical pain or have difficulty walking. He wanted to work with them, help them the best way that he could."

"That's remarkable," Harper said. "Most kids his age don't think in those terms."

"I'm a high school teacher in the Livonia district," Cindy said. "I'm one hundred percent biased, of course, but you're absolutely right, Mr. Harper. In thirteen years at Stevenson High School, I can count the number of kids like Max I've encountered on one hand."

"Please, call me Ray," he said. "Have either of you gone back to work?"

Cindy explained that classes started the following week and that she did plan to work. Jake said that he'd visited a few work sites around Plymouth and some of the other suburban Detroit locations.

"My head isn't there," he said. "I can't focus for more than about twenty minutes. I'm going to back away for a while."

"Classes are going to be tough, especially with football about to start," Cindy said. "Plymouth and Livonia are rivals. My students, the guys, liked to tease me about sacking Max or intercepting one of his passes."

"I understand," Harper said. "Have you all received support from your coworkers and friends?"

"I would have lost my mind without them," Jake said. "My brother works with me and helps run the business. I've leaned on him a lot, and our close friends from NorthRidge Church."

"I'm glad to hear that," Harper said.

"Sadie Rodgers has been great, too," Cindy said. "She lives next door. She was with us when Max passed."

That was news to Harper. His mind skipped back to his thoughts of commonalities between the hit-and-run and Doc Reston's murder. The Plymouth Police Department had been the biggest link between the two. Now Plymouth's mayor was also connected, even if it was in the benign role of friend to the victim.

Perhaps his mind was working too hard to link the two events when in reality there was no connection. Harper's heart sped up and he took a couple of long pulls from the bottled water, trying to regain his composure.

"Did Sadie offer insight into the police investigation before they arrested Lisa Ann Patton?" Harper asked.

"Between her and Chief Flaherty, I think they kept us in the loop as much as possible," Cindy said. "We knew the minute they had that Patton woman in custody."

"Jake, when we talked on the phone, you said you wanted to keep Max's story alive as a means of helping the police," Harper said. "Does that mean you're not convinced Patton was the one behind the wheel?"

"I was until I read your story Wednesday," Jake said. "Now I'm not so sure. The video you posted clearly showed the car had an oval rear window."

"It's possible that wasn't the vehicle that hit Max," Harper said.

"Why else would the driver have been speeding away and changing lanes so wildly?" Jake said.

"I can't explain it with any certainty," Harper said. "Cindy, what about you? Do you think the police arrested the right person?"

"She's a hooker," Cindy said, a look of fury and sadness etching her face. "I don't believe a word she says. But Jake and I looked at the video a hundred times. I'm just not sure, honestly. Why would the police charge her if there were any doubts? That's what I don't understand."

Harper scooted forward in his chair. "The department is under a lot of pressure," he said. "Your name carries a lot of clout in this town. Max's status as one of the biggest college football recruits in the country has also brought a lot of attention to the case."

"So, you think the spotlight made the cops cut corners?" Jake asked. "What about her neighbor turning her in? The damage to her car seemed to match what happened in the accident."

Harper shrugged. "As I said, I don't have all the answers. I'm going to keep investigating until I do."

Harper turned the recording app on his phone off. He had the Bells pose for pictures. Remaining seated on the couch, Cindy held an eight-by-ten portrait of Max in her hands and close to her chest. Jake got behind the couch and wrapped his arms around her shoulders. The look of devastation on the couple's faces was undeniable. Harper wondered if it would ever go away, if they'd ever recover.

He showed them the dozen frames he had shot and allowed the Bells to pick the one that would accompany the story.

Chapter 23

FRIDAY, August 21

After grabbing lunch from Taco Bell, Harper wanted to see the car that allegedly hit and killed Max Bell. Perhaps examining it from hood to bumper would jog his memory and confirm his theory. Then again, it could prove the police had it right. Either way, he wanted to gain clarity on the issue.

The Buick LeSabre was sitting in the lot of Keystone Auto Service, which had held Plymouth's towing contract for a decade. The business provided auto repair and towing services while also acting as a junkyard. Keystone sat on the city's far west side, adjacent to a massive landfill.

Harper exited Five Mile Road and pulled the Honda into a parking lot in front of a small office. A large mustard-colored rectangular sign trimmed in red hung above the office's door. keystone was written in oversized block capital letters at the top of the sign using the same shade of red.

As he got out of the car, Harper could hear barking dogs from a nearby Michigan Humane Society facility. When he was seven, Harper's family had adopted Charlie, a bichon, from the animal shelter. Charlie had seen him all the way through high school before cancer took his life weeks before Harper started college classes.

A seven-foot-tall fence with barbed wire at the top stood behind the office. It went back a few hundred yards and was screened on all sides, shielding operations from public view. A large six-bay repair shop sat west of the fenced junkyard. Pushing thoughts of Charlie aside, Harper could see the top of several piles of crushed cars toward the middle of the yard despite the fencing.

Keystone's front door was propped open. A man appearing to be in his midthirties, tall, with a military-style haircut and muscular build, stood at a counter writing on what appeared to be a form. Harper walked in with a steno pad and pen in his left hand and a business card in the other. He slid the card in the man's direction on the counter.

"Good morning. Ray Harper from the *Independent* newspaper."

"What can I do for you?" the man said.

"Are you the owner?"

"Nathan Glynn," he said. Glynn reached for Harper's hand and shook it without much conviction, despite his imposing physique.

"I've reported extensively about a hit-and-run accident that killed a Plymouth boy," Harper said. "I'm told the vehicle is here. I was wondering if I could look at it and snap a few pictures?"

Glynn set his pen down on the form. "Do you have written authorization from the cops, Mr. Harper?"

"No, but—"

"Then I can't help you," Glynn said. His tone was gruff and cold. "I'm busy right now."

"I only need a few minutes of your time," Harper said. "Just point me in the right direction and I'll be out of your hair."

A Keystone flatbed tow truck with a mangled Ford Explorer on its back like a wounded soldier pulled into the parking lot. Glynn turned his attention from Harper to the truck. He pressed a green button mounted in a box about the size of an electrical outlet, and a gated portion of the fence receded enough for the tow truck to pass. The Explorer was apparently dead on arrival.

"Hang on a minute," Glynn said, turning back to Harper. "I'll give the cops a call. It makes no difference to me if you see the car. But I'm not gonna piss them off on your account. If they say no, it's no."

"Got it," Harper said. "Thanks."

Glynn walked into a small office and closed the door behind him. Several minutes ticked by, and while Harper couldn't make out every word from Glynn's conversation, it sounded as if it was getting heated as the volume of the shop owner's voice rose on numerous occasions. Five more minutes passed before Glynn emerged from the office.

"No dice, pal," he said. "They told me to tell you, 'It's an ongoing investigation.'"

"The cops have already disclosed that the vehicle is a Buick LeSabre," Harper said. "What possible harm can I cause by snapping a few pictures of it?"

"They don't pay me to make decisions," Glynn said.

Frustrated, Harper turned to leave. Before reaching the door, he glanced back. "Were you threatened, Mr. Glynn?"

"Excuse me?" Glynn said, looking up once again from his paperwork. "Why in the hell would you ask me that?"

"Why? Because every step along the way, the cops' story doesn't add up."

"Why should I care?" Glynn said. "I don't know what crusade you're on, pal, but I got a business to run and you're wasting my time."

"If everything is so routine," Harper said, "why were you yelling into your phone a minute ago? My guess is, they're putting heat on you to stay quiet. What are they holding over your head, Glynn? The towing contract?"

The muscles in Nathan Glynn's jaw clenched. He looked around the office as if someone might be listening. "Listen, pal, I've got nothing to gain by talking to you and a whole lot to lose."

"There's where you're wrong," Harper said. He sat his notepad and camera on the counter before continuing. "They only have power in the dark. If you help me expose what's really going on, everything is brought into the light. The cops will not be able to make a move against you."

Glynn audibly exhaled. "I can't have my name in your article. I don't give a shit what you say."

Harper waited a beat before responding. At times, he could reassure a reluctant interviewee by talking about his experience as a reporter and promising their comments would be either fairly or positively portrayed in his article. It was often enough to get them to talk.

Glynn's reticence was different. It wasn't nerves or modesty keeping him from talking, it was fear. Despite the man's gruffness and drill-sergeant build, he was genuinely scared. It left Harper only one real option.

"What if we went off the record?"

"Off the what?" Glynn said. "Give it to me plain, pal, or beat it."

"'Off the record' means I don't quote you in the article and I don't attribute—"

Glynn smiled. "You think they ain't going to know where it's coming from just because my name isn't on it?"

"Let me finish," Harper said. "The information you give me will be on background. It means I'll find a way to get it into the record in a different way that doesn't involve you. Any pictures I take of the car don't get published. Now, what do you say?"

"The answer is, yes, I was threatened," Glynn said after what seemed like an eternity.

"On the phone just now?" Harper asked.

"When the Plymouth cops brought that car in, that little fireplug of a detective took me to my office, closed the door—"

"Detective Adams?"

"Yes."

"What happened?"

"Adams made it clear to me that he and his boss would use their influence around the county to get my other municipal contracts canceled."

"If you did or didn't do what?" Harper asked.

"Crush the LeSabre immediately and dispose of the scrap."

Glynn's statement hung there like a dark summer cloud ready to spew bolts of lightning. Without trying, he had confirmed the vehicle was a Buick and not the Ford Taurus Harper had been so sure about.

"How did you react?"

Glynn grabbed a bottled water from a small fridge beneath the junkyard gate open and close buttons. He took a long pull from the bottle, wiped his mouth with the back of his hand and shrugged his shoulders. "That wasn't the only threat."

"Did he threaten you physically?"

"Not me, my family," Glynn said. "Adams pulled a tiny notepad from his shirt pocket and then read out my address, described my son, my daughter and my wife."

"Are you kidding me?"

Glynn shook his head. "At that point, I said I'd do whatever he wanted me to."

"What I don't get is, why?" Harper said. It was a lie. He knew Flaherty wanted the evidence to disappear because it was fraudulent. He wanted Glynn to confirm his theory without influencing what he might say.

"You'd have to ask them. I've got no idea why they'd threaten my business and my family over an old beat-up car."

"Did you end up crushing the car that night?"

Glynn finished the water before answering. "The next morning. I was rattled by what happened with the detective. I went and had a few drinks to calm my nerves."

The last few minutes of conversation had been exactly the reason Harper hated going off the record. The information from Glynn would blow Flaherty and Adams out of the water. But he couldn't use it, at least not directly. He'd have to figure out a different way to get it on the record, one that didn't endanger Glynn or his family.

"What happened to the scrap metal from the Buick?" Harper asked.

"I have a contract with a shop on McNichols in Detroit," Glynn said. "They buy all my scrap."

Harper thanked him for his time and honesty. "I don't want you to worry about any of this showing up in my newspaper," he said. "You have my word."

Glynn held has hand out and, this time, shook Harper's hand firmly. "Your word better be good," Glynn said. "If it isn't and something happens to my family, I'll come after you, and it won't be to have another conversation."

Harper knew the man meant what he said, but the threat didn't faze him. It felt like there were still questions that needed to be asked, that Glynn was holding out on him. Harper made a mental note to circle back and ask them.

Chapter 24

MONDAY, AUGUST 24

As he sat in Darwin L. Burke's courtroom, Harper's thoughts bounced between his current assignment and his most recent date with Sophia. He'd texted her Sunday to say how much he enjoyed hanging out and hoped they could get together again soon. Sophia had replied with two thumbs-up emojis, told him he could pick the next restaurant and that she would be buying.

Harper hoped his luck would hold out through Lisa Ann Patton's preliminary examination. He was curious to see how much of its case the prosecutor's office would present and what, if any, defense Patton's attorney would mount. Short of a total whiff by the prosecutor, the case would be bound over for trial at the Wayne County Circuit Court in Detroit.

He sat in the first row behind the accused. Jake Bell was seated across the aisle to his right, his head locked in the direction of Patton. Rita Judson sat a row behind Bell, and Harper spotted Plymouth Detective Adams standing in the back of the courtroom. Since there was no jury for a preliminary examination, television news cameramen had set up in the jury box, a perfect spot to capture all the key players in the hearing.

Besides giving his statement to the police, Harper hadn't heard from either the prosecutor or defense attorney. Not that he relished the idea of testifying, but the fact that he hadn't even been deposed surprised him. He debated going to the defense attorney on his own.

The video he'd obtained from David Casey had sent Harper down a different investigative path than the official police version of events. It had started with the discovery of an oval rear window and was currently boiling with the revelations from Nathan Glynn a few days earlier.

While Harper still couldn't prove a Ford Taurus had hit Max Bell, he could cast reasonable doubt on the cops' case. Reasonable doubt was all Patton's attorney would need to win an acquittal at the circuit court trial.

Bringing such evidence forward meant Harper would have to bow out of coverage of the hearing and the circuit court trial. Perhaps Doc Reston had been right all along. Emily Jackson should've taken the story from the start. Harper cleared his throat, stood and leaned against the bar.

"Excuse me," he said. "Excuse me, Mr. Rosenthal?"

The defense attorney turned in his chair and Harper handed him a business card. Rosenthal glanced quickly at the card and stuffed it in a suit jacket interior pocket.

"We can talk after the hearing," he said. "I'm a little busy right now if you hadn't noticed."

"I'm the guy that rushed to Max Bell at the intersection," Harper said. "I've also been investigating and writing about the incident for the paper. I think I have evidence you need to hear about."

Rosenthal glanced at his watch. "We've got five minutes before the hearing starts. You better make it quick."

Harper gave him a condensed version of events. Rosenthal scratched at his closely cropped beard.

"Would've been nice if you brought this to my attention before game time," he said.

"Sorry. I thought for sure you would call me in for a deposition."

Burke walked into the courtroom and everyone stood. After acknowledging the judge, Rosenthal turned back to Harper.

"Do you have the thumb drive with you?"

"Yes."

"Good. Sit tight. I'm going to call you as a witness."

Jackson was sitting with a digital camera in the jury box. Harper motioned for her to come to him. She ducked underneath the row of television cameras and sat on his left.

"You've got to take over on this story right now," Harper said.

"What? Why?"

"I'm going to be called to testify." He handed her his steno pads and a couple of pens. "Don't worry about shooting any more photos. We have file pictures of Burke and Patton we can run with the story."

"I've already snapped several of her and her attorney and the assistant prosecutor."

"Okay, good. I should've planned this out better, Emily."

"I've got your back, Ray."

Burke called the hearing to order. He explained the purpose of the hearing for the gallery's benefit and then had the attorneys introduce themselves.

"Is the prosecution ready to proceed?" Burke asked.

"Yes, Your Honor," said Assistant District Attorney Samantha Waldon.

"And the defense, Mr. Rosenthal?" Burke asked.

"The defense is ready, Your Honor. If it pleases the court, a key witness has moments ago come forward that we believe will shed a different light on the facts of the case."

Burke motioned for the attorneys to approach the bench. Rosenthal said Harper had important evidence about his client's vehicle that would help exonerate her.

"Objections, Miss Waldon?" Burke said.

"None, Your Honor," she said. "The prosecution will more than meet the probable cause standard."

The attorneys returned to their tables and Burke told Waldon to call her first witness. She used Adams to establish the date, time, location and conditions surrounding the crash that claimed Max Bell's life.

Waldon was dressed in a navy blue suit and white blouse, and her straight light brown hair hung just past her shoulders. She was six feet tall and trim, and her movements in the courtroom were swift and confident. Her charge for the hearing was to prove a crime had been committed and that there was probable cause the defendant had committed the crime.

"Detective, what if any physical evidence was recovered by the Plymouth Police Department at the scene?" Waldon asked.

"Silver paint chips and several small pieces we believe are from the vehicle's side-view mirror," Adams said.

"Some of the paint chips were recovered from the deceased's body. Is that correct?"

"That is correct, ma'am."

"Were any bodily fluids of the deceased on the paint chips, detective?"

"Yes. There was blood."

Harper glanced at Jake Bell. His arm was around his wife's shoulders in a consoling gesture. Bell's chin quivered and he appeared to be near tears.

"Did there come a time when the Plymouth Police Department was able to match those blood and paint samples?"

"Yes," Adams said. He had ditched his normal casual suit for his full police uniform.

"Where were those samples located, detective?"

"We found blood and paint samples at the residence of the defendant on a vehicle registered under her name."

Waldon stood at a lectern facing Burke. She stepped away and approached Adams for her next question.

"The defendant's residence is located in the city of Belleville, is it not?"

"It is," Adams said. "After obtaining a search warrant, we received authorization and assistance from the Van Buren Township police department to conduct a search of the residence."

"Van Buren Township provides police services to the city of Belleville?"

"That's correct."

"Was the vehicle in plain sight?" Waldon asked.

"Upon our arrival," Adams said, "it was covered by a tarp."

"After removing the tarp, in what condition did you find the vehicle?"

"There was front-end damage, and the vehicle's side-view mirror was hanging, resting against the driver's door."

Waldon looked at Burke and then placed her hands on a wooden rail in front of the witness stand. "Can you describe the make and model of the vehicle?"

"It was a silver 1999 Buick LeSabre."

"What evidence, if any, was recovered from the LeSabre?"

"Our evidence technicians took paint samples from the vehicle. Dried particles of blood were also recovered."

"And was the Plymouth Police Department able to make a determination with respect to the blood samples? Who did those blood samples come from, detective?"

"From the deceased, ma'am. Maxwell Bell."

"You hit my boy and left him for dead!" Jake Bell screamed in Patton's direction.

Burke smacked his gavel. "Bailiff, remove that man from the courtroom."

A Plymouth officer reached Jake Bell before the bailiff, hooked his arm and yanked him into the aisle. He walked Bell out of the courtroom.

Burke hit the gavel again. "I will not tolerate any further outbursts. If I hear anyone speaking other than the attorneys and witnesses, I will clear this courtroom."

The judge looked from side to side as if he were scolding a rowdy room of third graders. He pointed the gavel at Waldon. "Do you have any more questions for this witness?"

"None, Your Honor."

"Mr. Rosenthal, your witness."

"Thank you, Judge. Detective Adams, did your investigation of the accident lead you directly to the defendant?"

Adams shifted in his seat. "The physical evidence allowed us to determine the make and model of the vehicle. We were in the process of examining video footage from the Ann Arbor Road corridor when we received a tip about the defendant's vehicle."

"That was certainly convenient," Rosenthal said. "Are you aware, sir, the paint used on the Buick LeSabre was also used on several other General Motors products? In fact, the same paint manufacturer supplied both General Motors and the Ford Motor Company in the late 1990s. How can you be sure, detective, the paint chips recovered weren't transferred to the body of the deceased by another vehicle or that another vehicle didn't transfer the paint to my client's Buick?"

"Maxwell Bell's blood was found on the defendant's vehicle," Adams repeated. "The odds that it ended up there by any means other than direct contact are astronomical."

"Astronomical, but not impossible," Rosenthal said.

Adams shot the attorney a look as if to say, *Seriously?* "Anything is possible, I suppose."

"No further questions, Your Honor."

Waldon called Rita Judson to the stand next. Her questioning was brief and to the point. Judson had called in her suspicion about her neighbor's car because it was the right thing to do. She felt bad for the Bell family and that poor boy.

Rosenthal's cross-examination consisted of one question. He asked if she was motivated by the $100,000 reward money offered by Crime Stoppers for information leading to an arrest. Judson rebuked the question, saying she hadn't accepted the reward money and emphasized how fond she was of Patton and her daughters.

As her final witness, Waldon called a forensics expert from the University of Michigan. After examining the evidence, it was his testimony that the blood samples from the defendant's Buick matched that of Max Bell.

Rosenthal didn't try to refute the testimony. After a short recess, Burke told him to call his first witness. He called Harper to the stand.

The defense attorney walked Harper through the accident step-by-step. Rosenthal asked if he got a look at the vehicle that hit Bell and Harper.

"A quick glance, perhaps a fraction of a second," Harper said.

"What do you recall about the car?"

"It was moving very quickly. I remember seeing a black taillight section on the back end."

"Anything else?" Rosenthal asked.

"No, the car disappeared into traffic."

"As a reporter, you started your own investigation of the accident, did you not?"

"I did. Even though I was involved, I believed it was my job to cover the story."

"I see," said Rosenthal. The attorney wore a gray suit, white dress shirt and red tie. Glasses and his salt-and-pepper beard gave him a professorial look. "During your investigation, did you come upon video of the accident?"

"Not the accident itself," Harper said. "The video picks up a second or two later, after the car passes by a gas station that's located at the corner of the intersection of Ann Arbor Road and Main Street."

"From whom did you obtain the video?" Rosenthal asked.

"I'm not going to reveal my source," Harper said.

Waldon stood and objected. "The People have a right to authenticate the video, Your Honor."

"Overruled," Burke said. "I'm not going to compel the witness at this point. You may proceed Mr. Rosenthal."

"Very well. Can you describe what happened in the video?"

"I first saw the silver sedan change lanes and cut off another driver," Harper said.

"From which lane did the silver sedan driver change?"

"From the inside to the outside lane," Harper said. "That was the point I got the clearest view of the car."

"Were you able to determine the make—"

"Objection. Calls for speculation," Waldon said.

"Overruled," Burke said. He looked down at Harper and nodded. "You may answer the question."

"I was able to slow the video down and view it frame by frame," Harper said. "Two things stood out to me. The taillights on the car were arrayed in a black panel just as I had remembered from the evening of the accident. Secondly, the shape of the rear window was oval."

"Why is the shape of car's window important?" Rosenthal asked.

"Because the shape of the Buick LeSabre's rear window is rectangular, not oval."

Noise from the court gallery arose as whispers and murmurs. Burke tapped his gavel once more and admonished the gallery to remain quiet.

"Based on your observations," Rosenthal said after taking a cue from Burke to restart questioning, "did you form an opinion on the make and model of the car?"

"Yes. From my research, it appeared to be a late-nineties Ford Taurus."

Rosenthal paused for dramatic effect. With his left arm folded across his chest and supporting his right arm, he pointed at Harper.

"Sir, do you have in your possession the video you're referring to?"

"I do."

"With the court's permission, I'd like to play the video from the witness's thumb drive."

"Objection," Walton snapped. "Judge, how can the court be sure of the validity of the video on this thumb drive? We don't even know where the video came from."

Burke thought for a moment. "Overruled, again, Ms. Waldon. It's not this court's job to determine the validity of the video or its evidentiary value. Mr. Rosenthal, you may play the video."

Burke nodded at a court clerk to dim the lights in the courtroom. Seconds later, the video played. After watching it, Burke told the clerk to play the video a second time, frame by frame. The clerk then turned the lights back on.

"Do you have further questions for this witness, Mr. Rosenthal?" asked Burke.

"The defense rests, Your Honor."

"Miss Waldon?"

Harper looked at the prosecutor. She appeared as if she had been blindsided by his testimony. She retook the lectern facing Burke.

"Good morning, Mr. Harper," Waldon said. "How did you obtain the video we just watched?"

"I canvased businesses in the immediate area around the accident scene."

"I know you won't reveal your source," Waldon said, "but how do we know you didn't doctor this video? Or are we just supposed to take your word for it, because lord knows the media has never done anything unethical to sensationalize a—"

"Objection," Rosenthal said. "Ms. Waldon is trying to testify here, Judge."

"I'll withdraw my last statement," Waldon said. "But my question remains. How does the court know you didn't doctor this video?"

Harper produced a second flash drive from his pocket. "This is a copy of the video. You're welcome to take it and have it analyzed for tampering, but they won't find anything. This video is directly from my source's outside surveillance camera."

The court's bailiff took the flash drive from Harper and walked it to Waldon. "That was thoughtful of you, Mr. Harper, thank you," she said. "Courtesy aside, I have to say I'm quite surprised you've continued to cover this story. The conflict of interest seems pretty obvious. Tell me, sir, don't journalists strive to be objective in their reporting?"

"Yes, it's something I take very seriously," Harper said.

"Yet you can see the conflict?"

"I had this discussion with my late publisher," Harper said. "He didn't want me on the story, so we made a little deal."

"Which was what, sir?"

"That if he even got a whiff of bias, he'd pull me off of it and assign it to a different reporter."

"With all due respect and acknowledging the tragic loss of Mr. Reston," Waldon said, "that safeguard is no longer available to you or your newspaper. Who is going to hold your feet to the fire now if you stray into compromised reporting?"

The question froze Harper for a moment. "Before I took the stand today," he said softly, "I did reassign the story, or at least the coverage of today's hearing."

"Sounds like you're waffling," Waldon said. "Doesn't journalistic integrity go to a newspaper's credibility, sir?"

"It does," Harper said.

"So, sir, are your journalistic ethics situational?"

"Objection," Rosenthal yelled. "Mr. Harper isn't on trial here, Judge. It's not the prosecutor's job to discredit the testimony of a witness at a preliminary examination."

"Sustained," Burke said. "Move along, Ms. Waldon."

"I have nothing further," she said.

Burke excused Harper from the stand. He waited a beat for the courtroom to settle and then tapped his gavel.

"We're going to take a fifteen-minute recess," Burke said. "I will render my decision when we return."

Harper and Jackson walked out of the courtroom into the lobby.

"How'd I do?" he asked. "Could you tell I was scared shitless?"

"You seemed fine to me," Jackson said. "What do you think about what the prosecutor said? Should I stay on the story the rest of the way?"

Harper rubbed his eyes and then focused them on the young reporter. "I'd be lying if I said I didn't have some doubts. I think I've been pretty straight up in my stories so far. But I'd probably be the worst one to make that call."

Jackson's phone buzzed. She pulled it from a back pocket, read the alert or message, whatever it was, and dropped her hand to her side. "You're going to have to make the call, Ray. And soon."

"I know," Harper said.

People started filing back into the courtroom. Harper and Jackson joined the flow of traffic and returned to their seats behind the defense table. Burke took his chair and tapped his gavel firmly to bring the hearing back to order.

"In making my decision, I want to call counsels' attention to a recent Kansas Supreme Court ruling," he said. "It held that when testimony conflicts on a key fact, or facts, the judge should find probable cause and leave it to a jury of a higher court to determine which witness to believe. I happen to concur. The authenticity of the video and its implications to the case are for the circuit court to sort out. Therefore, I am going to bind this case over to circuit court for trial. Bail is continued. Miss Patton will be remanded to the county jail until her next court appearance. We are adjourned."

Chapter 25

MONDAY, AUGUST 24

Harper hadn't smoked a cigarette since his freshman year at Central Michigan. Quitting the three-year habit was the hardest thing he'd done. Jennifer, his college sweetheart, had given him the extra motivation to kick nicotine to the curb with her constant admonishments about kissing an ashtray.

But Jennifer was no longer in the picture, and thinking about the implications of his testimony made his hands shake. The deaths of Max Bell, Doc Reston and Rob Snyder were connected to the Plymouth Police Department. Adams, at the behest of Neil Flaherty, had threatened Nathan Glynn to get him to dispose of evidence. Now Harper had just publicly debunked the department's criminal theory of the hit-and-run case.

Did Snyder have evidence that proved Lisa Ann Patton wasn't the driver of the silver sedan? Was that why Doc Reston and Snyder had been killed? It made sense, too much sense, perhaps. If Flaherty and Adams had killed Doc and one of their own officers to keep the driver's identity secret, would they really hesitate to make Harper disappear?

Theoretically, his job as a reporter acted as a shield. The threat of prolonged negative publicity was often enough to deter politicians and public officials from seeking retribution against the media. Harper knew the same rules of engagement didn't apply in his current predicament.

He pulled the Honda into a Mobil gas station on his way into the office and bought a pack of Salems and a lighter. Harper waited until he was back in the Honda to light up. After a couple of deep drags, it felt like he had never quit.

Harper put the car in drive and minutes later parked on Penniman Avenue. He smoked a second cigarette before making his way up to the loft. Emily Jackson was already pecking away on her laptop. Harper made himself a cup of coffee and then took a chair in front of his own computer. He waded through his email inbox, sifting through press releases, obituaries from funeral homes in Plymouth and a couple of letters to the editor.

"How's the prelim story coming?" Harper asked.

"Almost done. I sent you the pictures to edit. Not exactly my best camera work."

"Lighting in the court stinks. I'm sure we will be able to use one of them."

Getting into the rhythm of work calmed Harper's nerves more than the cigarettes. After forty-five minutes, his stomach growled. The banana he'd eaten on the way to Lisa

Ann Patton's preliminary examination had long since worn off. Harper's ability to think and remain productive was compromised when hunger pangs arose, a lesson he'd learned after flunking a college midterm in a journalism law class on an empty stomach.

He ordered lunch from a Coney Island restaurant a few doors down from the loft, a pair of hot dogs with chili, mustard and heavy onions. Jackson went with a Greek salad. Harper had her story to edit, the hot dogs and a mound of crispy French fries to dig into thirty minutes later.

Seeing himself quoted in his own newspaper felt odd. It reminded him of something Doc had said in his first week at the *Independent*: "You get pulled over for drunk driving or arrested for any other reason, you can expect to read about in the paper with a big, fat headline. You don't get a pass because you work here."

Being the snot-nosed, full-of-piss-and-vinegar young reporter that he was, Harper had fired back: "Do those rules apply to you, Henry?"

Doc gave him an incredulous look. "You bet your ass, kid. You can run my damn mug shot, too."

It was a speech Doc had given to every new reporter, including Jackson. It made Harper smile as he read her story on Patton's hearing. Aside from a few punctuation errors, the story was rock-solid. Her lead paragraph was taut and included a nice hook. She had nailed the story in less than five hundred words. Online, story length wasn't an issue. But Harper was used to worrying about column inches and Doc's credo of not "writing like a goddamn lawyer."

Henry Reston preferred shorter stories that got to the point for the print version. He crammed more news into his once-a-week edition of the *Independent* than some daily papers published in seven days. In five years under Doc's wing, Harper had adopted many of the same philosophies about the news business.

He wished he had more time to pass along the lessons he'd learned from his Obi-Wan Kenobi to the young Jedi, Jackson. But with less than five weeks remaining before the *Independent*'s lights went out, Harper would have to teach mostly by example.

"When do you think the circuit court trial will be?" she asked.

"Patton will be arraigned at the circuit court within two weeks," Harper said. "Trials are usually two to three months later."

"So, we won't even be around to cover it?"

"Not unless Victoria has a change of heart."

"That doesn't seem very likely."

"I agree. I haven't even heard from her since Doc's funeral."

Emily stood and walked toward Harper. "What do we do with the hit-and-run story?"

"We'll write a story announcing the trial date and any other court developments. I'm going to continue to pursue the angle on the cars."

"I thought I was taking over."

"If we're still around when the trial starts, yes, you will write about it. But not until then."

"That's bullshit," Jackson said. "You're part of the story now. You can't cover—"

"Yes, I can. This isn't just another story. I have a lot of skin in the game, and I'm not leaving it up to someone else—"

"To get it right?" Jackson said. "Is that what you mean? You don't want a rookie handling the story?"

Harper stood. His face was crimson. "You can get down from the high journalistic ethics horse you're on, Jackson. Yes, that's exactly the reason. You're good, and perhaps one day you'll be a great reporter. But you're also two months out of J-school. This is my ass that's in the sling, not yours. I'm going to do the investigating and the following up. Period."

She stormed back to her desk, grabbed her purse that was slung over the back of her chair and glared at him before descending the loft's stairs. "Screw you, Ray. Screw you."

Chapter 26

WEDNESDAY, August 26—Thursday, August 27

The doorbell rang at nine forty-five a.m. and John Harper figured it was probably a technician from Comcast. He had made an appointment to have the cable company remove its equipment from the house. Tired of constant outages and rate increases, he'd decided to give WideOpenWest a try. "WOW!" vowed to cut his television and internet prices by a third while providing its "industry-leading customer care."

John would believe it when he saw it. A man in a pair of beat-up jeans and a red T-shirt with a white "Santilli Brothers Construction" logo above the right chest stood on the other side of the screen door.

"I'm sorry to bother you, sir," the man, no more than thirty years old, said. Holding a construction helmet in one hand, he had long, curly black hair and a scruffy black beard. "I'm working with the crew next door and left my thermos at home. Can I trouble you for a glass of water?"

John hadn't seen the man before, but that wasn't uncommon. Tradesmen and laborers came and went. He'd stopped trying to keep track of them a month into construction.

"I'll get you a glass," he said. "But this isn't a watering station. You tell the rest of your crew. I'm not going to have you people knocking on my door all hours of the day."

"Will do, sir. And thank you. Thank you so much."

As he entered the kitchen, Ruth Harper came upstairs from the basement with a basket of laundry. "What are you doing?"

"Getting a glass of water, what does it look like I'm doing?"

"Since when did you starting drinking water instead of coffee?"

"It's not for me, smarty-pants. One of the fellas working next door forgot his thermos. I'm being, well, neighborly. Any law against it?"

Ruth walked past him and dumped the laundry on the dining table to sort and fold. "Go for it, Mr. Congeniality."

Both her and John's view of the screen door was blocked by the interior door. Neither had noticed when the man had cut the screen and let himself in. By the time John looked in that direction, it was too late.

The younger man sent him sprawling and the glass of water flying with a blow to the temple. The force of the blow knocked John unconscious.

The bearded young man closed the interior door with a swift kick. Ruth headed for the kitchen. He sprinted after her, but not before she grabbed a knife from a block on the counter.

She whirled around to strike him, but he caught her arm before it could descend. He forced her backward, and smashed her arm and then her head against a kitchen cabinet. She dropped the knife and he hit her viciously with a roundhouse right.

Ruth crumpled to the floor, dazed, and seeing stars. She looked at him for a second. His eyes were as dark as his hair and beard. There was nothing behind them, she thought. It was like looking into the eyes of a panther.

He pulled her to the middle of the kitchen, yanked her arms behind her and then secured her hands and feet with zip ties. As easy as picking up a bag of potatoes, he lifted Ruth from the floor, tossed her over his shoulder and deposited her on the living room couch.

He followed the same procedure with John.

"Why are you doing this?" Ruth asked. "Are you robbing—"

"Shut the fuck up," he said, "and I mean right now, or I will hit you even harder."

He went to the kitchen, rummaged through several drawers before finding what he was looking for. Ruth saw a pair of dish towels in his right hand and knew immediately what he planned to do with them.

"Got anything to write with in this dump?"

Startled by the question, she hesitated before answering. "China cabinet, top drawer on the right. There's a paper pad in there, too."

She wanted to ask what he intended to write but thought better of it. John started to stir at the other end of the couch.

The man walked to the door and picked up his construction helmet. He pulled out a small roll of what looked like duct tape to Ruth from his pants pocket. A few seconds later, he wadded up a dish towel and stuck it as far into her mouth as it would go. He secured the gag with the tape.

A groan escaped John's mouth. "What are you—"

The younger man sprang across the couch and sent a left hook into John's midsection. It doubled him over gasping for air. He was then pushed backward and gagged like his wife.

Neither of the Harpers moved a muscle as their bearded attacker went to the dining room table and began to write. A couple of minutes later, sitting in the same chair as their son had for dinner a week earlier, he rose and returned to the couch.

He ripped off a piece of duct tape with his teeth, slapped the note against Ruth's chest and taped it. Looking at his forehead, she could see the young man hadn't even broken a sweat. She realized then he made a living hurting people.

A sense of panic washed over her. Not for herself or John. Ruth worried this man's next target would be her son.

The bearded man went around the house closing curtains and shades. He found Ruth's cell phone and put it in his back pocket and then used one of her kitchen knives to cut the landline. A moment later, he grabbed his construction hat, put it on and left the house, locking the front door behind him.

WHEN RAY HARPER GOT HIS MOTHER'S VOICEMAIL for the second time in as many days, he tried the landline. He couldn't quite figure why she hadn't returned his call Wednesday evening, especially since they were supposed to meet for dinner at Buffalo Wild Wings. Being stood up by his parents was a first.

After five rings, the voicemail picked up and he heard his father's instruction: "You know what to do, so do it when the damn thing beeps." Harper waited an hour before trying the landline again. He left the *Independent* a few minutes before ten a.m. when he got the machine again.

He cut the drive time in half by speeding north on I-275 and then cutting across I-696 to the east. He called Royal Oak police on the way and asked for a safety check on his parents. Two uniformed officers stood at the front door as he approached.

"Are you the one that called us?" a female officer said.

"Yes, I'm Ray Harper. I'm their son."

"Sir, we've knocked three times without getting a response. Do we have your permission to enter the premises?"

"I have a key."

The officers parted; Harper opened the screen door and then unlocked the solid wood front door. He saw his parents bound and gagged on the couch.

"What the hell?" Harper screamed.

He went to his mother. A dish towel had been stuffed into her mouth as a gag. He removed duct tape that had held it in place. An officer aided his father while the other pulled her service weapon and searched the house for an intruder.

Ruth Harper's eyes were sunken, her skin dry and her breathing rapid as if she couldn't get enough oxygen into her lungs. He glanced at his father and saw similar symptoms along with a large bruise on the side of his face.

"They're both dehydrated," the officer said. "Sir, can you tell me what happened here?"

John Harper's eyes opened and closed rapidly as if he was trying to focus. "I don't remember, Officer. Why—"

"I know why," Ray interrupted, holding a piece of lined writing paper in his hand. He read it out loud. "'Publish another word, and they're dead. Then your girlfriend. I'll save you for last, and take my time making your death as slow and painful as possible.'"

He handed the note to the officer. The female officer returned to the living room and said the home was clear.

"Ma, are you okay?"

"No, I'm really not. Get your father and I a couple of bottled waters."

Ruth Harper detailed the incident to the officers and Ray listened intently. She gave a description of their attacker and fought back tears describing her husband's slipping in and out of consciousness. "I'm not a doctor, but I think he has a concussion."

"An ambulance is on the way, ma'am," the female officer said. "They'll take good care of you."

Beaumont Hospital was a five-minute ride from their home. Waiting for medics to arrive, Ray filled the officers in on the note's meaning.

"I'll reach out to Captain Chamberlain in Plymouth," the female officer, Sergeant Gina Gardner, said. "In the meantime, until this individual is caught, I strongly suggest you get your parents out of town when they're released from the hospital."

"My father will protest, but I will make it happen. Christ, they told me I should drop this story because they were worried about my safety."

"Clearly, these are very dangerous people," Gardner said. "You'd best take every precaution, especially if you intend to keep publishing the paper."

Ray heard the screen door open, and a pair of medics pushing gurneys filed into the living room. His parents were in the ambulance and on their way to Beaumont in less than five minutes.

Additional police officers arrived and secured the scene. Yellow tape was used to cordon off the little house from the rest of the street. A few neighbors and gawkers stood beyond the tape. Inside, evidence technicians pored over the living room and kitchen hoping to get clues about the assailant.

Ray gave his contact information to Gardner and then headed straight for the hospital. While he hadn't been clocked in the head like his parents, his temples throbbed nonetheless. As he pulled into the parking lot off Woodward Avenue, he found a parking spot, opened the Honda's door and retched.

The nausea in his stomach was soon replaced with rage coursing through his entire body. Ray knew exactly who was behind the attack. Though Neil Flaherty and Sadie Rodgers hadn't delivered the blows, the bearded man was simply a proxy.

Every fiber in his being wanted to haul ass to Plymouth city hall, find Flaherty and kick the living shit out of him and Rodgers. But that was probably what they wanted. He couldn't continue his investigation and publishing the newspaper from jail.

In their minds, they thought they had constructed a perfect plan to get the spotlight off them. Ray wasn't going to give them the satisfaction. He'd figure out a way to protect his parents, Sophia and Emily Jackson.

Ray looked in the rearview mirror and used a spare napkin from the Honda's glove box to wipe his mouth clean. He exhaled and then ran both hands through his hair. His mind whirled with all that had and could still happen.

A few long moments later, one thought settled. This was his battle until the end.

Chapter 27

FRIDAY, AUGUST 28

In just a few hours, the temporary fencing would come down and the charred remains of the *Plymouth Independent*'s Main Street office would be cleared. Though he had sifted through the rubble several times already, Dan Chamberlain owed Lieutenant Rob Snyder one last examination of whatever evidence might remain in the ashes.

He'd trained Snyder straight out of the academy and helped nurture his career. As captain, Chamberlain was responsible for all the officers under his command. In his twenty-five years on the job, he hadn't lost a single one until Snyder's murder.

With the investigation sputtering along in the two weeks since, Chamberlain was looking for a spark. Odds were against finding anything the fire marshal or his own investigators missed. They were highly trained and damned good at what they did.

Parked in the strip mall adjacent to the former newspaper office, Chamberlain leaned against his Ford Explorer and slipped a pair of fire department turnout pants on over his uniform trousers. He then stepped into rubber, felt-insulated boots. Over the years, he'd learned enough about fire service to lend a helping hand on rare occasions when the department was fully engaged.

Chamberlain unlocked a gate to the temporary fencing and then stopped a few feet away at stone steps that had once led up to a porch and the front door. He surveyed the scene, training his attention on areas of the office he, in his own estimation, hadn't spent enough time going through.

Framing for one of the office's side walls lay in the grass and looked like a set of rotten false teeth. Charred floor joists rested on top of a support beam in what had been the middle of the office. Chamberlain, walking around at ground level, carefully stepped around the joists on his way to the rear of the office.

In his mind's eye, he re-created the office and used it as an overlay to the remains. He went to the area where Henry Reston's office had been. Chamberlain used a gloved hand to sift through the rubble. The smell of smoke intensified the more he jostled the ashes. He found a stainless-steel tumbler with its lid missing underneath an inch of debris.

Knowing Reston's proclivity for fitness, Chamberlain guessed that it had held much more ice water than coffee. He put the tumbler into an evidence bag, including ash that filled it like some kind of satanic brew.

He found nothing else of interest and moved farther back in the office. A porcelain sink lay in rubble to his right. Chamberlain had gone through the kitchen area and didn't feel the need to revisit it.

Instead, he made his way to a second set of stone steps. They echoed the style of those at the front of the office and likewise had led to an entry door that was now gone. Using the steps as a spatial reference, he put the back of his heels against them and then stepped forward as if he were walking into the office.

Chamberlain crouched and looked at the debris, sweeping from his left one hundred eighty degrees to his right. He did some poking and unearthing but found nothing. He walked through what had been a hallway and then into the newsroom area.

Ray Harper's desk, at least the metal portion of it, remained intact. Chamberlain went to one knee and swept away the debris with his hand. As he pulled his hand away, he spotted a small piece of metal sticking up from the ash. Chamberlain bent forward for a closer look and saw a block "H" and an ampersand was etched into the metal.

He reached and pulled out what looked like a Swiss Army knife from the debris. Chamberlain shook the soot loose and it read, "H & H The Brand of High Quality." He took his fireman's gloves off and slipped on a pair of latex gloves. Chamberlain examined the H & H and pulled several of its tools out before determining it was a lock pick set.

Why in god's name would Ray Harper have a lock pick set? Chamberlain scoured the remaining area around the reporter's desk but, aside from a couple of half-melted ballpoint pens, found nothing. Another forty-five minutes of digging brought similar results.

Chamberlain walked away not knowing if his two finds were of any significance or just personal effects of Reston and Harper. One thing was certain: he wouldn't make either object an official part of the investigation.

Neil Flaherty had ordered Chamberlain to stand down the night the Bell boy was run down on Ann Arbor Road. He'd allowed Detective Adams to handle the scene and the follow-up investigation. Adams was also lead on the murders of Snyder and Reston.

The move had sent red flags up in Chamberlain's mind. But he had already put the paperwork for his January retirement in, and Flaherty had signed and approved them. The documents were as close to ironclad as you could get in the world of municipal employment. He was virtually untouchable and immune to the political winds that constantly blew in Plymouth.

Had Snyder not stopped by his house the next morning, Chamberlain would've buried the red flags. Instead, he'd listened intently over a cup of coffee on the back deck as Snyder detailed Adams's bungling of the hit-and-run investigation.

"Damn it, Dan, that intersection should have been shut down all night, not a couple of friggin' hours," Snyder told him. "And MSP should've been out there. I don't know what Adams and the chief are trying to pull here."

Less than a day later, Snyder was gone, and the red flags had turned into tornado sirens in the back of Chamberlain's head. He couldn't turn them down, let alone off. Retirement be damned, he was going to get answers for his friend and colleague of nearly two decades.

"RAY HARPER."

"Hey, Ray, it's Captain Chamberlain. Where are you working from these days?"

"We've set up shop in Henry's loft," Harper said. "What can I do for you?"

"I'd like to stop by if you have a minute."

"Sure. Can I ask what this is about?"

"I'll be there in a couple minutes," Chamberlain said. "We can talk then."

It was eight thirty in the morning. Jackson wouldn't be in until later. She was out interviewing new teachers getting ready to start their first school year. Harper thought Chamberlain might have news about the investigation into the attack on his parents.

He didn't have to ponder long. As he placed a breakfast blend coffee pod in the Keurig, the doorbell to the loft went off. Harper buzzed Chamberlain through the security door facing the back alley and then heard him coming up the steps.

Before extending his arm to shake hands, Harper noticed Chamberlain carrying what looked like an evidence bag. "Good morning, captain. Get you a cup of coffee?"

"I've already worked up a pretty good sweat this morning," Chamberlain said. "You got a Diet Coke or something else cold?"

"You're in luck," Harper said. "My colleague is a big Diet Coke fan."

Moments later, Harper returned and set a soda can and a glass filled with ice on his worktable. He took a sip of his own coffee before speaking and then nodded in the direction of the evidence bag.

"What do you have there?"

Chamberlain drained a portion of the Diet Coke and then poured the remainder into the cup of ice. "Forget that for a minute. How are your folks?"

"Better. They should be released from the hospital tomorrow."

"You're not letting them go back to that house, right?"

Harper shook his head. "They're going to a hotel room for a couple nights and then down to their friends' house in Texas. Nobody is going to bother them there."

"Good," Chamberlain said. "That's the smart move."

"Any updates on the investigation from Royal Oak?"

"Unfortunately, there isn't much," Chamberlain said. "The perp knew what he was doing. Your folks gave an excellent description of him but there were no hits from any of the databases."

Harper exhaled then closed his eyes.

Reading his frustration, Chamberlain handed Harper a clear evidence bag. "We do have something of interest in our other case."

The item in the bag looked like a wine bottle opener but was dingy, like it had been pulled from a trash can.

"Ever seen this before?" Chamberlain asked. "Found it by your old desk a little while ago."

Harper leaned in for a closer look. "No wonder you smell like smoke. I can't say that I have. What is it?"

"It's a lock pick set," Chamberlain said.

"It's not mine. How in the hell would that wind up near my desk?" Harper said. "I never saw Doc with that thing, and I'm pretty sure our new reporter wouldn't be carrying a lock pick set. You think somebody used it to break into the office?"

"Possibly. We'll know more after testing it for prints."

Harper pulled out his iPhone. "Mind if I take a picture?"

"It can't go in the paper right now," Chamberlain said.

"Why not?"

"Rob Snyder was more than just my subordinate. He was a friend. I know he spoke with you about his problems with the Bell investigation. He told me, too. After he talks to me and then you, he winds up dead at your office a few hours later."

"And you don't think it's a coincidence," Harper said.

"No," Chamberlain said. "I don't believe in coincidences."

Harper shared his ideas about commonalities between the hit-and-run and murder cases. "The question is, what did Rob know that got him killed?"

"You're assuming he was the target," Chamberlain said. "While I don't believe in coincidences, there's not enough evidence to conclude whether Snyder was the target or if it was Reston."

Harper thought for a moment. "I see your point. The list of people who had motivation to kill either Doc or Rob seems pretty small. I'm guessing nobody was motivated to kill both of them, which makes one the target and the other collateral damage."

Chamberlain let out a sigh. "There's another factor at play here," he said.

"I'm listening."

"Flaherty and Sadie Rodgers have been involved for more than a year," Chamberlain said.

"Whey you say 'involved,' you mean romantically?"

"Yes. It's fairly common knowledge at city hall."

"Jesus," Harper said. He paused before continuing. "It all makes sense now. Flaherty is covering for Rodgers for obvious reasons."

"Rob was investigating it, investigating the chief before he was killed," Chamberlain said.

"Knowing that, you still don't think there's enough to say the lieutenant was the target?"

"I'm leaning that way, but no. I do think we can say that with certainty. Listen, we could sit here and speculate all day. That's not productive. I'll work on the prints; you see if you can track down who might have purchased it."

"Is there a serial number on it?"

Chamberlain picked the evidence bag off the table then pointed to a tiny inscription on the back side of the lock pick set. "Zoom in with your camera and take a picture. See what you can dig up."

Chapter 28

TUESDAY, September 1

From the very start of his job with the *Independent*, Harper had written a personal column at least once a month. Doc had insisted on it. The column was the only place in the paper where he could share his opinions on events or issues, whether they were about Plymouth or something going on in Lansing, Washington, D.C., or somewhere in between.

The column served several purposes. It allowed for interpretation, not just the reporting of facts. It could help put news into a context that a news story often couldn't. Personal feelings were not off-limits, either. The idea, according to Doc, was to let the readers get to know the people who wrote about them every week.

Harper often featured Plymouth's "everyday" people in his column space. A postal worker. The group that ran the old-time movie theater. A homeless man who worked the off-ramp at I-275 and Ann Arbor Road. The community was much more than what happened at city hall.

He'd rarely strayed into personal topics, but the column he was currently writing was very personal. It was news Plymouth residents should know. And publishing it in the next day's paper carried risks. Hell, publishing the paper at all was a risky proposition if the threatening note taped to his mother's chest was to be believed.

But now was not the time to play it safe. He wanted to send a clear message to his adversaries:

As sad as it is to write, a middle-aged couple being attacked in their own home isn't big news these days. The pages of the Independent and other news publications are filled with crime stories often worse than what happened to a Royal Oak couple a week ago.

Now, you might ask, why is this guy writing about a crime in Oakland County? It's a fair question. The answer is, because that middle-aged couple are my parents.

I grew up on Houstonia Avenue in a modest ranch-style home, and that's where John and Ruth Harper still live. Until last Wednesday, it had been their refuge, their safe place in the world. That all changed at the hands of a man Royal Oak police describe as being in his late twenties or early thirties, with a muscular build, black hair and dark brown eyes.

The suspect, who police believe is approximately six feet tall and 190 pounds, didn't steal anything from my parents. The house wasn't ransacked. Police say the motive for the attack is unclear.

What is clear is that my parents will never be the same. The bruises this man left with his punches will heal. I have to wonder, though, will they ever feel safe? Anywhere?

Harper completed the column with a few more details about the attack and its aftermath. He tossed in some of his heartfelt feelings. As much as he wanted to tell the world who was responsible, he couldn't. Not yet.

Still, the column did what Harper wanted it to do, which was to put Neil Flaherty and Sadie Rodgers on notice. He hoped it made them angry. He hoped it would make them angry enough to get sloppy because sloppy criminals got caught.

And that's what they were: criminals. Rodgers and Flaherty's respectable titles as mayor and police chief didn't mean squat. They were no better than street thugs, dope slingers or grifters. In a sense, they were worse, Harper thought.

Thousands of people relied on their integrity, that they would look out for their best interests and do all they could to make Plymouth a better place to raise their families. That trust had been shattered irrevocably.

It was killing Harper to not tell the whole story. He took solace only in the belief that one day, one day soon, he would be able to write the truth. Hopefully, it would be enough to excise the cancers currently residing at city hall.

Chapter 29

WEDNESDAY, September 2

Sadie Rodgers didn't bother knocking before she entered Neil Flaherty's office. Wearing a gray business suit, a light blue blouse, and block-heel pumps, she carried the printed edition of the *Plymouth Independent* newspaper in her right hand.

Rodgers tossed the paper at her lover and hit him square in the chest. "Once again, your strategy backfired. You've read Harper's column, I assume?"

Flaherty shot her a sarcastic look. "Funny, I didn't see either of our names in there."

"That's not the point and you know it," Rodgers said, taking a seat in front of his desk. "Harper is calling our bluff."

"Bluff? What makes you think I'm bluffing? Have I bluffed up until this point?"

A bead of cold sweat traveled from the back of her neck down past her shoulder blades to the small of her back. While she put on a strong front to the outside world, inside stress and nerves were taking a toll.

She had dropped seven pounds since hitting and killing Max Bell. Her face looked more and more gaunt by the day. Rodgers's mind was constantly going, assessing her next moves. While she still believed a path out of her current predicament existed, doubt was creeping in.

"I suppose not," Rodgers said. "But be practical. Our own police department is investigating, and now Royal Oak PD is looking for the guy you used to put heat on Harper. If we leave enough breadcrumbs, pretty soon, they're going to lead to us."

Flaherty leaned back in his chair as if pondering her words. "I'm really uncomfortable doing nothing. I'm inclined to eliminate threats."

"You still think like a soldier," Rodgers said. "That's useful only to a point. We have to be a lot more tactical if we're going to get out of this in one piece."

Flaherty's normally erect posture loosened. He shrugged his shoulders, lifted his hands off the desk and turned them palms up, as if to say, *What now?*

Rodgers came around the desk and massaged his shoulders. "I think we should delay our plans for the time being. Let things cool off."

"It's too late for that. The longer this drags out, the more exposure we have."

"I get that, I do. But—"

"Going after a member of the media was probably a mistake," Flaherty said. "I agree. I'll put that on ice for now."

"Why do I still hear a 'but' in there?"

"I'm not leaving other loose ends out there to come back and bite us."

Rodgers spun his chair around and straddled his legs with her own. He looked uncomfortable, but she didn't care. "Still have to think you're in charge, don't you?"

Flaherty half-heartedly tried to push her off. He stopped resisting when she kissed him hard.

The fact that his secretary or another city hall staffer could walk in on them at any point turned her on, and she continued to kiss him. After an intense few minutes, Rodgers came up for air. She smiled a wicked smile.

"Okay, then. Have it your way," she said. "Take those chess pieces off the board."

Chapter 30

MONDAY, SEPTEMBER 7

After seventeen years as a jail officer for Wayne County, Eldon Turner had his pick of shifts and facilities to work in. Rookies had no choice and often did years of hard time at Division II, better known as the old county jail.

If hell on earth existed, Turner was convinced its epicenter was 525 Clifton Street. Ironic, considering the jail sat in the middle of Detroit's touted Greektown, a section of the city known for its restaurants, bars and nightlife. In the decades since the jail's 1929 opening, the city had risen to become the Arsenal of Democracy in World War II, swelled to nearly two million residents at the height of the baby boom, and been ripped at the seams by rioting, left for dead in the 1980s and reborn from the ashes of bankruptcy in 2013.

Through it all, the jail had stood unchanged. From its rat-infested lower levels to the floors of dingy jail cells with peeling paint, its walls were pregnant with human suffering. Contrary to popular fiction and movies that portrayed inmates as belonging to a kind of brotherhood whose members thrived with lively discussions, games of basketball and studying the law in the jailhouse library, Turner knew better.

Life for the inmates under his charge was about the same mind-numbing routine day after day after day. Hushed talking. Dark cells with glorified mats for beds. Endless rows of steel bars painted sickly beige and peeling. Humming fluorescent lights. Overheated by old radiators in the winter and sweltering on summer days with nothing but a few oscillating fans to push hot air around.

Division III? A glamorous hotel by comparison. Plentiful lighting. Freshly painted walls. Air conditioning. Cleanliness so acute the floors shined. The jail's main hall looked like a wing of half the high schools across America. It was where Turner had been posted the past five years, until a few days ago.

He had taken a temporary transfer back to hell. His sentence was six months. With the jail short of staff, Turner was pulling doubles. The routines of the place came back to him like an old nightmare. The faces of the inmates had mostly changed since his last tour of duty. But the eyes of the damned were the same. Hollowed out. Cold. Lifeless.

As he stood outside the jail keeping an eye on a small group of female inmates that included Lisa Ann Patton, Turner wondered if $50,000 was adequate compensation to kill an innocent woman. He sipped black coffee from a paper cup while leaning against a wall. The women were walking laps around a cramped courtyard enclosed with brick and topped with barbed wire.

On Labor Days past, Turner would've been relaxing with a glass of single-malt whiskey at eight in the evening, his belly full of smoked brisket, artisan-crafted mac-and-cheese and a slice or two of cornbread lathered in butter from his favorite restaurant, Slows Bar BQ. Not tonight. He had no appetite.

As the half-dozen women completed a loop at the far end of the courtyard and turned to face him, Turner made a slight gesture of tipping the cup of coffee in their direction. A tall white woman pushed a Black woman's shoulders and sent her to the ground. A moment later, the two women were scrapping, pulling hair and punching for all they were worth.

Patton stepped away from the fracas and then found herself surrounded by three women. One grabbed her arms and pulled them back. Patton struggled to free herself but was hopelessly overmatched. The two remaining women pulled plastic shanks fashioned from toothbrushes and stabbed her chest without mercy.

Turner radioed for backup and sprinted across the courtyard. He drew his service weapon and ordered Patton's attackers to the ground. Three other officers arrived seconds later and separated the two women still fighting. All of the women, except Patton, were handcuffed and led away.

Blood poured from a dozen wounds to Patton's chest. Turner applied pressure to two near her heart, but it was like sticking fingers in a dam ready to burst. She struggled to form words as blood gurgled from her mouth. Turner lowered his head to within inches of her face while keeping pressure on the wounds.

"Tell them," she said, gulping air, her words sodden with blood. "Tell them. Tell my girls. Tell them their mama loved them."

Though he had killed women before, though he had killed white men and Black men, pimps, drug lords, businessmen and even cops for money, Eldon Turner had never known remorse. Yet as Lisa Ann Patton's last breath escaped her, tears formed in his eyes.

"I will," he said.

This wasn't just another hit. For reasons that he couldn't yet grasp, it wasn't the same. He wasn't the same. He closed Lisa Ann Patton's eyes and laid her arms gently at her sides.

A medical staff member helped Turner to his feet while two others tended to his victim. His well-choreographed play had been successful. The target was eliminated, and the money would be waiting for him, cash in a duffel secured by his longtime partner and ex–Detroit police officer Dwight Alexander.

He would pay the murderous actors' families what he had promised. There would also be favors to impart to the inmates during the remainder of his stay at the old county jail. Turner prided himself on his professionalism and would, despite his feelings of angst, keep his word.

That word would also be extended to Patton's daughters. Alexander would protest. It might, in fact, cost him their working relationship. Didn't matter. Eldon Turner had made his last hit. As he scrubbed the blood from his hands, he vowed to keep not a nickel of the money.

People in his now former line of work rarely got to leave on their own terms. Most wound up dead or in jail. And wouldn't it be fitting in his case? To wind up on the other side of the bars, to become one of the bedraggled living corpses?

Chapter 31

<u>TUESDAY, SEPTEMBER 8</u>

A 36-year-old Belleville woman charged in the hit-and-run death of Plymouth resident Maxwell Bell was killed Monday as the result of an attack at a Wayne County jail. Lisa Ann Patton was pronounced dead at the scene after suffering numerous chest wounds in an attack by two female inmates, according to a sheriff's office statement.

Patton was awaiting trial on two felony counts in connection with the August 14 hit-and-run that took the life of the 16-year-old Bell. The attack happened at about 8:15 p.m. last night at the county's Division I jail in Detroit, authorities said. Patton leaves behind two children, both currently under the care of child protective services.

"The system failed my client, pure and simple," said Matthew Rosenthal, Patton's defense attorney. "The evidence would've proven her innocent beyond a reasonable doubt. Now her girls will grow up without a mother, orphans and wards of the state."

Jake Bell, the father of Maxwell Bell, declined to comment on the incident. Plymouth Police Chief Neil Flaherty said he considers the hit-and-run case closed, despite conflicting evidence presented at Patton's preliminary examination hearing last month at the Thirty-Fifth District Court.

"What happened to Miss Patton is tragic," Flaherty said, "but we think the case against her was very strong. We believe it would be a waste of taxpayer funds to continue investigating the case at this time."

Harper recapped the hit-and-run accident and the events leading up to Patton's arrest before finishing the article and uploading it to the *Independent*'s website. Not exactly the story he was expecting to write the day after a holiday.

Any remaining doubts about a conspiracy to cover up the identity of the driver of the car that killed Max Bell were erased in Harper's mind. Given the relationship between Flaherty and Plymouth Mayor Sadie Rodgers, little doubt remained about who was being protected.

The problem was proving it. Flaherty had made a tactical mistake in closing the case, Harper thought. The department wouldn't be able to hide behind the "ongoing investigation" exception to any Freedom of Information Act requests he made. Harper's intention was to gather every report, communication and piece of evidence he could get his hands on.

He had no doubts Flaherty and Adams would redact as much as legally permissible. Time was also not on his side. The *Independent*'s last issue was in three weeks. Flaherty could simply run out the clock on any information request. Harper could continue to pursue the story as a freelance reporter, but without the backing of a news organization, his job would be even more difficult.

Complicating the last few weeks of life at the *Independent* was Emily Jackson's upcoming departure. Despite her initial pledge to stay until the final issue, she would be heading north for a reporting job in Traverse City at the end of the week. Victoria Reston-Coble had given him the green light to hire another reporter, but Harper hadn't found any takers for such a short stint. Odds were, he'd be a one-man show until the doors closed.

Harper went to the kitchen and searched Doc's pantry for something to nibble on. He found a box of Ritz crackers and peanut butter. He grabbed a small plate from the cupboard and made four Ritz and peanut butter cracker sandwiches. A fresh cup of coffee from the Keurig and he was ready to edit a story from Jackson on the fate of Plymouth's beloved Kellogg Park fountain.

He had pulled the story up and read the first paragraph when his iPhone rang. He checked the screen and Sophia's smiling face popped up. He answered the call.

"How goes the first day?" Harper asked.

"Great. I just got out of my reading class."

"That's like twelve credit hours on its own, right?"

"Yeah, it's a bear. But I'm looking forward to getting in the classroom. It will be a nice warm-up for student-teaching this winter. How's your day going?"

Harper filled her in on the hit-and-run story developments. Sophia had taken a keen interest in his work. She had written for her high school newspaper for two years and still had a taste for journalism, despite her career choice.

"I could do a few freelance stories for you, you know."

It wasn't the first time Sophia had nudged him about writing. Harper had reviewed a few of her news stories from the *Perspective*, the Plymouth-Canton school district's monthly student publication. He was certain she could handle a city commission meeting or several other assignments but resisted the idea.

"Your plate is already full, isn't it?"

"Yeah, so? What's your point? I think you're just afraid I'll show you up."

"Without a doubt," Harper said. "How's it going to look when a college kid comes in here and kicks my butt?"

"Kid?"

"Sorry, you know what I meant."

"I'll accept your apology on one condition."

"What's that?

"Lunch at the Sidetrack Bar & Grill tomorrow. You're buying."

Sophia's appetite was one of the things he liked about her. She wasn't afraid to throw down a steak or a plate of nachos. He was only starting to discover some of her other appetites and was hoping they were equally voracious.

"The Sidetrack sounds great," he said.

"I've got to get to my next class," Sophia said. "See you tomorrow, handsome."

"Can't wait," Harper said.

He disconnected the call, then gathered a pair of empty coffee mugs from his desk and took them to the kitchen. Harper set them inside a stainless-steel dishwasher and smiled at Jackson as she approached. She didn't return the smile.

"I've got to run a few errands," he said. "You need anything while I'm out?"

Jackson took a chai tea from the pod tree next to the Keurig and snapped it into place. She added sugar to her cup and shot Harper a cold look.

"I'm fine. I don't need anything," she said.

"Okay. Any other stories coming today?"

"I'll have a police blotter late this afternoon."

"Anything interesting?"

"A robbery at Bode's."

"What did the thieves get, cod or corned beef?"

Jackson rolled her eyes. "The manager got jumped in the parking lot after leaving the restaurant around midnight on Saturday."

"Was he hurt?"

"Thankfully, no. They got the night deposit bag that had a couple thousand bucks in it. Pulled a gun."

"Do the cops have any leads?"

"Better than that, they have the punks locked up."

"That was quick," Harper said.

"The geniuses got hung up by a train on Mill Street, the one just south of Ann Arbor Trail. Instead of turning around and going a different way, they waited for the train to pass. The cops blocked them in and arrested them without incident."

Harper laughed. "Nice to hear the trains were actually useful for once."

Plymouth was nearly encircled by train tracks. The city had locked horns with CSX for decades about stalled engines tying up crossings, sometimes for hours, largely to no avail.

Fines and harsh letters from politicians were just the price of doing business for the company. Harper counted it as a good day if he wasn't delayed at least once heading in or out of town.

"That will be a great lead item for the blotter," he said.

A smile finally broke across Jackson's face. It was a nice thaw from the icy turn Harper's relationship had taken with her after his hit-and-run story edict. While their paths were not likely to cross again once she left for Traverse City, Harper didn't want the young reporter's lasting impression of working at the *Independent* to be negative. She needed to go into her new job with the right attitude.

"You've done excellent work here," Harper said. "The *Record-Eagle* is getting a hell of a reporter."

The compliment caught Jackson off guard. She seemed almost embarrassed. "Thanks. I appreciate it. Do you have any leads on a job?"

Harper shook his head. "No. I've been so wrapped up in everything going on, I haven't looked. Honestly, I've barely even thought about it."

"I'm sure you'll land on your feet," Jackson said.

"I've got a few bucks saved, so I'll be okay until I find something," he said.

Sensing the conversation's awkward turn, Harper smiled, excused himself and left the loft.

Chapter 32

THURSDAY, SEPTEMBER 10

Cup of coffee in hand, Harper made it to the bottom of his apartment stairs without spilling a drop, a rare occurrence he took as an omen of a good day ahead. Harper opened the interior door to leave but stopped dead in his tracks when a brown envelope toppled over and fell against his shin.

He set his computer bag and coffee on the steps and opened the envelope. Harper pulled the contents out, a two-page report and a handwritten note.

Sorry about the delay, Dan Chamberlain wrote. *Flaherty is well connected around here, so I took the lock pick set to a friend up north. His resources are limited and he's not the speediest at processing fingerprints. But you can take his findings to the bank. Call me on my personal phone when you're done digesting the report.*

Harper grabbed the computer bag and coffee and went back upstairs. He set everything down on the kitchen table, an oval-shaped piece made of oak and handed down to him by his parents when they upgraded.

The report included a written one-page summary of findings. Its second page showed a latent print from the lock pick set on the left side and a comparison print on the right.

The quality of the latent print was good despite the conditions Chamberlain had found it in, according to the report. Using various methods, Chamberlain's unnamed friend was able to overcome "significant background interference," meaning the debris and soot from the *Independent*'s torched office.

Red lines pointing to various spots on the magnified fingerprints were numbered one through twenty-one. Each of the numbered ridges identified in the latent fingerprint appeared to match the comparison fingerprint, at least to Harper's untrained eye.

The report came to the same conclusion, in excruciating scientific detail. Every profession had its own lingo and acronyms, from football coaches, engineers and attorneys to doctors and teachers. Cops took it to a whole new level, and the report was even a notch above regular police jargon.

With the help of Google, Harper discovered what "SWGFAST" meant "Scientific Working Group on Friction Ridge Analysis." "ACE-V" was the term for the scientific method of analysis, comparison, evaluation and verification. But the only acronym that really mattered to Harper was "IAFIS."

The Integrated Automated Fingerprint Identification System, run by the FBI, contained millions of fingerprints from known criminals nationwide and had come into existence in the late 1990s. The system was available to most law enforcement agencies. It crunched analysis data and spit out matching suspects about 80 percent of the time if prints were good. Harper wondered what reporters did before Google.

The latent print from the lock pick set had been queried on IAFIS earlier in the week, according to the report. The comparison fingerprint was its match. The individual the print belonged to, however, had been blacked out by Chamberlain.

"What the literal fuck?" Harper said out loud.

Seeing red, he dialed the captain's personal phone number. Chamberlain picked up on the third ring.

"Why did you give me the report if you were going to redact who it identified?" Harper said.

"Well, good morning to you, too, Ray."

"What the hell, Dan? Whose print is on the lock pick? Adams? Flaherty?"

"No. It's not anyone from the Plymouth Police Department."

"Then who?"

"I'm not going to tell you who at this point," Chamberlain said. "Additional investigation needs to be done."

"Unbelievable. You've got a lock pick and the identification of the person that used it and that's not enough? Are you kidding me? Whoever used that lock pick is the son of a bitch that killed Henry and Rob. What other explanation could there be?"

"Settle down, Ray. It's solid evidence, no question. But we're still a long way from connecting all the dots."

"Are we?" Harper said. "Flaherty and Rodgers are a couple, that's well established. Flaherty lied about the make and model of the car that hit and killed Max Bell, which I testified to in open court. He had that car crushed and sold for scrap. Then—"

"That's news to me," Chamberlain said.

"Hell yes he did. The Keystone Auto Service owner told me off the record he was threatened by Adams and Flaherty to crush the car and get rid of it or they'd ruin him financially. They threatened his family, too."

"So, he's scared and won't go on the record?"

"Of course not," Harper said. "Nathan Glynn is scared. I'm almost certain he put two and two together long before I got there to talk to him."

"You believe the car that hit Bell was an older-model Ford Taurus?"

"It's the only vehicle that matches what I saw at the scene."

"So, where is that car?" Chamberlain asked. "Glynn tell you anything about that?"

"No," Harper said. "If he knew, he didn't say. From Flaherty and Adams's perspective, wouldn't it make sense to keep Glynn out of the loop on the location of the Taurus?"

Chamberlain waited a beat before responding. "Yeah, it does make some sense. Kind of like street gangs keeping dealers in the dark about operations above their pay grades."

"Then Lisa Ann Patton winds up dead in the jail," Harper said. "She claimed she was being framed by the cops. You were there, you heard what she said."

"But she was an admitted prostitute, so who's going to believe her."

"Exactly," Harper said. "I'll give Flaherty and Adams that, she was a good patsy."

Chamberlain sighed. "One thing you've got to keep in mind," he said. "When we come for the chief and Adams, this thing has to be rock-solid. As coherent as it all looks, what we've got mostly is supposition."

"You don't have enough evidence to go straight to the Wayne County prosecutor's office?"

"We've got a print but it's not from the murder weapon," Chamberlain said. "We don't have the Taurus with any associated forensic evidence. You're alleging a conspiracy to kill Patton but we've got no evidence of—"

"What about the inmates who killed her?"

"For all we know, Patton was killed for something she did or didn't do in the jail. And even if she wasn't, you think those women are going to just tell the sheriff's office they were paid in some way to take out Patton? You're dreamin'."

"Oh, for fuck's sake," Harper yelled into the phone.

"I understand your frustration, Ray," Chamberlain said. "I'm right there with you and I do believe we're on the right track. But it's too soon to move. The prosecutor would laugh me out of her office and then the chief would be onto us."

"And I'd get my ass sued off if I printed what we know."

"What we think we know," Chamberlain said, correcting him.

"Where do we go from here?"

"Have you gotten anywhere with the serial numbers off the lockpick?"

"Why does that even matter? You've got the fingerprint ID."

"It never hurts to have additional proof."

"No, I haven't got shit," Harper said. "It's a common set sold by a couple of dozen retailers on the web and at brick-and-mortar stores. Best I can tell—and I even called the manufacturer—that serial number is really a batch number. Lock picks from that batch went all over the country. There's no way to trace it down farther than that."

"Needle in a haystack, I get it."

"I would assume you're going to investigate the 'individual' identified by the prints?" Harper asked.

"That's the next step."

Chapter 33

FRIDAY, SEPTEMBER 11

Incoming calls to the *Independent*'s landline had dwindled to a trickle in the past few weeks. With just a few editions left and advertising schedules locked in, there were fewer calls from local businesses.

Harper had streamlined the subscription cancellation process on the paper's website. Still, the *Independent*'s battalion of loyal print edition readers, most north of fifty years old, preferred talking to a real human being. Since he was the circulation department—Jackson had offered help, but Harper wanted her eyes on the editorial prize—he took the calls.

Inevitably, his lunch was interrupted each day by a sad customer sorry to see local news coverage going away. When the phone rang at 12:50, Harper's eyes rolled.

"*Independent*, how can I help you?"

"I live at the corner of Sandalwood and Ann Arbor Trail," said a woman with a voice made raspy by decades of smoking, Harper guessed.

"Are you calling to stop your subscription?"

"No. It's on fire, the golf course."

"Golf course? Are you talking about Hilltop?"

"Yeah, I'm talking about Hilltop. The clubhouse is on fire. Better get a photographer out here and a reporter, too."

"When did the fire start?"

"I was outside watering my flowers and saw smoke, maybe ten minutes ago. Flames shot up a couple minutes after that."

"Can I get your name?"

"I don't want my name in the paper."

She hung up before Harper could ask another question. Jackson looked up from her computer.

"What's going on?"

"Fire out at the golf course on Ann Arbor Trail."

Jackson stood, grabbed a notepad from her desk, a couple pens and her camera. "So much for a quiet last day."

"Well, now, that would've been boring. Leave your camera. I'll shoot stills and video. I want you to talk to as many people as possible."

"Somebody's stogie explode on the ninth green or what?" Jackson asked.

Harper checked the charge on his camera and grabbed a long lens from a gray photographer's bag at the edge of his steel and glass workstation. "Nah, it's the clubhouse. Hope the fire department is already out there. It's got a shit ton of historic stuff."

"You ready?"

"Let's roll."

Jackson had parked her Ford Fusion on Penniman Avenue in front of the loft. Since it was closer than going to the deck to retrieve Harper's Honda, they took hers. She zoomed down Penniman to Main Street, hung a right and then waited less than patiently for pedestrians to cross from Kellogg Park to the restaurants lining Main.

Seconds later, they were headed away from downtown traveling west on Ann Arbor Trail. Jackson gunned the Fusion and cut the drive time to the golf course from ten to five minutes.

Police blocked the road about a quarter mile from Hilltop. Jackson parked on the gravel shoulder, and a moment later she and Harper were grabbing their gear and hurrying out of the car.

A patrolman recognized Harper and waved both of them past the roadblock. Golfers and gawkers were cordoned off across Ann Arbor Trail and watched as firefighters battled the flames.

Harper clicked the camera's long lens into place and started snapping shots in rapid succession. Jackson made a beeline to Plymouth's fire chief, who was standing in the middle of the golf course parking lot. He was dressed in turnout gear and coordinating firefighter movements on a walkie-talkie.

An aerial truck sprayed the center of the clubhouse from above. Harper circled around the truck to get pictures of the firefighter's face as he worked to douse the flames.

Meanwhile, other firefighters were attacking from the ground at the rear of the clubhouse, where a formal dining hall stood. Its roofline was raised, and the walls were bumped out as if a single-family home had been fused into the structure.

The bulk of the historical items were in the dining hall. Several firefighters rushed paintings, old photographs and other items out a side door. Harper chronicled their movements on video. After taking a few more stills, he backtracked to the chief. A scrum of reporters from local television and radio stations had gathered around him.

"How long before the fire is under control?" a reporter asked.

Fire Chief Scott Shaw glanced from left to right at the television camera operators. "All of you good to go? I only want to do this once."

After a small chorus of "ready" and "all set," Shaw cleared his throat. He rattled off the basic facts of the incident in a firm but monotone voice.

"At this point, the fire is about seventy percent contained," Shaw said. "We should have it completely under control and extinguished within in an hour. We'll keep units on-scene for a few hours after that to take care of any hotspot dustups that may occur."

"Has a cause for the fire been determined?" asked Jackson, who was front and center in the scrum.

"We believe it started in the kitchen as a grease fire."

"Chief, I saw your guys hustling antiques out of the dining hall," Harper said. "How much were they able to recover and what is the extent of the damage to the hall?"

"We didn't get much, unfortunately," Shaw said, "and the hall is a complete loss. The fire snaked its way in there mighty quick. We did the best we could, but as some of you may know, the walls of that hall were made of fine wood more than a hundred years old. Once it caught, it was kindling. Damn shame."

Every mayor since the early twentieth century had been sworn in at the dining hall. An incalculable number of important community meetings, hearings and official events had been held within in its walls. High school graduation parties, wedding receptions and baby showers for Plymouth's elite kept it busy year-round. Now it was gone in a matter of minutes.

Harper snapped several shots of Shaw, and the impromptu news conference was over in less than fifteen minutes. He headed back for the Fusion while Jackson gathered reactions and quotes from bystanders.

They had returned to the loft by two thirty. Jackson went to work on the story while Harper uploaded and edited his photos. The story, photos and video were on the *Independent*'s website a few hours later.

"God, what a depressing way to go out," Jackson said, standing and stretching.

"For you or the Hilltop dining hall?"

"Both. People were genuinely upset. I talked to one couple that had an anniversary celebration planned for next month. They were married right on the golf course and then held their reception in the hall. They were in tears."

"That sucks," Harper said. "You still feel like dinner and drinks? My treat."

"Sophia coming?"

"Yeah."

"Good. I'll give her a few tips on how to handle you as a boss."

"Is that right?"

"You can be a prick. Has she seen that side of you?"

Harper smiled and Jackson blushed.

"Not talking about your anatomy," she said. "It's your personality I'm worried about. Sophia is all kinds of cool. You'll screw things up."

Harper raised his hand. "Hang on just a minute there, Action Jackson. I haven't even agreed to let her write a word for the paper."

"Oh, please. She's a better writer than you."

"And you would know this how?"

"She asked me to read some of her clips."

"I've heard enough. You're fired."

Jackson looked at her phone. "You can't fire me. My tour of duty has expired."

"Technicalities."

For the occasion, the trio met up at Barrio Cocina y Tequileria at the end of Forest Avenue on the outskirts of downtown Plymouth. Known for its street tacos and adult refreshments, the joint was hopping every night of the week, not just on Fridays.

Harper had been smart enough to make reservations the day before. He'd chosen outdoor seating, one, because the weather was still spectacular, and two, because Barrio's indoor acoustics made conversations at moderate volumes difficult.

Sophia wore a bright yellow sundress. It provided a gorgeous contrast to her dark brown hair, and Harper loved how the sun glinted off her green eyes. He had changed into jeans and a turquoise polo shirt. Since it was her party, Jackson had decided to go casual with white capri pants and a dark blue V-neck blouse with a floral print.

"She tells me you got drunk on power," Sophia said. "A real—"

"That's false," Harper said. "I only get drunk on the finest British ales."

Jackson clinked margarita glasses with her female cohort. "Don't let him bully you off a story you want to go after."

A waitress took their orders, fish tacos for Harper, carne asada for Sophia and a Fiesta Bowl for Jackson. They snacked on queso and chips while they waited for their entrées.

"What are you going to be covering in Traverse City?" Sophia asked.

"General assignment to start. I'm really hoping to get the cops and courts beat at some point. What about you? How much are you going to be able to squeeze in between teaching classes?"

"I'll determine that," Harper said, taking a swig of his beer.

"Does that mean you've finally come to your senses?" Sophia said.

“Depends on your perspective,” Harper said. “But I am going to give you a shot if that’s what you mean. I’m giving you a feature story. Let’s see how you—”

Sophia rapped on his skull like she was knocking on a door. “Don’t patronize me, Bud. What you’re doing isn’t rocket science.”

Jackson held out her fist and bumped Sophia’s. “Girl, I don’t need to tell you anything. You got it going on.”

“I know that’s right.”

The playful banter continued through dinner and several additional rounds of drinks. Around nine, Harper decided he’d had enough of being ganged up on.

“In all seriousness, Miss Emily Grace Jackson,” he said, “I hate to see you go. You’ve taught me a thing or two, and I have no doubt you’ll do the same up north. Bon voyage.”

Chapter 34

WEDNESDAY, SEPTEMBER 16

Keshawn Stokes opened the door of Amato's a few minutes after noon and was hit with the smell of pizza sauce, cheese and pepperoni. It was as if the walls were infused with the stuff. He locked the door behind him, turned and made his way past the prep line, an old brick oven, a pair of walk-in coolers and a dishwashing area to the office.

It was two hours before his usual arrival time at Plymouth's oldest pizza joint. As manager, he prided himself on always being the first to arrive. Cleaning whatever the previous night's crew missed. Oiling pizza pans, making dough, stocking extra bags of mozzarella. Being prepared was who he was, a trait he hoped would suit him well in the courtroom as an attorney in the not-too-distant future.

Every shift he worked at Amato's, every pizza he tossed, brought him one step closer to that future. It kept him going, kept his attitude upbeat. Eyes on the prize. He took satisfaction from maintaining the pizzeria's reputation as the city's best, too. The *Detroit Free Press*, in fact, ranked it among the metropolitan area's top ten annually.

However, there was one duty even "Better Call Stokes," as some of his teenage staff called him, didn't relish: reviewing a month's worth of internal and external security camera footage. He put it off as long as he could, but any further delay would mean days' worth of video wouldn't get recorded. The system's hard drives were maxed out.

The recordings rarely revealed much. Since workers knew they were being recorded and also knew there were no blind spots except in the restrooms, most didn't try to pilfer or even take a quick vape hit. Vince Amato didn't hesitate to fire anyone stepping out of line or prosecute a worker with light fingers.

As a new hire seven years ago, Stokes had seen his share of firings and a couple of arrests. His boss was tough but treated those who worked hard and kept their noses clean very well. Amato paid staff $12 an hour to start, $15 after a year. When Stokes was promoted to the managerial ranks, his pay jumped to $40,000 per year.

Fast-forwarding with occasional stops for closer looks, Stokes made it through the internal video in a little more than an hour. Nothing out of the ordinary. He usually took even less time with the video shot outside the shop.

A never-ending parade of cars pulled in and out of the lot, to pick up either their pies or beer, chips and lottery tickets at the next-door Mayflower Party Shoppe. The camera on the other side of the building caught some of the same scenes from a different angle. It also captured the occasional comings and goings of reporters and old Henry Reston from the *Independent*, the little newspaper that wrote about Stokes's hometown.

Damn shame what had happened. Burned to the ground and Henry killed along with a cop. Stokes couldn't count the number of pizzas and calzones he had made Doc over the years, always with anchovies and black olives. Couldn't get enough of either.

That detective, Adams, a ham, mushroom and onion guy, had interviewed Stokes and his staff. Nobody saw anything or realized something was happening until they smelled smoke. Adams had taken the hard drive with the recording of the outside video and returned it a week later. Said he didn't see anything suspicious on it.

Nevertheless, Stokes was going to review it. He made himself a steak and cheese grinder and grabbed a bottle of water from the cooler before sitting down to watch. One perk of being the manager, he could eat and drink as much he wanted with the owner's blessing.

He gnawed off a large bite of the grinder, savoring the melted Parmesan and mozzarella and the creaminess of the mayonnaise. Stokes knew it wasn't the healthiest of lunches, but at twenty-four, he rationalized that he could get away with it without clogging his arteries.

The recording started the day before the fire at the newspaper. He breezed through the first day in minutes. He kept the recording flying until ninety minutes before the fire. It was one of those slow but steady summer nights at Amato's. Just busy enough to keep him and his staff occupied.

From the account Ray Harper and Emily Jackson had written in the *Independent*, Stokes knew the cop had stopped by the office sometime after nine that Wednesday night. He watched the recording as the cop parked in the paper's rear lot, next to Doc's vehicle, and walked around the office, presumably to enter through the front door.

Stokes paused the recording and scolded himself for assuming the cop had gone in the front door. The newspaper's back door was enclosed. A side entrance led to stairs that went up to the door. The only chance for detection was through a window in the enclosure that faced the camera. With a blind covering the top half of the window, only the door handle and a small section of the door below it were visible. It was at least twenty yards from the camera.

Adams would've caught someone entering from the back door. He was the trained detective and Stokes just a second-year law student. Still, his curiosity was eating at him. He played the recording at normal speed and kept his eyes fixed on the back door.

The cop never appeared, meaning he had gone to the front door. Stokes reasoned that whoever killed the two men and torched the place had to have come in through the back.

Doc wouldn't have let his killer or killers in through the front door, he thought.

Stokes hit play on the recording again, and twenty minutes ticked by with nothing happening. At 9:35 p.m., he saw a glimmer of light in the enclosure's window.

Stokes first thought it was the parking lot lights kicking on as the sun fully set. He rewound the recording and played it three more times. It couldn't be the parking lot lights, because once they were on, the window would've shown nothing but a constant reflection of the light.

It didn't. It was a quick flash, nothing more. Stokes zoomed the recording to enlarge the area around the door handle. It made the recording a fraction grainy but after the flash of light, he could clearly make out someone's head and then their hands.

The person appeared to have cornrows on his head and was fiddling with the door's lock. The object that caused the quick flash of light was in his hands. A second later, the cornrowed man pushed open the door and stood.

Stokes saw him and then a second person, probably a man, walk through the door. Dim light bled out from the door, coming from the newspaper's kitchen. He had been in the office enough to know its layout. The kitchen went dark as the door closed.

After several minutes of stillness, Stokes hit fast forward on the recording once more. About thirty minutes after the two men had entered through the back door, flames became visible from the street and soon the entire structure was engulfed.

The cornrowed man and his partner had to have murdered Henry Reston, Stokes thought. Too bad the recording didn't capture the killers leaving. Still, he had a hard time believing Adams had missed what he had just witnessed. What should he do about it?

As a future officer of the court, the obvious answer was to take the recording to the police. It was evidence that could help lead to the suspects. But Adams had already bungled it once. Would he do it again?

Stokes looked at an old-fashioned analog clock on the office wall. It was two forty-five p.m. The Wednesday evening crew wouldn't start showing up for at least forty minutes. He had enough time to run a copy of the recording over to Harper and Jackson at Doc's old loft, the temporary home of the newspaper.

Stokes took his work apron off and set it on a hook in the office. He tossed the remnants of his lunch in a garbage can near the prep line, locked the door to Amato's and jogged to his Ford Fiesta. It was facing the lot where the newspaper office had stood. Demolition crews had already cleared the debris and backfilled what had once been a basement. A fresh layer of soil had been hydroseeded and grass would eventually emerge. It would be as if the office had never been there.

In less than five minutes, Stokes was parking the Fiesta on Penniman Avenue. He rang a doorbell to the loft and told Harper via an intercom he had a special delivery.

"I don't see any pizza, Ke," Harper said.

"I've got something even better," Stokes said, stepping into the loft. He looked around and smiled. "Damn, Doc did all right for himself, didn't he?"

"That he did," Harper said. "What's on your mind?"

Stokes pulled a green Lexar flash drive from his pocket. "I think you're going to want to see what's on this."

Harper motioned for Stokes to sit at his workstation. Stokes filled him in and then showed him the recording. The editor's eyes went wide and what little color he had seemed to vanish.

"I've seen that guy before," Harper said.

Chapter 35

WEDNESDAY, SEPTEMBER 16

Before leaving the loft, Harper copied the Amato's recording to his laptop's hard drive. He grabbed the flash drive and his phone and walked to the parking deck to his Honda. As he pulled onto Harvey Street, he picked up the phone, went to his favorites list and dialed.

"I was about ready to call it a day," said Dan Chamberlain, answering on the second ring, "and get nine holes in at Whispering Willows."

"Sorry," Harper said. "But I've got something you're going to want to see."

They agreed to meet at Twelve Oaks Mall in thirty minutes. The regional mall sat about ten miles north of Plymouth and was always packed with shoppers at its Apple Store, Nordstrom and an array of trendy shops and restaurants.

Twelve Oaks was far enough away to avoid unwanted attention, Harper thought. He made his way to the food court and ordered a chicken quesadilla, nachos and a Pepsi from Taco Bell.

About halfway through his feast, Chamberlain sat down in a chair across from him. Harper reached into his backpack, pulled out his MacBook Pro and inserted a flash drive. He queued up the video from Amato's, then turned the laptop to face Chamberlain.

"Hit play."

"What am I looking at?"

"The manager from Amato's brought me a CCTV recording of the night Snyder and Doc were murdered," Harper said. "It shows our parking lot and the back door as well as the traffic on Main Street."

"Why haven't I already seen that footage?"

"Because Adams beat you to it. He snagged it early on. But he was stupid enough to return it to Amato's."

"Probably figured they'd record over it without looking."

"I think you're right. Lucky for us, Keshawn Stokes did look at it. He brought it to me a little while ago."

A look of confusion crossed Chamberlain's face. "Why would he bring it to you?"

"Got to know him over the years, the two of us working next door to each other. Real personable. We hang out on occasion."

Chamberlain returned his attention to the laptop. Before he could hit play on the video, Harper came around the table and took control. He zoomed the picture to focus on the back door as seen through the entrance enclosure's window.

"You can see the door handle."

Chamberlain stopped the recording when he saw light reflecting off something being held by a dark pair of hands. "Holy shit."

He repeated the phrase after seeing the cornrowed man's head and a second man entering through the back door that had just been picked. Chamberlain took his glasses off and rubbed his temples.

"It gets better," Harper said. "I've seen the guy picking the lock, actually talked to him."

"Wait. What? When?"

Harper filled him in on his encounter at the Penniman Deli. He gave him a thorough description of the Black man with cornrows and his partner.

"They were casing the loft and you," Chamberlain said. "I'm surprised you're not dead. A couple of pros. No doubt about it."

Harper felt the hair on the back of his neck stand up. Fear gave way to frustration in a flash.

"You ready to tell me whose fingerprints were on the lock pick set? We're talking about the same guy, right?"

Chamberlain sighed. "Has to be. You can see it in his hands in the video."

"Well?"

"Milton Johnson. Last known address is in Detroit. Arrested several times in his late teens and early twenties."

"For what?"

"Shoplifting, home invasion. Never served any time."

"Why did you say 'last known address'?"

"Milton Johnson appears to have gone off the grid in the mid-1990s, or at least he stopped committing crimes and using credit cards. His criminal and financial histories came to an abrupt end."

"So, you think what?"

"Changed his name, maybe. Moved out of the country. There's a lot of possibilities."

"But even if he changed his name, he can't change his fingerprint, right?"

"No, of course not. About the best you can do is alter them. I've seen a few people mangle their own hands, cut 'em up, really disfigure the shit out of them. Read about criminals that'll go as far as using acid to burn the prints off their fingertips."

"That can't be the case here," Harper said. "The report showed a clear match with this Milton Johnson. Apparently, he's back on the grid. So, what do we do?"

Chamberlain rewound and watched the break-in at the *Independent* again, shaking his head the whole time. "We're going to get a sketch artist on this pronto," he said. "You're going to describe every detail you can remember about Johnson and the other suspect to the artist. She's a damn good one, so I suspect we'll have a pretty close depiction. Better than what we can get off of your video."

"How are you going to do that without Adams or Flaherty getting wind of it?"

"We'll work at her place."

"Which is where?"

"State police post in Northville. Relax, I've worked with this gal a long time. She'll do a bang-up job, and then I can issue the BOLO right from there. It'll be out before either one of those pricks knows a thing."

Harper's body language screamed apprehension.

"Why are you getting cold feet now?" Chamberlain asked. "You've been pushing to get this into the paper at every step."

Harper picked up the cafeteria tray in front of him and sat it at an adjacent table. He looked around and noticed the food court was starting to fill up. He glanced at his watch and saw that it was a quarter after six p.m. He wished he had a cigarette.

"What if we're wrong? Hell, what if we're right and those goons come after me?"

"The best thing for you is to hide in plain sight," Chamberlain said after a brief, uncomfortable silence. "The sketches will be sent to all the media outlets in town. That's not something Flaherty can control. Once it's out, once those two guys' faces are plastered everywhere, they're burned."

"Yeah?"

"Absolutely. Those dudes will be so toxic, there's no way they'll show up anywhere near you or Plymouth."

"What's going to stop Flaherty from sending someone else? You know, like the guy that beat up my folks?"

"Too much heat, at least in the short term. But we're going to have to finish the lot of them off in a hurry. They've got more resources and manpower than us. The odds are in their favor. You get me?"

Harper nodded. "How long do I hold off on writing the story?"

Chamberlain stood and motioned with his head that it was time to go. "You call Flaherty twenty minutes after I issue the BOLO. All the media will have it by then, but you'll be the first one to get to him. You play it straight, like you don't know a damn thing except what's on the bulletin."

"I'm going to enjoy that call," Harper said. They walked toward the mall exit at a fast clip. "Gonna make that bastard squirm."

Chapter 36

<u>WEDNESDAY, September 16</u>

Adams dumped the remainder of his coffee in the sink, squirted dishwashing soap in the glass Bunn decanter and filled it with hot water. He swished it around, emptied the water and rinsed it clean. He repeated the process with a second decanter and then made coffee so strong it would put the finest Turkish blend to shame.

Officers began filling the patrol room for the evening briefing. A few grabbed cups of the brew. Adams filled his own mug, a white ceramic piece adorned with Plymouth's city logo. As lead detective, it was his job to keep up on what was happening at the street-cop level.

Sworn officers were divided into three shifts: mornings, seven a.m. to seven p.m.; overlap, ten a.m. to ten p.m.; and midnights, seven p.m. to seven a.m. Adams worked all three shifts a few times each month to brief each squad on the detective bureau's current investigations.

A pair of computer workstations were set up in the back of the squad room. Patrol officers shared them to check email and news from other city departments or to make use of various law enforcement tools. Adams parked himself at one of the workstations and pulled up Michigan's version of the Law Enforcement Information Network.

There was the usual plethora of Detroit Police Department posts. Lookout notices for suspects in crimes committed in Dearborn, Redford Township, Royal Oak and Shelby Township also appeared, many with mug shots attached. "Shitheads," or suspects, all looked the same to Adams. White. Black. Latino. Arab. The names changed; the cold, punkish look of criminals never did.

He took a sip of his black coffee and, in his mind, declared it nectar. He kept scrolling down until a BOLO from the Michigan State Police stopped him cold. A sketch of two men appeared. One an African-American man with tight cornrows and the other a white guy with a thick mop of gray hair and a bushy moustache of the same color.

Adams exited LEIN and returned the computer to its intranet home page. He picked up his coffee mug as calmly as he could and gave slight nods to a few officers as he made his way out of the patrol room. He continued until he was out of the building and standing in front of his unmarked Ford Edge.

Adams unlocked the vehicle with a fob and pulled a burner cell phone out of his pocket. He got in and closed the door. He dialed the number to his old Detroit Police Department partner.

"Yeah," said Dwight Alexander.

"You've been made," Adams said.

"What are you talking about?"

"You and Turner have been made. I just saw the BOLO with two very accurate sketches."

"Goddamn it. How?"

"You've been retired too long. You know as well as I do the 'how' isn't on a lookout. Doesn't matter how anyway. The two of you have to get out of here right now."

"Well, no shit, Sherlock. We got contingency plans in place."

"Turner at work?"

"Yup."

"Wonderful," Adams said. "You better hope nobody down there has looked at LEIN."

"When did the BOLO go out?"

"Less than an hour ago. Christ, they've probably got him in a room down there right now. He won't talk, right?"

"Let's not go assuming anything," Alexander said. "I'll try him now."

"Do it."

Alexander hung up without another word. Adams was sweating. He reached for the coffee but spilled it on the passenger seat. He pulled a wad of napkins from the Edge's center console and began blotting the coffee up. Adams yanked an evidence bag from the glove department, put the soaked napkins in and sealed it. He'd dispose of the bag later.

THE CHIME FROM ELDON TURNER'S IPHONE went off at 7:10 p.m. He was making his rounds on the third floor of the old Wayne County jail. A reprieve from a mid-September heat wave had made the ninety-one-year-old structure comfortable for a change. Turner bantered with some of the inmates as he walked, sharing details of his previous night's meal—a prime piece of steak and roasted vegetables with sweet potato pie for dessert—with men who had dined on a concoction of rubbery chicken and over-boiled noodles.

He turned the corner into a hallway without jail cells. Turner glanced around before pulling his personal phone out from a case on his duty belt. He swiped the screen to life and then punched in his six-digit security code. The chime was an alert for a new text message. He opened the app and read the message, which consisted of just one word: "SUNSET."

Turner abandoned his rounds and made his way down two flights of stairs to the first floor. His heart raced as he tried to figure out which scenario had made Alexander activate their emergency plans. The list of possibilities wasn't long: the police or other law enforcement agency was closing in or their identities as hit men had been exposed, perhaps publicly.

A decision about how to play his current situation had to be made in seconds. Should he bolt out the door without explanation or come up with a diversion to ease his escape? Turner reasoned he would've already been detained if the jail's command officers or a sheriff's deputy liked him for one of his extracurricular "jobs."

He decided to test his theory and opened a door to the administrative suite. The jail commander and his deputy occupied offices in the suite, while a few lower-ranking administrators had desks in an open area. Turner approached the commander's administrative assistant with as big of a smile as he could muster.

"Good evening, Jocelyn," he said. "You're working late. Hey, I'm going on a Starbucks run. Wondered if you and the chief—if he's still here—wanted something."

"He's still here," she said, rolling her eyes, "which is why I'm here late for the second straight night. Let me check. Hold tight."

The midthirties woman, with medium-length light brown hair, hazel eyes and an efficient soccer-mom aura, left her desk, knocked on the commander's door and poked her head in. Turner scanned her desk, reflexively looking for anything incriminating. A stack of file folders sat to the left of her computer and a printout of a report showing incoming and outgoing prisoners rested on top of a desk calendar.

"Sergeant," Jocelyn said, turning toward him, "the commander would like to talk to you."

Turner's heart rate rarely exceeded one hundred while he was carrying out a hit. But he was sure his Fitbit was registering about one hundred fifty at the moment. He smiled at Jocelyn as he walked into Commander Ryan Franklin's office.

"Take a seat, sergeant."

"Good evening, sir. What can I do for you?"

"Internal affairs is planning on interviewing you again about the Patton incident. I've made you available at zero nine hundred Friday morning."

"I thought we had gone through it pretty thoroughly the first time, sir," Turner said.

"I'm not privy to their reasons, sergeant. I want to make sure there's nothing you left out of your report or failed to brief me on. I don't need any blowback right now for a screwup by anyone under my command. So now is your chance to set the record straight."

Well, sir, the Patton incident was actually a well-planned hit on a suspect who could've implicated one of my clients in a criminal act. In fact, sir, I've murdered thirty-seven people over the years for money. Why, you ask? Well, sir, it's because of the bullshit salary you and the county pay me. And you know what, sir? I was really good at it until a few months ago. My heart hasn't been in it like before. So, I've messed up and dragged my partner and myself down a crap hole. I think that about covers it, sir.

Turner pushed the self-flagellating thoughts away. "Yes, sir."

"Patton was obviously executed," Franklin said. "From what I've gathered, she kept a low profile around here. No way she pissed off enough of her fellow inmates to that degree. You must have heard something by now."

"Would've been nice to talk directly to her attackers," Turner said, "before the state shipped them off to different facilities."

"That was never going to happen. What about their friends still under our watch?"

"Rumor was that she was trying to start some type of Aryan group for women. Sisters didn't take kindly to it, sir."

Franklin stood up from his desk and glanced out a window overlooking Beaubien Street. "I thought we had stamped the gang shit out of here."

"Never can get rid of it completely, sir," Turner said. "It's like a handful of worms. You slice their tails off and they all grow back."

Franklin turned to him. "Don't offer that up to IA. Make them ask the questions. You hear me, sergeant?"

"Copy that, sir. Loud and clear."

"Very well. If you're going over to Starbucks, get me one of those espresso Fraps. A large."

"That's a lot of caffeine, sir."

"I need it, sergeant I'm dealing with another round of budget cuts. The unions are already up my ass, and the county executive is pressuring the hell out of my boss. Shit runs downhill."

"Yes, it does, sir."

Turner stood and turned to leave.

"One more thing, sergeant." Franklin slid a BOLO sheet across his desk. "That perp looks just like you. What are the odds?"

Turner glanced down and looked at the sketches of himself and Alexander. "The nose is off. They gave that brother a white man's nose. Otherwise, yeah, I can kinda see it, too.

Guess we all got a twin somewhere."

He slid the sheet of paper back toward Franklin and left the office. He walked out of the jail onto Clinton Street and took it to St. Antoine. He passed people heading toward the Frank Murphy Hall of Justice, a circuit court, and then reached Starbucks at the corner of Monroe a few minutes later. He kept his pace even, not wanting to draw attention.

He turned left onto Monroe. A few moments later, he entered the Greektown Casino parking garage and went straight to a bank of elevators. His getaway ride was a silver Honda Odyssey parked in long-term on level five.

The space was registered to Milton Johnson, the name given to him at birth. He'd shed that identity long ago in favor of Eldon Turner, the guy who appeared to be the salt of the earth, albeit with refined tastes.

Cameras were everywhere in the garage, so there was no point in trying to conceal his identity. When authorities, including his nitwit boss, put together that he was the man from the BOLO sketch, they would have a clear line of breadcrumbs to track him. Well, at least until he ditched the minivan.

A second vehicle would be waiting for him at an Ohio Turnpike rest area. Turner pulled the Odyssey onto southbound I-75 and drove for about thirty minutes. He exited onto Telegraph Road near the city of Monroe and pulled into the parking lot of a Walmart. He changed clothes, stowed his jail uniform in a duffel and set it on the floorboard behind the passenger seat.

By now, Franklin might have had an inkling that he'd let a suspect walk right out the door. Turner wasn't waiting to find out. He got back on the highway and continued south. After switching vehicles, he'd get off the turnpike and take back roads all the way into Kentucky.

He'd meet up with Alexander in Harlan County near the Virginia border and lie low for a few days in a well-stocked, run-down trailer. Alexander would stay there among his "kin," while Turner would drive to a hole-in-the-wall apartment in a not-so-nice section of Memphis. In a few months, they'd quietly exit the country separately into Mexico.

Chapter 37

FRIDAY, September 18

Everything was so still, all the time, like a valley of death occasionally punctuated with fleeting signs of life. An old beater driving too fast on the winding mountain blacktop. Teenagers walking down the same road saying "hey" to people passing time on porch swings. The chirping and cawing of birds flying overhead and an occasional gunshot off in the distance, echoing like a boulder falling in a canyon.

And wretched morning fog, every day. As if the dead were yawning and yearning for the lives they once had. It had only been a couple days since Eldon Turner's arrival deep in the heart of Harlan County, Kentucky. Yet each hour between the dark and the light seemed like an eternity.

Stilted conversations with his hit-man partner, Dwight Alexander. A television set locked to Fox News. There was no escape. Turner had known this day was always a possibility in his line of work. He just hadn't known how tough being the hunted instead of the hunter would be.

The emergency getaway plan he and Alexander had created years ago and tweaked only slightly since was a joke. No way they were going to make it into Mexico. Hell, it had taken quick maneuvering just to get through Ohio. If he hadn't ditched the Honda Odyssey in favor of an old Ford sedan, he wouldn't have made Kentucky.

Turner grabbed the remote and turned the television off. He rose from a pea-green velvet couch, whose origin dated to the 1970s, and went to the kitchen to make breakfast. The place was stocked, he had to give Alexander that much. Granted, it wasn't what his epicurean palate was accustomed to, but it wasn't exactly hard rations either.

He pulled Bob Evans sausage and a dozen eggs from the fridge. Much of the pan bread Alexander had concocted for the previous night's dinner, which consisted of smoked pork chops, green beans, salad and fried apples, remained and would be splendid with a fried egg and sausage between two thick pieces.

In minutes, the sausage was sizzling, and the eggs were nearly done. Alexander walked into the kitchen shirtless with his gray mop of hair sticking up in all directions. Damn if he didn't look like a redneck version of Albert Einstein.

"Hungry?" Turner asked.

"How long have you known me?"

"Too long," Turner said. "Lucky for you, there's enough here for both of us."

Alexander yawned. "Whatever. I don't smell any coffee."

"If you're talking about that mud you make in the old range pot, well, I've got my standards."

Alexander pulled a clean glass pot from a dishwasher on the other side of the kitchen. "Make it myself. I ain't down for any of that prissy shit you drink, professor."

In minutes, Alexander had coffee boiling on the stove, so pungent it overpowered the smell of the frying sausage and eggs. He poured a large mug full, smelled it as if it were a prized bottle of Bordeaux and drank. No sugar, milk or half-and-half.

Turner looked at his partner, and his mouth curled like he had just bitten into the world's most sour apple.

"Good to the last fuckin' drop," Alexander said. "Now, I know how much you enjoy my company and all, but my kinfolk are startin' to talk, what with me holed up in this trailer with the likes of you."

"You mean a Black man?"

"Now, me, I'm a freethinking man of the people. And by that, I mean all the people. Black, white, Latino, Asian—"

"You've killed them all without impunity, I must admit," Turner said. "You're an equal-opportunity hit man."

"Damn straight," Alexander said. "The only color that matters to me is green, my friend. But these simple folk around here ain't as progressive as I am."

Turner handed him a sausage and fried egg sandwich. He then finished his own and took a seat at a small, circular table.

"What I'm trying to tell ya, partner, is it's time for you to move on to Memphis. Have you talked to your people down there? They got your place set up?"

Turner took a second mouthful of the sandwich and savored the egg, which had taken on an even better taste having been fried in bacon grease. He studied Alexander's face and debated how to play his next few words. After dabbing the sandwich in egg yolk drippings from his plate, he decided honesty was the best policy.

"I haven't talked to 'my people' because I'm not going to Memphis."

Alexander chewed the last bite of his sandwich but didn't bother to swallow it before speaking. "You going straight to Mexico? That wasn't part of the plan, but it's your neck."

Turner shook his head as he wiped his mouth with a napkin. "I'm not going to Mexico, either."

Tiny bits of bread and egg clung to Alexander's mustache. His face contorted into a mask of confusion. He wiped his mouth with the back of his hand. "Fuck you talkin' about? You got someplace better to go?"

"As a matter of fact, I do."

"Stop playing games, goddamn it. Where do ya think you're goin'?"

"Home. Detroit. I've got unfinished business to—"

Alexander pushed his plate and coffee mug to the side. "What? Have you lost your fuckin' mind? What business?"

"I made a promise to someone," Turner said. "I intend to keep it."

"I have no idea what in the hell you're talking about," Alexander said. "Every cop in the state of Michigan is looking for us and you want to go back? You'll get your stupid ass caught."

"I don't care. It's about time I did something right in this world."

Alexander stood, looked around the trailer and then leaned against the kitchen counter. "I knew it. Goddamn it, I knew it. I could tell on the last few jobs. You put on a good act with that newspaper guy and cop, but I knew. How long you been feelin' this way?"

Turner took a sip of his black tea, which he had doctored with milk and Splenda. "A year, maybe. I'm not sure I even know why it changed for me. I mean, all this time, the killing was never the main thing. It was just a means to an end. I liked the money and the lifestyle."

"You shoulda got out soon as you started having second thoughts," Alexander said. "This fix we're in, it ain't all your fault. We both got sloppy, I guess."

Turner shrugged. "It is what it is."

Alexander nodded. He reached into his jeans back pocket and pulled out a TAC Force knife. He made no effort to conceal what he was doing from his partner. He used his free hand to extend the knife's three-and-a-quarter-inch black blade. He then got into a defensive posture, like he was a basketball player getting ready to guard a ball handler.

"This ain't exactly how I pictured our partnership comin' to an end," Alexander said. "I respect the hell out of what you just said, but I can't let you do it. You'll end up in jail before you get a chance to make whatever amends you're aimin' for. Then you'll give me up, sure as the world."

Turner had anticipated Alexander's move. Having worked with the man for as long as he had, he knew him inside and out. Even when he wasn't on a job, Alexander always carried the TAC Force knife. If a problem arose, he was prepared.

Turner thought back to a trip to New Orleans he had taken with his partner five years earlier. After back-to-back jobs, the Dynamic Duo had decided a dose of fun was in order and Mardi Gras was just what they were looking for, with copious amounts of food, women and booze, and not necessarily in that order.

After a night of partying, they'd ambled back toward their hotel. A trio of young street thugs thought they had found easy marks with the two slightly inebriated middle-aged tourists. The leader pulled a switchblade and advanced on them, demanding money and their watches. Alexander grabbed the TAC Force from his front pants pocket and gave the younger man fair warning to back off.

Instead, he lunged with the switchblade, going for Alexander's throat. Alexander used a roof block to stop the move, sliced the thug's knife-holding arm, and then did an inside sweep, cutting the younger man across the chest in a long horizontal line. The leader fell to the ground, blood seeping through his T-shirt. His cohorts turned tail and ran.

While Turner could take care of business with an inexperienced knife fighter, he knew he was no match for Alexander. But he had two distinct advantages in the current situation: the timing of his announcement and the ability to plan for it. He had given no indication that he would not follow the emergency escape plan; in fact, he'd talked up its virtues.

Before starting breakfast, Turner had executed his plan by strapping his Sig Sauer SRD45 with silencer to the underside of the cheap dinette table. He carried a Glock 43, a nine-millimeter weapon, in an ankle holster as backup.

As Alexander pulled the TAC Force, Turner reached under the table and yanked the Sig Sauer free. His partner's eyes went wide when he saw it aimed at his chest.

"All this time," Turner said, "I looked up to you. The Gray Ghost, the best hitman in Detroit. I just can't believe that you, you of all people, would be stupid enough to bring a knife to a gunfight."

Alexander sprung out of his defensive position and launched himself at Turner. Without flinching, Turner put his first shot in Alexander's chest, a second into his forehead. And, like that, the partnership was dissolved before Dwight Alexander's dead body hit the floor.

Chapter 38

FRIDAY, September 18

Sadie Rodgers surveyed her walk-in closet for a more casual suit to wear to the office. With nothing on her schedule until after lunch, she didn't care that it was approaching ten a.m. It was Friday, which was casual day at city hall by design.

For five dollars donated to one of Plymouth's official charities, employees were allowed to wear blue jeans. Rodgers didn't wear them often despite the way they accentuated her trim figure. She decided on a pale-yellow two-piece suit. She slipped on the slacks, picked a long-sleeved white blouse, and finished her ensemble with gold earrings. Rodgers checked her look in the mirror and liked what she saw.

"Sadie?" Tim Rodgers called. "You dressed?"

It took her a dozen strides to emerge from the closet, which featured forty pairs of shoes positioned precisely on shelving, and a dresser/jewelry showcase in the middle. The space was Rodgers's favorite in the home. She didn't bother replying to her husband. She walked past him, sat at a white antique-style vanity, pulled a blue tube of It's a 10 firm-hold gel from a drawer, squeezed a dab on her hands and ran them through her hair.

Tim walked up behind Sadie and tossed a large brown envelope on the vanity's left side. She glanced at him in the mirror as she continued to fiddle with her hair.

"I've filed for divorce," Tim said. "You might want to look through that packet. Our first court date is in a month. I'm guessing you're not going to fight me on this?"

Sadie opened a second drawer in the vanity and pulled out La Mer sheer pressed powder. She applied it with a soft-touch bristle brush for about a minute before responding.

"Why would I?" she said. "Our marriage has been dead for a long time."

"If you believe that, why did we bother going through marriage counseling? Why did you promise me four years ago you would give it your best shot to save us and keep our family together for Sara's sake?"

She finished applying the powder and turned to him. "It wasn't about Sara. She's a strong girl."

"Then what?" Tim said. "I don't get it. You tried for about a month, then poof, you were done. What did I do?"

"You didn't do anything wrong."

"Then I'm at a complete loss."

A slight smile curled on Sadie's lips. "That's because you're dense, Tim."

His jaw went slack, and his mouth opened slightly, but no words came out.

"Let me clue you in," Sadie said. "Four years ago, I had a serious challenge from a former Plymouth mayor. I *needed* you. I needed to project the right image to the voters."

"So, Sara and I, we're all about the optics?"

"Not Sara. She's my daughter. I love her, and if you're looking for sole custody of her, I will fight you tooth and nail."

Tim's face flushed. His hands went from his hips to a questioning, pleading motion before he spoke. "So, basically, I was a prop to help your campaign. Why keep me around after that? Why didn't you file for divorce after the election?"

"Oh, I wanted to, trust me."

"You thought it would be better to treat me like a leper for years? Are you really that cruel?"

"I was advised not to seek a divorce."

"By whom?"

"The party. Plymouth isn't going to be my last political stop. Not by a long shot."

"Hard to spin a candidate that dumps her husband for no good reason, right?"

"You're finally catching on."

Tim stepped closer to his wife and invaded her personal space. He kept his hands at his sides. "I don't suppose an adulterous whore is the image you want to project for the upcoming election, either."

Sadie's facial expression went from cold and vacant to a malevolent icy stare. "I have no idea what you're talking about."

"I know about you and Flaherty," Tim said, his voice dropping a couple of octaves. "I'm not blind and I'm also not without resources. The two of you are utterly despicable."

He stepped away from Sadie and went to his own closet. He pulled a second large brown envelope from underneath a stack of winter wool sweaters on a top shelf. He opened the envelope and pulled out three eight-by-ten photos as he walked back toward Sadie.

The first photo depicted Sadie in a tender embrace with Neil Flaherty outside of a hotel. The second and third photos showed Flaherty and then Sadie exiting the hotel room.

"There's more if you'd care to see," he said. "Well, shit, there goes your image, hon."

Sadie went back to the vanity. She opened the envelope and glanced at the first few pages of documents. She nodded as if she was agreeing with what she was reading. A few minutes later, she set the documents down.

"We can do this quietly and the information and photos I have stay out of the public eye," Tim said, "or we can do this the hard way. Your choice."

Dealing with a potential threat from her husband was the farthest thing from Sadie's mind. She had been so engrossed in finding a way out of the hit-and-run mess, she'd turned a blind eye to what was happening in her own home.

Whatever. Just another obstacle to overcome, Sadie thought. In a nanosecond, she decided how to play it.

Contempt for her husband rose in Sadie's chest as she opened the vanity drawer with her powder and other makeup and pulled out a black and silver Ruger .22-caliber pistol. She moved at a quick but steady pace toward her husband, keeping the gun at her side. She walked a step past him and then swept her right foot into his left ankle. He fell hard onto his back.

She pounced on him like a panther. Sadie sat on his chest and shoved the Ruger under his chin. He tried to push her off, but at five-seven and one hundred forty-five pounds, he couldn't muster enough strength to buck her.

"I will blow your brains out right here, right now," she said. She pulled the hammer back and put her finger on the trigger. "You'll get your divorce after I'm re-elected in November. You will not go to the press. You will not take full custody of Sara. If you try, you will be dead. There is no place I can't get to you. Do you understand me?"

Tim's face was turning purple. "Can't breathe," he moaned. "Get off, I can't—"

Sadie took her left hand and raked his face with her fingernails. She then ripped her expensive jacket and her blouse and messed up her hair. She finally got off his chest and backed away. She kept the Ruger trained on her husband, picked up her cell phone and punched in 911.

"Think carefully about your next move," Sadie said. "I can call my cops right now and have you arrested. You attacked me. I fought back and was able to get to my gun. My word against yours, and guess what, they're going to believe me."

Tim Rodgers got to his feet and breathed hard. Blood trickled in small beads down his face. It wasn't the first time Sadie had gotten physical with him. Along with charm and beauty, she had an explosive temper. Despite their years together, he couldn't always predict when it would blow.

It had gotten progressively worse as Sadie's political career advanced. He was usually able to fend off anything serious but had taken more than one punch and several slaps to the face. Tim internalized the aggression, believing if he resolved to do better, to not beef about petty issues or air his own frustrations, his wife's physical outbursts would stop.

And they had for a time. He'd thought it was his extra effort at first. Sadie was facing the same pressures at city hall, but with his support, perhaps she was getting better. Then came late-night texting when she thought he was asleep. Meetings at all hours, even on the weekend. Unexplained gifts.

A year ago, Tim had hired a private investigator. Within a few days, his worst fears were confirmed: his wife was having an affair. When he saw who her lover was, Plymouth's police chief, a man who smiled at him and shook his hand at public events, it made his flesh crawl.

After he saw the cheating wasn't going to stop, he contacted a half-dozen divorce attorneys before settling on a Southfield specialist in the field. He wasn't interested in being vengeful, he just wanted it over.

Tim wanted his daughter living with him. Without him as a target for Sadie's anger, he feared Sara would become the new recipient. He was certain she hadn't hit their daughter. On the issue of custody, he wasn't willing to budge. He didn't care that Sadie had just raked his face, cut off his airway and pointed a gun at his head.

Given her frenzied, irrational state, now was not the time to push it. He would fight with everything he had in court. He would try to survive the next few months until November. He could keep the charade up for Sara.

Tim raised his hands in a surrender motion, then bent over at the waist, putting his hands on his knees, still trying to catch his breath.

"Okay, Sadie, okay."

"Okay, what?" she said, still pointing the gun at him.

"No divorce until after the election. I'll call my attorney and have him stop the proceedings."

Sadie uncocked the Ruger and put it in her handbag. She looked at her ripped clothing. "See what you made me do, stupid ass?"

She walked back into her closet and closed the door behind her.

Chapter 39

SUNDAY, SEPTEMBER 20

Sophia Casey filed her first story for the *Independent* Sunday morning from Harper's apartment. The subject was all too familiar, Plymouth's ongoing parking problems.

Harper was eager to see how Sophia had done with the story. He wondered if she could breathe life into a topic city officials and residents had both grown weary of. As evidenced by her high school articles, Sophia had some talent and natural instincts as a reporter.

But she hadn't had any journalism classes in college. Term papers and lesson plans had been the extent of Sophia's writing over the past few years.

Her intentions were good. She wanted to contribute and relieve some of the pressure on Harper since Jackson's departure. Still, anxiety built as he double-clicked the Word file on his desktop.

Harper decided a beer was in order before he started to edit. He pushed away from his computer table and walked slowly into the kitchen. After a blissful weekend of making love, eating carry-out and watching football, he kept waiting for Sophia to walk up from behind, wrap her arms around him and squeeze tight.

Funny how quick he'd gotten used to all the little touches and interactions with her. Two nights and one full day was all it took. She'd left for her father's home a few hours before dinner and after they'd watched the Detroit Lions lose yet another game.

Harper felt a void in her absence. Though he was charged up to continue his investigations, though he understood their potential impact on the community and his own career, it all seemed less urgent than his need to be with Sophia. Was he in love with her?

He let out a long breath. Asking himself the question was a first for Harper. Sure, he had had crushes as a teenager. He'd used the word with his college girlfriend but knew he hadn't really meant it.

While he was brutally honest with himself about his professional career, about what he needed to do to improve and grow as a journalist, he didn't shine the same light on his personal life or feelings. He compartmentalized.

It was what had allowed him to have several one-night stands and brief flings before meeting Sophia. Those "relationships" were for fun, for satiating his needs as a man and nothing more. He thought about how he treated other people, too. They were simply a means to an end with very few exceptions. Over the years, Harper had had a golfing buddy, a softball buddy and a drinking buddy. The buddies came and went. There were no permanent friends.

Now this, with Sophia? Not what he'd expected. She was making him feel. She was making him care about something other than his next byline. It scared the living hell out of him.

He took his phone out of his back pocket, swiped it to life and hit the phone app. He went to favorites and then stopped his index finger a half-inch from Sophia's face and phone number. Harper wanted to talk to her but hesitated. Should he? Wouldn't he be surrendering the upper hand to her if he acted so... so clingy?

He clicked a button on the side of the phone and the screen went dark. Harper grabbed a bottle of Corona from the fridge and returned to his desk to edit Sophia's story. He read the first paragraph:

Cultural events and a hot downtown are a few of Plymouth's biggest strengths. Cultural events and a hot downtown are also a few of Plymouth's biggest issues, at least from a parking perspective. A local developer is hoping to solve the city's problem and keep downtown buzzing by building a three-story parking deck at the site of a former lawn care center.

Not exactly how he would have played the lead paragraph but not bad either, Harper thought. Doc would have screamed at him for writing like a "goddamned lawyer" and demanded he cut the three sentences down to one.

After a long-winded quote from the developer in the second paragraph, Sophia got into the nuts and bolts of the story. The city was currently "stuck" with a lone parking deck on Harvey Street and a couple of large surface lots, both in the downtown area, she wrote.

For a community whose cozy downtown depended on dining and nightlife, it simply wasn't enough. Numerous trial balloons for parking expansion had been floated over the years but all had been shot down. Sophia deftly explained how factions within the community fought over keeping the downtown vibrant and maintaining Plymouth as a family-friendly, quiet hamlet.

The latest parking expansion idea was for a second parking deck. The developer wanted to put a three-story structure at the corner of Ann Arbor Trail and Union Street, kitty-corner from Kellogg Park.

The lawn care center had been razed a few years earlier and the city had purchased the land. It had paved the remaining lot and used it for overflow parking or as a staging area for events like Art in the Park in July and the September Fall Festival.

Sophia's article went on to detail concerns of residents in the neighborhood adjacent to the old lawn care center. Homeowners on Maple and Wing streets were quoted as saying it would hurt the value of their property. Noise, trash and public urination were among their concerns. Advocates said a new garage would help keep restaurants, bars and the city's other shops full. What was good for business was good for Plymouth.

All in all, it was a solid effort, Harper thought. Sophia had done a thorough reporting job that required very little in the way of editing.

The anxiety he had felt before reading the story vanished. He admonished himself for doubting her abilities.

Harper uploaded the piece to the paper's website and then put it in a queue of stories to get into Wednesday's print edition, the *Independent*'s second to last. He downed the remainder of the Corona and got a mouthful of pulp from a lime wedge he had squeezed into the bottle.

This time, he didn't hesitate when he grabbed his iPhone.

"What did you think?" Sophia answered.

Harper didn't sense any nerves in her voice, which annoyed him a little. "Well, I've got to be honest. I—"

"Don't even go there," Sophia said. "It was good, and you know it."

Harper waited several beats before saying anything. Her cockiness was off the charts.

"You know what, hon, you're right," Harper said. "It was good. So good, in fact, I may nominate it for this year's Pulitzer Prize."

"Ha ha, smart-ass."

"You had that coming."

"No, you just have a problem with confident women."

Harper pulled the phone away from his ear and stared at it as if it were an alien artifact, his face slightly flushed. "That's a pretty broad statement, don't you think? I mean, let's be real. Yes, it was a good piece for someone—"

"Oh, here it comes," Sophia said, "you've got to throw in a few qualifiers."

"Why are you being like this?" Harper said. "I keep trying to compliment you and you're throwing it back in my face."

"I don't want to be patronized. Would you even tell me the truth if it sucked? Or would you just throw out a few superlatives, rewrite it and hope I didn't notice?"

For one of the few times in his life, Harper didn't know what to say. Her questions hit a nerve, which meant there was probably a large element of truth in them.

"Are you still there?" Sophia asked.

"Yeah, still here. If I've treated you that way, I'm sorry. I know what being patronized feels like. Your story was damn good, no qualifiers. I believe you would be a fine journalist if you decided to make it your career."

"Thank you. Honesty is all I'm looking for, Ray. I want our relationship to be based on honesty. Don't hold back to spare my feelings. I'll do the same for you, promise."

At that moment, Harper realized he was all in, not only with his work, but with Sophia, too.

Chapter 40

MONDAY, SEPTEMBER 21

Every minute of every day since the hit-and-run, Sammy Bell had lived with the idea that he'd caused his brother's death. If only he hadn't challenged him to a race. If only he had heeded the pedestrian signal's blinking red hand telling him to stop before trying to cross Ann Arbor Road.

If only.

Sammy had wished a thousand times over he had been the one to get hit, not Max. Then there would be no more pain, no more guilt. His parents hadn't blamed him, instead focusing their rage on the person who hit Max. He was pretty sure his father would kill that person, whoever it was, with his bare hands if he got the chance.

It didn't mean there wasn't friction. His parents had returned to work, slowly at first but now pretty much back to their normal routines. They expected the same of him, only Sammy wasn't up to the task. He couldn't just carry on. Though they didn't say anything, he could see frustration in their eyes.

He just couldn't bring himself to play football or hang out with his friends. His grades at school were in the toilet. Despite their encouraging words, Sammy couldn't shake how he felt: it was his fault.

A few weeks ago, his parents had taken him to see a psychologist. She'd asked a lot of questions and wanted him to talk about how he felt. She was a super nice lady, but it felt weird talking to someone he didn't know about the worst thing that had ever happened to him. He hadn't gotten very far with Dr. Covington, another disappointment to Sammy's parents.

Wanting to please them, he'd agreed to try hypnotherapy. A few minutes before nine a.m., Sammy sat in the back of his father's Lincoln Navigator as they pulled into Dr. Covington's parking lot.

The office was set back off a busy road, almost hidden from view by evergreen trees. On his way to the front of the onetime single-family home, Sammy walked over a short bridge and noticed several small fish swimming in a stream below. He liked the sound of water as it gurgled through and around a pile of branches in the middle of the stream.

The office's appearance provided Sammy with a measure of comfort. Its outside walls were made of large chunks of granite, quartzite and basalt, rocks he'd learned about last school year. The roof was constructed of wooden shingles that had seen many Michigan winters and summers. When they reached the front of the office, he looked at his mother and pointed to a pair of doors that faced the sky.

"Those are cellar doors," Cindy Bell said.

"What's a cellar?" Sammy asked as he walked up the porch stairs to the front door.

"They were much smaller than basements that are built in new homes today. They were used mostly for storage. Your great-grandmother had one. She canned a lot of food in the fall and stored the jars in her cellar."

Sammy nodded. "I like this place. Why didn't we come here our first few visits with Dr. Covington?"

"Doctors like her usually work out of several offices. She works here on Mondays. Are you nervous about doing this?"

Sammy walked into the old home's front room, which served as its lobby. He pushed a button near a closed door to let the doctor know they were there.

"Yeah. What if this makes it worse?"

Jake Bell spun his son around and put his hands on the boy's shoulders. "We wouldn't let you do this if we didn't think it would help. One thing you're going to discover about life, it's better to confront problems head-on instead of letting them fester. Mom and I know this will be painful, but you said yourself, it feels like there are things about the accident you can't quite remember."

Sammy looked up at his father. "This will help me remember?"

"The doctor thinks so," Cindy said, rubbing his back.

The family found seats and waited ten minutes before Elise Covington opened the door and ushered a woman and her daughter out. In her mid-sixties with silver hair that framed an elegant oval-shaped face and crystal-clear blue eyes, she smiled and motioned them in.

The office was sparsely furnished with a pair of comfortable-looking small couches sitting perpendicular to each other. Sammy sat alone on one and grabbed a red cushion with a velvety texture and placed it on his lap.

The room was dimly lit, and soft jazz music was turned low enough to be barely audible. Covington explained in detail how the hypnosis process worked and the possibilities of what could be achieved.

"It's just another therapeutic tool," she said, "and like all techniques and tools psychologists use, results vary from patient to patient."

"Are there any lingering effects?" Jake Bell asked.

"No, none at all," Covington said.

"Will I remember what I said?" Sammy asked.

"Most of my patients don't. But we're recording this session, so you can listen later if you choose."

Covington rolled her office chair around her desk and positioned it directly in front of Sammy. She led him through several relaxation exercises before pulling out a shiny silver pocket watch. Covington placed it about ten inches from his face and started swinging it back and forth like a pendulum.

"I want you to focus on the watch and only the watch," Covington said. A couple of minutes passed before she spoke again. "You are relaxed and comfortable. You're safe and your parents are right here. Do you understand, Samuel?"

He answered in the affirmative as his eyes remained fixed on the watch. His breathing was slow and rhythmic, as if he were asleep with his eyes open.

Covington took him back more than a month in time to the night of the hit-and-run. She asked him the name of the restaurant where he and Max had had dinner and what they had eaten.

"Silverman's," he said. "I had a hamburger and fries. Max had a chicken stir-fry."

"The two of you ate alone, didn't you?"

"Yes."

"Where were your parents?"

"Dad was still at work. Mom dropped us off because she had errands to run."

"She was going to pick you up at the restaurant, correct?"

"No," Sammy said. His facial expression didn't change, and his voice was flat. "At the drugstore on the other side of the road."

"You were going to get school supplies. Is that right?"

"Yes."

Covington looked down at a yellow legal pad before continuing. She scanned through questions she'd written out before the session started.

"After you finished dinner, you and Max decided to race to the drugstore, didn't you? You wanted to see who was the fastest."

"Yes," Sammy said. "He said he would win. I told him, 'No, I'm way faster than you.'"

"Where did the race start, Samuel?"

"In the parking lot. We ran across Main Street when there was an opening in the traffic."

Cindy Bell's chin started quivering and she put her hand over her mouth to keep sound from escaping and interrupting the session. Her husband took her other hand and squeezed.

"When you got to the other side of Main Street," Covington said, "were the cars on Ann Arbor Road moving?"

"No. The light was red. They were stopped."

"So, you continued to run. Who was winning the race?"

"Me. Max stayed close for a while, but I pulled ahead when we started to cross the other road."

"Did you see the cars start to move while you were running across Ann Arbor Road?"

"No."

"But when you got to the other side, you looked back to see where Max was? Was he right behind you?

"No. He was in the middle of the road. I saw him right before—"

Sammy's breathing had quickened, and his facial expression changed. He was clearly under stress.

"What happened next?" Covington prompted.

"The car hit Max," the teenager said, tears flowing from the corners of his eyes despite his hypnotic state.

"Pull him out of it," Cindy Bell said. "Doctor, I'm telling—"

Covington switched the watch to her left hand and used her right to make a "stop" gesture to Cindy.

"We're almost done, Samuel," Covington said in a calm, even voice. "Are you still with me?"

"Yes."

"Very good. You're still relaxed, you're still safe. Focus on the watch. Now, tell me, what happened to Max?"

"The car knocked him into the air. He landed hard on the pavement. A man came running toward Max and then helped him."

"What color was the car that hit Max?"

Sammy hesitated before answering. "Silver. But I see another color."

"What is it?" Covington asked.

"Blond. I see blond."

"Where do you see blond?"

"Inside the car. The person driving the car has blond hair."

"Do you recognize this person, Samuel?"

When he didn't answer, Covington repeated the question.

"She looks familiar, but I don't know her name."

"It's a woman? Are you certain?"

"Yes. Her hair is short, but it's not shaped in a man's style."

"Did you watch the car drive away after hitting Max?"

"No. I couldn't take my eyes off of Max."

Covington talked to Sammy for a few minutes before bringing him out of his hypnotic trance. He stretched, looked at his parents and then at the doctor.

"Are we going to get started or what? I'm hungry."

Cindy got up from the couch and hugged him tight. "We're all done, honey."

"No way," Sammy said. "How can we be done? I don't even remember starting."

Covington explained how she had instructed him to feel refreshed upon coming out of hypnosis. It was not uncommon for patients to have no memory of the event.

"Did I do good?"

Jake patted him on the back. "Let's get you something to eat. We will fill you in."

Chapter 41

MONDAY, SEPTEMBER 21

The lack of exercise was catching up with Harper. While he'd never been a gym regular, he usually got to Planet Fitness enough to keep a semblance of muscle tone in his chest and his arms. But working nearly around the clock and hanging out with Sophia had left him feeling like a plate of overcooked spaghetti.

He let out a yawn and then stretched. Against his better judgment, he dropped to the floor of Doc's loft, got on his knees and then leaned into a push-up posture. The first few repetitions were torture. His shoulders ached and he could feel every last pound he'd gained in the past month. Harper got in fifteen reps before resting on his gut.

He started a second set and heard footsteps on the loft stairs. With any luck, it was the assassins coming back to put him out of his misery.

"Your face is beet red," Sophia said. "Better stop that before you stroke out, honey."

Harper increased his pace until he hit twenty reps. Breathing heavily, he walked over to Sophia and jabbed his index and middle fingers into his left pectoral muscle. "Feel this, babe. Hard as a rock."

Sophia set her school backpack on Harper's desk. She made a fist and knocked three times on his forehead with her knuckles. "You're right. Hard as a rock."

"Is that any way to greet your editor?" Harper said, rubbing his forehead.

"Better watch yourself," Sophia said. "I might just sue you for sexual harassment."

Harper laughed. "Go ahead, you won't get much. The clerks at my credit union look at me like, *Seriously, dude, this is your paycheck?*"

Sophia grabbed him by the waist and pulled him in. "Shut up and kiss me, you broke fool."

Harper obliged. A minute later, he pulled back from the embrace. "You ready for your first Plymouth City Commission meeting?"

Sophia shot him a scowl that would've made Clint Eastwood proud. She pulled her phone out and after a few swipes turned the screen toward Harper.

"Have you looked at the agenda?" Sophia asked. "I'm not a seasoned reporter, obviously, but I don't see a whole bunch of breaking news here."

"Welcome to community journalism," Harper said, smiling like a Cheshire cat. "On paper, you're right. It looks like a snoozefest. Budget amendments, a rezoning over on

York Street and the ever-popular traffic control order."

Sophia shrugged as if to say, *What am I supposed to do with this?* Harper read her expression with ease because he had been in her shoes many times before. Prior to the Bell hit-and-run and murders of Doc Reston and Rob Snyder, culling news that would capture at least a portion of the newspaper's audience was a constant challenge of small-town journalism.

"There is something here I think will make a decent story," Harper said.

Sophia, who had walked into the kitchen, opened a bottle of water and downed a quarter of it before replying. "I'm all ears, chief."

Harper followed her to the kitchen. "I like the sound of that," he said. "Chief. Supreme leader. The head honcho. The big cheese."

"I think those push-ups cut off the oxygen to your brain," Sophia said. "Can you just fill me in on what you think you see as a story, please?"

"There's something that might make a good follow-up to your parking deck story. Look at the other rezoning item on the agenda. That's for land around the proposed deck along Ann Arbor Trail and Maple. Did you read the backup material to the agenda?"

"Honestly, no. Between school and helping Dad at the store, I haven't had time."

"I get it," Harper said. "The city is working with a developer on a small condominium project for the site. Ten single-family condos and rehabbing the historic building that faces Ann Arbor Trail. It's actually not a bad story."

"You think those same residents that moaned and groaned about the parking deck will be at the meeting?"

Harper snagged his own bottle of water from the fridge. "I would be surprised if they weren't."

"What do you think their reaction will be?"

"Hard to say. I'm sure the city will argue the condominium development will mitigate the new deck as far as the aesthetics of the neighborhood. Either way, whether they like the condos or not, residents will be vocal about it."

"I guess this is why you're the editor," Sophia said.

"It's just experience. I've been to dozens and dozens of meetings like this. After a while, you learn how to spot stories. Believe me, I whiffed on a lot of opportunities the first few years of my career."

"Did Henry give you a hard time about it, when you missed things?"

"Depended on what it was, but he was generally pretty cool about it. He called them 'teachable moments.' I think he really enjoyed being part journalism professor, part editor and publisher."

Harper let out a long sigh before taking a drink of water. “I miss the hell out of that old man.”

Sophia rubbed his shoulders. “I know. But I think he’d be proud of the job you’re doing.”

He kissed her softly on the lips. “Thank you.”

“I was thinking,” Sophia said. “I should try to get an update on those two alleged hit men from Captain Chamberlain, or have you already talked to him?”

“No, actually I haven’t. That’s a great idea. If you go up to city hall a little early, he’s usually in his office before the commission meeting.”

Sophia pulled her phone out of her jeans back pocket and checked the time. “I better go then. I’m going to grab a tuna sub over at Jimmy John’s before I try Chamberlain.”

Harper pulled his wallet out and tried to hand her a twenty-dollar bill.

“You don’t need to do that, I’ve got money,” Sophia said.

“Nonsense. You’re on the job. The newspaper can buy your dinner.”

She smiled and took the cash. “Look at me, professional reporter.”

“Another Sophia Casey byline is going to look really good in print. Are you sure you want to do the teaching thing?”

She walked over to a hutch near Emily Jackson’s old desk that held supplies. She took out two skinny reporter’s notepads and a pair of ballpoint pens.

“I have to admit,” Sophia said, “seeing my name in print was awesome. I know it was just a story about parking. But interviewing those people and seeing the story come together kind of gave me a rush.”

“It can definitely give you a rush,” Harper agreed. “Just wait until you cover some real breaking news on deadline. It gets the adrenaline flowing like nothing else, trust me.”

Chapter 42

MONDAY, SEPTEMBER 21

Sophia crossed Main Street and glanced at an old-fashioned street clock stationed about a hundred yards away from the Ann Arbor Trail intersection. The section of Main between Penniman and Ann Arbor Trail resembled a divided boulevard with planters full of colorful annual and perennial flowers.

Coupled with Kellogg Park's lush, green grass and tall shade trees, it was a visual feast for Sophia. The street clock read 6:25, meaning she had very little time to enjoy the sights of downtown Plymouth. As she reached the other side of the street, a tall older man stood up from a bench facing the park.

"Claire, is that you?" the old man said. Tears came to his eyes and he took hold of Sophia's arms. "Good lord, Claire, you're so beautiful and I haven't seen in you in so long."

"Excuse me, sir?" Sophia said, trying to pull away. "I think you must have me confused with someone else."

"Claire, don't you think I recognize my own granddaughter? Why, I'm not that senile yet."

He let go of Sophia's left arm and reached into his khaki pants pocket. The man's hand grasped an injector filled with Rohypnol.

"My name is Sophia, sir, and you need to let go—"

He pulled her close. "Give your old granddad a hug, Claire."

Sophia decided to play along. Perhaps a brief hug would be enough for the old man and she could go about her business. She wrapped her free arm around his back and immediately felt his strength as he returned the embrace.

A second later, Sophia felt a pinprick in the middle of her left thigh. She shrugged it off when she saw a bee buzzing a few feet away. Little bastard got her good. She pulled away from the old man's embrace and smiled.

"It's good to see you, too, Grandpa," Sophia said.

"Can you sit with me for a couple of minutes?" the old man asked. "I've been so lonely since your grandma passed."

The old man's eyes were wet. She wasn't sure who Claire was but thought she must be a poor excuse for a granddaughter, or the old guy was, in fact, senile. Either way, she could forgo the Jimmy John's tuna sub and head straight to the police station to talk to Chamberlain after playing make-believe for a few minutes.

The old man led her to the bench and then held her hand after they sat down. He looked around the park and smiled, seeming to enjoy the people walking by and others seated at the fountain in the middle of the park. "Tell me what's going on in your life, Claire. It has been ages since we caught up."

Sophia had taken a few drama classes in high school. She wondered if she could pull off the dutiful granddaughter this man seemed to need so desperately.

"Well, Grandpa, my studies are coming along really well at Eastern Michigan. I'm hoping to have a teaching job lined up before I graduate."

The old man put his hands to his face. "I'm so proud, Claire. I always knew you would end up working with the little ones."

She smiled and a wave of drowsiness washed over her. Sophia yawned.

"I see you've been working too hard, my dear," the old man said. "You better turn in early tonight."

"You're right, Grandpa. I will."

"As pretty as you are, Claire, I bet you have to beat those young fellas at EMU off with a stick."

"Well, there is one special guy I'm seeing," Sophia said.

"Oh, really? What's his name?"

Sophia's eyes were becoming heavy. "Um, his name is Ray. Ray Harper, perhaps you've heard of him? He's the editor for the—"

"For the newspaper," the old man said. "Yes. I'm very familiar with his work. In fact, he's a real thorn in my employer's ass."

Sophia was puzzled at the remark. "What, uh, what do you mean?"

Her words were slurred and the world seemed to be spinning. The old man put his arm around her shoulders and grasped her hand with his free hand. He helped her stand.

Sophia stumbled. "I think I'm going to be sick."

The old man, at a solid six foot one and one hundred ninety pounds, had little trouble escorting her to his car parked in front of the Penn Theatre. "Everything's going to be okay, darling, Grandpa will take you home."

A couple in their early thirties pushed a stroller by the old man and Sophia as they neared his black BMW. "Everything okay, sir?" asked a tall, thin man with a closely cropped beard and curly dark hair. "Can I help you?"

"My granddaughter has had too much to drink, I'm afraid. If you could help me get her into the car, that would be a big help, young man."

A few seconds later, Sophia was strapped into the passenger seat of the BMW. The old man thanked the bearded young dad for his help, went to the driver's side of the vehicle and got in. A moment later, the BMW was rolling toward Union Street. Sophia fidgeted in her seat as the old man steered his way out of downtown Plymouth.

"Where, uh, where we goin'," she said unevenly.

"Not to worry, Sophia," the old man said, his voice sharper. "I'm taking you to your father."

DREADING THE EMPTINESS OF HIS APARTMENT, Harper decided to work late. He edited a batch of obituaries sent earlier in the day from the area's funeral homes and then posted them to the *Independent*'s website.

Next came a round of rewriting sports briefs submitted by parents of the Steelers football teams and youth soccer game scores and highlights. He closed out the session by editing a piece from a freelance reporter on an all-state swimmer at Plymouth High School.

Harper hated relying on submissions for sports or any kind of coverage. Truth was, the newspaper had less than two weeks left to live, and he couldn't write about everything going on in the community.

He fought the urge to check in with Sophia. He had thoughts of walking down to city hall to see how it was going. Intuition told him it was a bad idea. Finally, at nine fifteen, Harper texted her.

The commission meeting was running late, but it wasn't a surprise. The residents were most likely giving Plymouth's top legislative body an earful on the condo development. Harper hoped Sophia wasn't too bored.

He returned his attention to his laptop and opened a story he'd written earlier in the day about the opening of a new coffee shop in Plymouth's Old Village. He smoothed out sentences that needed it. Harper's biggest problem as a writer was dropping words. Coupled with his tendency to write quickly, it led to sentences like the one he found in the third paragraph.

The 1,500-square shop is location at 475 Libety Street between and Starkweather. He corrected it to read, *The 1,500-square-foot shop is located at 475 Liberty Street between Mill and Starkweather.* Harper's brain often worked faster than his fingers.

He checked his phone for a reply from Sophia at nine forty-five. Nothing. That was unusual. His girlfriend—funny to think of her in those terms—always replied within a few minutes of his texts.

Considering all of the craziness of his life over the last month, Harper decided he'd gladly take a snappy rebuke from Sophia to know that she was safe. He closed his laptop, checked his pockets for keys and wallet and put his iPhone in his back pocket.

The streets were still active with people at the watering holes on Penniman and late evening diners on Main Street. Harper navigated his way through them, past a long line at Dairy King and finally to city hall. He pulled on the front door, but it was locked and the lights in the building were off.

He tried one more pull and then, with his heart beating hard, went nextdoor to the police station. He was hoping Chamberlain would still be around. Harper walked into the lobby and over to the desk sergeant, whom he didn't recognize.

"Is Captain Chamberlain in?"

"And you are... ?"

"Ray Harper from the *Independent* newspaper."

The sergeant picked up a desk phone and dialed Chamberlain's line. Harper could tell by his facial expression the captain wasn't picking up.

"He's not answering. Is there something I can help you with?"

"Do you know what time the city commission meeting let out?"

The sergeant swiveled in his chair, got up and walked over to a pair of cubicles where the night dispatchers worked. He nodded after speaking with them for a few seconds.

"The meeting let out a few minutes after nine."

Harper looked at his name badge. "Thank you, Sergeant Holcomb. Do you know if a female reporter was in the audience?"

Holcomb turned again and asked the question without standing. Both dispatchers shrugged. "Have you tried calling your reporter?"

"I've texted twice in the last hour without getting a response."

Holcomb picked up the phone receiver again. "I'm going to try Captain Chamberlain on his cell phone. He was at the meeting and should know if she was there. What's her name?"

"Sophia Casey," Harper said.

"Why don't you call Sophia's phone?"

Harper nodded and pulled his iPhone from his back pocket. Sophia's phone went straight to voicemail. He looked at Holcomb and shook his head to indicate his call had failed to get her.

"Captain, it's Holcomb. Did a Sophia Casey from the *Independent* newspaper talk to you at the commission meeting tonight?

"No? Sir, Ray Harper is here and can't seem to locate the young lady. Uh-huh, okay."

Holcomb handed Harper the receiver.

"Describe Sophia to me," Chamberlain said. "Perhaps she was just a little gun-shy about introducing herself to me and the commissioners."

Having to give him a description of Sophia made Harper's stomach roil. A hundred possibilities of what could've happened to her went through his mind. He gave Chamberlain specifics about Sophia's build and what she was wearing.

"She was going to try to talk to you before the meeting about the manhunt for those two guys involved in Doc's death."

"Well, that didn't happen. I don't recall seeing anyone taking notes either. I'm assuming she'd have come with notepads."

"Yeah, she had a couple," Harper said. "What do I do here? Do you think this is related—"

"Stop right there, Ray. Let's not jump to conclusions. Where does she live?"

"Here in Plymouth with her father, David Casey. She stays at my place sometimes, too."

"Okay. That's a good place to start. I'll have our dispatch sends units to your apartment and Casey's house. You sure you aren't jumping the gun on this? It's only been about an hour since the meeting ended."

Harper's face went red. He couldn't believe what was happening. Was Sophia really missing or was it just his nerves getting the best of him?

"Maybe? It's just with what went down with Doc and then my parents—"

"I get it," Chamberlain said. "But you know, our policy isn't to start a missing person investigation for twenty-four hours. I'm doing you a favor here."

"I appreciate it. What do you want me to do?"

"I want you to sit tight right there at the station. If something is going on, I don't want you walking into the middle of it. Do you want to authorize us going into your apartment?"

Harper answered without hesitation. "Yes, yes, of course. Whatever you need to do."

"Good. Give the phone back to Holcomb. And, Ray, plant your ass in my office. I'll be there in fifteen minutes."

Chapter 43

TUESDAY, SEPTEMBER 22

Sophia Casey felt her hair being stroked. She remembered how it had comforted her as a child when she would rest her head on her mother's lap as they watched television together. She often fell asleep to her mother's gentle touch, which told her how much she was loved without a word ever being spoken.

It was as if she were inside one of those memories. In the fog of being somewhere between sleep and consciousness, she was eight years old again, her mother was still alive, and she was safe. Sunlight from above tickled her closed eyes. A few minutes later, the fog lifted, and her eyes opened. It was her father stroking her hair.

She looked around the room, confused as to where they were and how they had gotten there. Sophia tried to move her hands but realized they were bound together with a zip tie, as were her feet. Her father's hands and feet were also bound.

"What's going on?" she asked. A wave of nausea washed over her, and she felt as if she might vomit. "Where are we? Who is that man?"

"Lower your voice," David Casey said. "We do not want to make that gentleman nervous."

"Who is he? I don't understand any of this."

Sophia looked around the room. It appeared as if they were in a basement. Light was coming through a window at the top of a foundation wall from a corner. One half of the window was covered with plywood and the other half with glass. She counted three additional windows, all partially covered with vertical strips of plywood.

A man in jeans and a hooded sweatshirt with the arms cut off sat a table at the far side of the room. A handgun sat on the table next to him. He wore black, army-style boots and had a matching black belt that appeared to hold extra rounds of ammunition and a gun case. A large knife was sheathed adjacent to the gun case.

He had long, curly black hair and a scruffy black beard. He sat with perfect posture, his back ramrod straight. He appeared to be texting someone on his phone.

"He came into the store late last night with two other men," David Casey said. "They checked to see if I had any other customers. When they didn't see any, they killed the lights and locked the front door. This gentleman pulled his gun, and I thought they were going to rob the place.

"I thought, *Well, at least I'll have you bastards on video.* But they didn't rob me. He held a gun on me, and one of the others bound my hands and put a black hood over my head. They led me out the back and put me in a car or SUV, I'm not sure which. About thirty minutes later, we were here. They didn't take the hood off until I was down here where we're sitting now."

Tears came to Sophia's eyes. "Did they hurt you, Pop?"

"No, honey, I'm fine."

"Have they said anything?"

"I tried talking to this one, but he wouldn't speak to me. Just told me to shut up and take a seat. I think his name might be Joshua. I heard the three men whispering when they thought I was asleep."

Sophia took her father's hands and held them firmly. "When did they bring me here? The last thing I remember, I was on my way to Plymouth city hall. I was supposed to cover a meeting for the paper."

"You were already here when I got here, honey. You were out cold on this crappy old couch. When I saw you, I figured I better do what Joshua told me, so I took a seat and kept my mouth shut."

"Have they demanded money?"

"No. I don't know why they're holding us here or what they intend on doing with us."

Feeling the aftereffects of the Rohypnol, Sophia stood unsteadily. "I'm going to throw up," she yelled to Joshua.

He pointed to a sink a few feet beyond the table he sat at. He grabbed his gun but didn't bother to look up from his phone. "Make a wrong move, I put a bullet in your dad's skull. Understood?"

Sophia nodded and put her hand over mouth as if trying to hold back an eruption. She moved as quickly as she could toward the sink, but it amounted to a series of short hops, like she was an oversized bunny. She didn't think she would make the sink.

Finally, she reached it and her body expelled the contents of her stomach, which were surprisingly sparse. Acid and other fluids burned her throat as they came up. After several rounds, she stopped heaving. Sophia turned the faucet on to rinse away the mess. She cupped her hands and caught some of the cold water, lapping it up like a kitten.

Sophia felt a strong hand squeezing her left upper arm. "You're done," Joshua said. "Go sit back down."

She looked at him for a second. His eyes were as dark as his hair and beard. He had a certain kind of coarse handsomeness. Raw. Ruthless. There was nothing behind his eyes,

Sophia thought. It was like looking into the eyes of a panther. The idea of going for his knife and maybe sticking it into one of those eyes crossed her mind for a split second. Then she thought better of it and made her way back to her father.

Joshua returned to his seat and his phone without a word.

"What's going to happen to us?" Sophia asked her father.

"Nothing good, I suspect."

AT SEVEN A.M., HARPER'S IPHONE ALARM WENT OFF. He had spent a few fitful hours trying to sleep in a spare bedroom at Doc Reston's loft.

The search by the Plymouth police hadn't turned up anything on Sophia. Officers had discovered David Casey wasn't at home and found the back door of his party store open after being notified by an alarm company.

There were no obvious signs of foul play, but the store's CCTV cameras had been smashed and the recording system inside of Casey's office removed. A BOLO for Sophia and David Casey had been issued by eleven thirty the previous night.

Harper showered and was dressing when his phone buzzed.

"Any news?" Harper asked Captain Dan Chamberlain.

"Unfortunately, none. We sent patrol cars to the Caseys' house several times overnight. Neither of them showed. No leads off the BOLO, either. I'm assuming you didn't get any calls or texts?"

"Nothing. Believe me, I would have called you already if I had. Are you someplace where you can talk freely?"

"Negative."

Harper heard Chamberlain speak away from the phone. "Detective Adams, I want you to take a seat in my office. I want the latest on the Casey investigation."

"Okay, I get it. Adams is in your grill," Harper said. "You don't have to say anything but we both know what's going on here. No way Sophia and her dad just up and vanished on their own."

Chamberlain waited several beats before answering, presumably giving Adams time to walk away. "Not likely."

"I know you don't want to move on Sadie Rodgers or your boss until the case is airtight. But they keep upping the ante. That's exactly what this is, right?"

"Uh-huh, yes, I think that's a good bet."

"They're forcing our hand, Dan. You've got enough to arrest her for sure and maybe Flaherty, too. So what if it doesn't stick? It might be enough for them to call their dogs off, to get Sophia and David back."

"Nope, don't agree."

"All right, let's finish this conversation later when you can talk."

"Good idea."

Harper disconnected the call. His mind was racing, trying to come up with answers. Why snatch Sophia?

No doubt, Rodgers and Flaherty were sending him a message. But why hadn't they made their intentions known? Why no back-off-or-else threat? Was it all for plausible deniability?

Harper couldn't prove they had anything to do with the Caseys' disappearance any more than he could prove they'd sent a goon to rough up his parents.

The uncertainty was eating him alive. Harper went back to the kitchen and made another cup of coffee. He turned to a junk drawer and grabbed a pack of Salem cigarettes. He opened the box and let one of the smokes slide between his lips. He pulled a lighter from the junk drawer and lit the smoke.

Harper took a long drag and then a gulp of coffee as soon as it finished brewing. He walked to the windows overlooking Penniman Avenue and pondered his next move. His first instinct was to go to city hall and wring Flaherty's neck.

He'd orchestrated Sophia's abduction without question. That was the only explanation that made sense. Taking Sophia and David was a desperate move by someone afraid of losing something important, like a long law enforcement career or a lover.

It meant Harper's investigation was getting close.

Chapter 44

THURSDAY, SEPTEMBER 24

Harper thought of Thursday as a day of fresh starts. It was the first day in the publishing cycle of the *Independent*, a day to formulate story ideas and start working them for publication the following Wednesday. There was a rhythm to the cycle, a choreography, like a Broadway play that begins rehearsals and months later opens for the world to see.

For the tiny newspaper, it was the first day of its final act. At five a.m., Harper gave up trying to sleep. It was the last night he'd spend at the loft. While he had adjusted to working in Doc Reston's home, he'd never gotten used to occupying it. Harper got out of bed, rubbed his eyes and walked slowly to the kitchen for coffee.

He was sure half the blood circulating in his body was infused with Green Mountain Dark Magic. At the moment, he didn't care about regulating his caffeine intake. His thoughts were intertwined with Sophia and the newspaper. He was responsible for both, and they were pulling him in different directions.

Harper finished the cup before he got to the shower. He sat the mug on a chestnut vanity and then flung the white T-shirt he'd worn to bed across the expansive bathroom toward a clothes hamper. His boxer shorts followed. Both shots missed the mark. He turned the water on and waited for a puff of steam to rise before stepping into the shower.

The harder he tried to work out a plan of attack for the day and for the week, the more Harper's mind jumbled. He noticed his skin starting to tint red from the hot water and dialed it down until it was almost cold. The rush of water felt like sleet against his back.

His limbs began to tingle, as if he had lain on all of them until they fell asleep. He was gasping for air as he opened the shower door and stepped out with the water still running. The glass door clanged closed as he stumbled across the bathroom. He couldn't stop his chest from heaving and knew he needed to sit down before his legs gave out.

Harper grabbed a towel, tried wrapping it around his waist but couldn't get his hands to work well enough to accomplish the task. He exited the bathroom into the bedroom and sat at the end of the bed. Besides the fact that his limbs were tingling, the room was now spinning around him. For the first time in his life, he did not feel in control of himself.

Tears came to his eyes and then his body convulsed into sobs. Harper grabbed a pillow, put it against his face and let loose with a howl like an animal snared in a steel trap. All his fears, all his worries, rushed out of him. The pillow fell to the floor and the volume, and tone of the screams made his heart race even faster.

He knew he was acting like a lunatic, like someone coming down off a bad drug trip, but he couldn't stop. Harper heard someone walking up the steps into the loft. He saw a figure rushing toward him but the man, if it was a man, was distant, as if he were at the end of a long tunnel.

"Ray," the figure called out. "Are you all right?"

Harper continued to wail. He tried to formulate words, but all that came out was, "Gone, gone, all gone." Images of Doc, his parents and Sophia raced across his mind's eye. "Got to find, got to find her, got to—"

Captain Dan Chamberlain reached for the Motorola handset of his police radio. He had come to the loft to talk to Harper about the case but became alarmed when he found the door ajar. "Male subject found at 821 Penniman Avenue," he said to a dispatcher. "Appears to be having a stress-related attack. Requesting an ambulance at the location."

Chamberlain picked up the towel from the floor and covered Harper's groin area. "Hold tight, help is the on the way."

Harper's sobs ebbed. He looked around the room, the walls spinning a little slower and Chamberlain's face becoming clearer. "Where is Sophia? We've got to find Sophia. Got to —"

"We'll find her," Chamberlain said. "Right now, we're going to get you some help."

Chamberlain looked about the room for clothing and found a pair of jeans lying on a chair in a corner of the bedroom. He opened a closet door and grabbed the first button-up shirt he found. Harper looked at him, puzzled.

"Let's get some clothes on you," Chamberlain said.

Moments later, paramedics came into the bedroom and took Harper's vitals. His blood pressure was sky high, and his heart raced at more than a hundred thirty beats a minute. He was no longer hyperventilating, but his breathing was still rapid and shallow.

Harper was loaded onto a black and yellow stretcher and strapped in. "Am I crazy?" he asked one of the paramedics.

"No, sir, you're not crazy," the paramedic said. "You've had a panic attack, a pretty bad one by the looks of it. You're going to be fine."

Chamberlain helped the two paramedics negotiate the steep steps down to the alley behind the loft. With lights and sirens blazing, they whisked Harper to St. Mary's hospital in Livonia.

HARPER AWOKE DISORIENTED. He looked around the room and realized that he was in a hospital. The room was dark, as was the world outside, leaving him to wonder how long he'd been out. He spotted an old analog clock on the wall. It was partially obscured by a television and he was able to read the time only after leaning to his left.

It was nine forty-five p.m. He had lost most of the day, assuming it was still Thursday. Despite the rest, his body cried out for more. The panic attack that had knocked him down for the count wasn't far off, perhaps standing in its corner waiting to pounce and send him to the canvas again.

His memory flooding back, he rang for a nurse. Harper remembered talking to intake workers at the hospital and he had had a short session with a psychiatrist. He couldn't recall the name of the medication he'd been prescribed. A nurse with long, curly blond hair and deep blue eyes entered his room, tapped a wall-mounted dispenser of hand sanitizer and smiled.

"How are you feeling?"

Harper stretched and yawned. "Like I could sleep for about a year. What was I given?"

"Restoril and Celexa," said the nurse, Cora, according to her name tag. "One was to help you sleep and the other for anxiety."

She took his pulse, put a blood-oxygen reader on his index finger and then checked his blood pressure. "All of your readings are within a normal range."

"That's good, but I don't exactly feel normal."

"It will take a few weeks for the medication to take full effect," said Cora, who Harper guessed was in her mid to late thirties.

"Weeks? Why do I need to stay on this medication? It's not like this has ever happened to me before."

"That decision will be between you and your doctor."

"Then why did you start talking about weeks of medication?" Harper asked.

"I've seen a good number of patients with similar symptoms," Cora said. "A majority of them end up on medication to help control their anxiety. Severe panic attacks are often a symptom of a larger underlying condition."

She smiled and continued. "I'm sorry. I don't mean to alarm you and I shouldn't speak out of turn."

Harper took his hand off of a rail and gently gripped Cora's. "No worries. I appreciate your perspective. Am I allowed to check out?"

"The doctor authorized your stay through tomorrow morning. But, yes, you are free to leave."

"The look on your face is telling me that might be foolish."

Cora pulled a pair of fresh pillows from a closet, walked back to Harper's bed and motioned for him to lift his torso up. He complied and she fluffed the pillows after laying them on the bed.

"Do you live alone?"

"Yes," Harper said.

"Then I would advise staying here at least through tonight," Cora said. "In my opinion, you need someone to look in on you. Whatever factor or factors led to your panic attack could intensify again. If you have another one or even a smaller attack, you'll get help here immediately. We have an excellent staff."

"I don't have any doubts about that," Harper said. His thoughts returned to Sophia and the *Independent*. But he realized he would be of little use to either if his brain went back into meltdown mode. "I'll trust your judgment, Cora."

She smiled again and patted him on the shoulder. "Smart man."

Chapter 45

FRIDAY, SEPTEMBER 25

By ten a.m., Harper had been discharged from the hospital and was at his apartment working on a three-egg omelet at the stove. He carefully placed diced ham in the eggs and then added green pepper, onions and a sprinkling of sharp cheddar cheese. In less than ten minutes, the creation was done and on his plate, along with sliced cantaloupe and a piece of rye toast with butter.

A second round of medication the night before left him feeling groggy as he bit into the omelet. While his thoughts remained on the paper and Sophia, he felt more in control. The full boil his brain had been on the day before had been reduced to a manageable simmer.

It felt good to eat something wholesome. He was sure weeks of fast-food meals and too much coffee had contributed to his panic attack. Toss in the bucketloads of stress he'd been under and it was no wonder he'd broken down, according to Dr. Deepak Patel.

Harper would visit Patel on a weekly basis for the next month. If it kept him from having another panic attack, he'd see the man daily. The loss of control had left doubts in his mind. How hard could he push before breaking down again? Would he always need medical supervision to live a "normal" life? Would he recognize signs of psychological trouble if they arose again?

He finished the last bite of eggs. Just as he got up to take the plate to the sink, his phone rang. Harper sat the plate back down on the kitchen table and glanced at his iPhone. It was Victoria Reston-Coble. He picked up after the third ring.

"Are you all right?" she said. "Dan Chamberlain called me last night and said you were at St. Mary's. Something about a panic attack?"

Harper filled her in as succinctly as possible. "This whole thing is embarrassing. I feel like I've let everyone down. I'm—"

"Stop right there with the pity party," Victoria said. "You didn't let anyone down, least of all me. You're human. That's all this proved. You might still be in your twenties, but you're not bulletproof."

"That's for sure."

"Listen to your doctor and to what your body is telling you," Victoria said.

"How do I do that and still do what I need to do? Sophia's gone and we don't have all the answers about your father's murder. I mean, I want to the finish the job. I've got to. But I'd be lying if I said I wasn't scared shitless."

"Anybody in your shoes would be. These people you're investigating and writing about have no qualms about doing whatever's necessary."

"Yeah, and now I'm not only fighting them but myself, too."

"I wish I had some nugget of wisdom or experience to pass on," Victoria said. "The only thing I can tell you is, I believe in you. Dad believed in you."

"Chamberlain believes that I'm being watched and that if I keep digging, they'll know it," Harper said. "I may not get a chance to write these last stories."

"They're not the only ones watching you. Chamberlain is paying very close attention. Are you at the loft now?"

"No, my apartment."

"Well, I wouldn't stay there long," she said. "You'll be safer at the loft in downtown. I'm going to hire a private security company, too."

Harper felt the need for a cup of coffee and a smoke. He fought the urge and considered Victoria's offer before speaking.

"You still there, Ray?"

"Yeah, just thinking. Listen, I appreciate the offer, but I don't want it. I can't do my job with some bald dude in black talking into his wrist hovering near me twenty-four/seven. I'm going to do this. I'm going to nail these bastards, but it's got to be my way. I don't want you flying in from Arizona, either. You've got a family."

It was Victoria's turn to go silent. "Not smart, but okay. Let me know if you change your mind."

"I will. Any chance we could print the *Independent* a few more weeks after Wednesday's edition?"

"I was wondering when you were going to get around to asking that question," Victoria said.

Harper stood, grabbed his dish and rinsed it off in the sink before putting it in the Bosch dishwasher.

"Is that a yes or a no?" Harper asked.

"I've thought about it," Victoria said. "While I understand it would probably be helpful from a journalistic standpoint, I've got to say no. Pushing it another few weeks or a month comes with added risks for you, for me and for other people. And while I have financial resources, they're not limitless. We've got no backing from advertisers to print more papers. I'm sorry."

Harper let out a sigh. "I get it. What about the online edition? Doesn't cost much to keep it going."

"Don't make this harder than it already is," Victoria said. "You know how much the *Independent* means to me. It was my father's lifework, his dream job. But that dream ended the day he died. Wednesday is it, end of story."

Harper felt like an ass for pushing. She was a strong woman, a good woman, with every right to do as she saw fit with the newspaper. He was just being selfish. "Sorry, Vic. I—"

"I know your intentions are good," she said. "But my family and I, well, we need closure to this nightmare."

Chapter 46

SATURDAY, SEPTEMBER 26

The thought of returning to the loft was less than appealing to Harper. He had never considered himself superstitious, yet he took the clothes he had worn into the hospital on Thursday and threw them in the garbage. He would never wear jeans with a gold-colored shirt again. Nor would he shower at the loft or sleep there despite the warnings from Victoria.

As the rolled into downtown Plymouth, Harper spotted a man at least six-five and two hundred and seventy-five pounds walking a Yorkie. A few months ago, he probably would've parked the car, jumped out and snapped a few pictures. You could never go wrong with a picture of a dog on the front page of a community newspaper. He would've run the picture as "wild art," meaning there would be no corresponding story, on the front page and given it the title "Odd Couple Out for a Walk" or some other trite heading.

There was no time for such frivolities now. Harper also needed every column inch of front-page space for hardcore journalism. The *Independent* was going to go out with a bang. He skipped his usual stop at Panera Bread or Starbucks and headed straight for the loft after parking the Honda. He flipped his keys around in his hand as he walked toward the entrance, fishing for the mail key.

He opened the back door to the building Doc's loft shared with the Irish pub. The mailbox was to his left and he opened it in one motion, despite a little resistance. Two days' worth of mail was jammed inside. Harper yanked it out, a yellow legal-size envelope ripping at a corner. He leafed through a dozen smaller envelopes before coming to one with no return address.

The yellow envelope appeared to have something inside. As he unlocked the door to the loft and walked upstairs, he felt the contents of the envelope. It appeared to be a set of keys, one with a rectangular fob and the other something akin to a house key.

He started to tear the envelope as he reached the top of the stairs. Harper turned to his left to set the mail down on his glass worktable. His eyes spotted a gun lying on the table before he noticed an African-American man sitting in his chair.

"Good morning," the man said. "Glad to see you're feeling better."

Harper froze. The man had short gray dreadlocks. He flashed back to their first encounter, at the Penniman Deli. He had called himself Patrick, and his alleged husband was Barney. Harper now knew his real identity, insomuch as it was depicted in a BOLO issued by the state police. He was one of the men who had murdered Henry Reston and Rob Snyder.

Harper finished setting the mail down. "Come back to finish the job, 'Patrick'?"

The smile on Patrick's face grew even wider. "Yes, sir. I am here to take care of business."

Possible moves dashed through Harper's mind. Could he reach the gun before Patrick? Could he get down the loft stairs before Patrick put a bullet in his head or back? If this was his time, he wasn't going to go out like a coward.

Harper lunged for the gun. Patrick grabbed his wrist before he could touch the weapon. The man had a vise grip. Harper lost his balance and fell on top of the table.

"Relax, my man, relax."

"Fuck you," Harper grunted.

"You'd be dead already if I wanted to kill you," Patrick said. "Seriously, I'm not here to hurt you, but you don't get to play with my junk, so to speak."

He loosened his grip on Harper's wrist and helped him get up from the table. Patrick pulled a seat out from the table and motioned for him to sit.

Harper unruffled his shirt and complied. His heart was pounding. His anxiety level was through the roof. He prayed he wouldn't hyperventilate into another panic attack. "Then why the hell are you here?"

"I thought you might like to hear what I have to say. I'm here to set the record straight. Isn't that what people say before they spill their guts to a reporter?"

"Set the record straight?" Harper said. "Are you kidding? You sick fuck, you and your partner murdered my boss and another good man."

"True," Patrick said.

"You realize I'd have blown your brains out if I got to that gun first, right?"

Patrick smiled, almost politely, as if he were there pitching a story about an upcoming speaker at the next chamber of commerce luncheon.

"Well, thank goodness you didn't. I like my brains right where they're at. Now, why don't you pull out a pad of paper and start taking notes or turn on a recording device, whatever it is you do to write your stories. I've got a lot to tell you."

Harper ran a hand through his hair without thinking about it. A hit man was sitting at his table, begging to be interviewed about killing people. It was like someone aiming a pistol at a police officer to commit suicide by cop. What did Patrick have to gain? What were his motivations? The last five minutes simply didn't compute.

Not believing his own actions, Harper actually reached for his phone and opened the voice recording app. He then got up and walked over to the supply hutch for a fresh pad of paper and a pen. He sat back down and glanced at Patrick's face, which was still oddly cheerful.

Under normal circumstances, he'd offer an interviewee a bottle of water or can of soda. He laughed out loud as the thought crossed his mind. Patrick laughed right along with him, which creeped him out even more.

"Okay, then. Can I start by getting your real name? I know it's not Patrick. Milton Johnson?"

"My, my, you are good, aren't you? But I haven't gone by that name in many years. Eldon Turner."

"And your partner?"

"Dwight Alexander. I'm surprised you don't know already. It's been all over the news the past few days."

"I've been a little busy," Harper said. "You'll have to forgive me."

"Why were you in the hospital?"

"Never mind that, Eldon. Where is my girlfriend?"

"That, I don't know," he said, holding his hands up in a surrender gesture. "God's truth. I wasn't part of that operation."

"Who was then?"

Turner steepled his fingers together and then laid them on the table. "If I knew, I would tell you."

Harper let out a heavy sigh. "So, you're confessing to murder but not kidnapping? This is unbelievable."

"Shall we continue? What is your next question?"

"Oh, sure, why not? Can I get you a coffee? Water? How about a sandwich? You can't confess your sins on an empty stomach, can you?"

"Your anger and contempt are justified," Turner said. "I don't know how long your girl has been missing, but every extra minute we spend talking is a minute you could be trying to get her back. Now, let's get to it."

Harper shook his head, smacked the table with both hands and gestured as if to say, *Whatever*. "Where's your partner? He have cold feet about talking to a reporter?"

"Like I said, I'm surprised you haven't heard about him. He's dead. I put a hole in his chest."

In this Twilight Zone interview, Harper didn't even blink at the words. "Why did you put a hole in his chest?"

"He didn't want me coming back to Michigan to take care of my business. Thought I'd get us both caught. He's probably right about that. He tried to silence me. Luckily for me, he brought a knife to a gunfight."

Harper grabbed his phone and opened the *Detroit Free Press* app. He scrolled down and found a story from a few days ago talking about the discovery of Alexander's body and the possible connection to the double murder in Plymouth. Maybe Turner was legit?

"Take me back to the beginning," Harper said. "How did the two of you get involved?"

"We were hired to do a job, to kill that cop."

"Who hired you?"

"An old buddy of Alexander's, name of Michael Adams. He's—"

"Also a Plymouth cop," Harper interrupted. "Why?"

"Most times, you don't get the whys in our line of work, and we didn't this time either. We were given a description and his work schedule. That's it."

Harper shifted in his chair and cleared his throat. "If Snyder was your target, why'd you kill my boss, too?"

"We followed Snyder to the newspaper. Our research indicated Mr. Reston and you were causing problems for our client and his boss. So, when Snyder went to his office, we saw it as an opportunity to increase our payday."

"And how much was this payday?"

"It was supposed to be twenty-five thousand dollars each. Ended up being forty thousand dollars each."

Harper shook his head. "That's all a man's life was worth to you, twenty-five thousand dollars?"

"I've killed people for less."

"Did the two of you have real-life jobs?"

"Me? I was a corrections officer for Wayne County. Alexander was a Detroit cop before he retired years ago."

"That's pretty ironic, don't you think?"

"I suppose," Turner said. "We didn't make squat, you know?"

"So why not be a bouncer or do some other kind of security side gig like every other cop?"

"It was all about the return on investment for us."

It was the coldest comment Harper had ever heard, and Turner said it like he was a portfolio manager. He couldn't fathom being so disconnected from his humanity as to justify taking lives year after year for a healthier bank account.

"Did you and Alexander travel to make hits, too?"

"Generally, no. There was plenty of work for us in the metro Detroit area."

Harper detected a hint of irritation in the man's voice for the first time. He didn't care. "I'm assuming you got paid per job?"

Turner sat his right elbow on the arm of the chair, put his hand on his chin and rubbed for a few seconds. "Yeah, that's right."

"Adams have you guys on retainer to harass me, keep me from reporting the truth?"

"Something like that. When we weren't available, I suspect they snatched your girl for leverage."

"Yeah, I figured that much out. You've got no idea who Adams would've turned to?"

"It's not like we belonged to a union local of hit men or something. We didn't carry UAW cards."

"Right. So, you and Alexander hightailed it after the BOLO came out."

"We had a plan in case something like that ever happened, yes."

"The article I just saw said your partner was found dead in Kentucky?" Harper asked.

"Dwight has family down there. They kept a close eye on his trailer, for a price, of course. We were lying low until—"

"You got the idea of coming home. I don't get it. Why the hell did you want to come back?"

"It's like this, Ray. I arranged for Lisa Ann Patton to get shanked to death at the jail. I know she had two little girls. I guess I had remorse about those girls' growing up without a mama. I've already visited them since I've been back. They'll both have some money to get started when they turn eighteen."

"Talking to me was part of this plan?"

"Yeah. Pretty late in the game for someone like me to get a conscience or whatever. But that's the way it is. I can't atone for all the shit I've done, and I don't feel like I need to. Most of the people Dwight and I took out were lowlifes, scum that the system hadn't caught up to."

"So, the two of you were, what, evil Batman and fuckin' Robin?"

"Oh, I like that. You're a bright boy, but I think we've covered everything."

Turner lifted the gun from the table and stuck it in his waistband at the small of his back. He walked toward the loft's stairs.

Harper followed him. "So, now what? You going to turn yourself in?"

Turner went down several steps before answering. Looking back at Harper, he smiled.

"Oh, hell no. I ain't about to make it that easy. They'll have to catch me. I've got a whole new life waiting and a clean conscience to get it started."

"You're not clean," Harper said. "You'll never be clean. I'm not the Pope. I can't absolve you and wouldn't even if I could. Tell me, why shouldn't I call the cops right now?"

"That's your decision," Turner said. "I'm not going to stop you. But you got more important things than me to worry about, don't you?"

Chapter 47

SATURDAY, SEPTEMBER 26

After Turner's departure, Harper looked around the room and then to the glass table that doubled as his workstation. He picked up the half-torn yellow envelope and finished opening it. He slid its contents into his hand.

It was, indeed, a set of keys. One was a Ford Motor Company car key, not a fob. It suggested to Harper the vehicle it belonged to was an older model. The second key was gold-colored and stamped with the manufacturer's name, "Master." It appeared to be a padlock key.

A small note from the envelope had fallen onto the table. Harper picked it up and read it. *1551 Church Street, Detroit. Take the keys with you and go to unit 455. You'll know what to do.*

Harper's stomach, already churning from his encounter with the hit man, started doing backflips. Should he take the obvious next step and investigate whatever was at the Detroit address?

For all he knew, it could be a trap. The old car key could be nothing more than bait to lure him in. Eldon Turner, if he was to be believed, was not the only killer on Sadie Rodgers and Neil Flaherty's payroll.

The flip side? What if the key fit the car that killed Max Bell? Assuming DNA evidence could be found on the car, it would be the last piece of evidence both he and Dan Chamberlain needed to nail Flaherty and Rodgers.

While he pondered, one thing was clear to Harper: whoever had sent him the key knew the stakes. He wanted to believe he had done a thorough job of reporting the story from the start. But he was convinced that no reader or concerned citizen could read between the lines well enough to conclude Sadie Rodgers was the target of his investigation.

And even if they had, what motivation would someone have to lead him on a wild goose chase? Harper reasoned the keys came from either the Rodgers/Flaherty camp or Nathan Glynn, the Keystone Auto Service shop owner.

Glynn had admitted off the record he destroyed Lisa Ann Patton's Buick LeSabre. Wasn't it reasonable to assume Rodgers and Flaherty would use him to crush and dispose of the real hit-and-run vehicle?

He decided he'd come this far and had to risk the possibility this was a trap. His money was on Glynn as the supplier of the envelope. Either way, he wasn't going to be stupid about it.

Harper grabbed his phone from the table and dialed Chamberlain. He filled him in on the encounter with Turner and, more important, the set of keys.

"This is really pretty convenient, don't you think?" Chamberlain asked. "If it's Glynn, why would he wait until now to give you the literal key to this case?"

"Hard to say," Harper said. "Perhaps they threatened him again and he sees this as the way to get them off his back once and for all?"

Chamberlain exhaled. "That's a possibility. But this feels too good to be true."

"So, let's find out."

"Your youthful exuberance could get us killed."

"Dan—"

"Oh, relax. I'll be there in ten minutes."

Chapter 48

SATURDAY, SEPTEMBER 26

As of Friday morning, Detective Adams was on a two-week vacation, gone to northern Michigan for the start of bird season. He'd loaded up his Ford Edge with camping gear, two Coleman stoves, several lanterns, canned food and three oversized containers of beef jerky. Then there were multiple boxes of Budweiser and several bottles of Jack Daniel's.

He'd even made a production of stopping in the police station in his full hunting uniform, including Wrangler jeans and a red and black checked flannel shirt punctuated with a matching hat that screamed Elmer Fudd. The ruse was plausible because he had, in fact, gone bird hunting in late September every year for the past decade, often with other Plymouth officers.

This time was different though. He'd told anyone who'd listen he needed the tranquility of the woods all to himself. The death of the Bell boy had really gotten to him, not to mention the loss of one of his own colleagues. Adams had driven an hour north of Plymouth before doubling back after a late breakfast at Tony's in Birch Run.

In Adams's mind, this deception was needed for one specific reason: he had failed to contain the hit-and-run situation with Sadie Rodgers from the start. Adams had let Neil Flaherty down, something he'd sworn would never happen to the man who'd saved his life in Afghanistan, Lieutenant John Flaherty, Neil's older brother. Guilt and pride had led him to his current location, outside the loft formerly occupied by Henry Reston.

Ray Harper was there. Adams was not going to let some piece-of-shit reporter bring Neil down. Oh, he was plenty pissed with the younger Flaherty. He'd warned him not to get involved with Sadie Rodgers. She was a climber who'd use him and then kick him to the curb when he was no longer useful.

And it was playing out just as Adams had predicted. He seethed at doing her dirty work, but it was the only way to keep Neil safe. All because little brother couldn't keep it in his pants.

Soon, Neil would see. Adams was a man to reckon with, a man who did his job, no matter what it took.

Adams ditched the Edge in Howell with an old Detroit Police Department pal. He borrowed an extra car, a well-maintained, older-model BMW. It fit right in on Penniman in Plymouth with its upscale shops, restaurants and condos. Adams had also changed clothes and now wore a pair of beige khakis and a white polo shirt. He blended as much as he could for a man of his girth.

He parked the BMW a couple spots west of the loft. Penniman was a one-way street with diagonal parking spaces in front of shops and restaurants. A limited number of parallel spots were across the street in front of a coffee shop, a former post office converted into a swanky grocery, and the Penniman Deli. While one of the parallel spots would've given Adams a better look into the loft, he couldn't risk being made by Harper.

Still, he had a clear view of the loft through its many second-story windows. Adams could only see a few feet into the space because of his close proximity to the building. He was still worried about being seen, so he held the Saturday edition of the *Detroit Free Press* up past the steering wheel and placed a cup of coffee up on the dashboard as if he were a patient husband waiting for his wife to return from shopping.

Every couple of minutes, he'd change newspaper pages, bringing the newsprint down as he glanced up at the windows. Adams got a glimpse of Harper as he stood near what looked like a hutch. Adams glanced at his watch, which read eleven forty-five a.m. Despite his oversized omelet at Tony's, his stomach was starting to rumble, and the smell of fresh-cooked burgers and other sandwiches wafting his way from the deli and its outdoor seating didn't help.

Adams knew Harper was parked in the deck behind the building. Another fifteen minutes passed and he decided to change positions, driving the BMW to the deck. He spotted Harper's Honda, which faced the alley and the back of the building. Adams pulled into a spot facing the opposite direction. He had a clear view of the Honda via his rearview mirror.

He sipped the last of his coffee and grabbed a few pieces of beef jerky from a sandwich bag on the passenger seat. The first piece was gone in two bites. Adams shoved another piece in his mouth, and when he glanced into the rearview, he spotted Harper and a man he recognized as Dan Chamberlain walking toward the Honda.

Why in the hell was Chamberlain with Harper? He choked a little on the jerky before spitting it out the window. They were on the move, and Adams decided he'd follow and see what was going on.

Harper turned left out of the parking area onto Harvey Street and then made another left minutes later onto Ann Arbor Road. They were heading for the freeway. Adams stayed several car lengths behind and had to gun the BMW to make it through the traffic light at Haggerty Road to not lose the Honda.

Harper went north on I-275 and then east a few miles later on I-96. When they sailed through Livonia, Adams realized they were headed for Detroit.

The Honda exited at Martin Luther King Junior Boulevard on the city's west side. Harper followed the service drive to Michigan Avenue. Harper turned left and was soon in Detroit's Corktown neighborhood, the former home of the Detroit Tigers at the corner of Michigan and Trumbull Avenue. Adams glanced around and looked to his left with envy at Slows Bar BQ.

It finally hit Adams, what Harper and Chamberlain were up to: they were going to rescue Harper's girlfriend. They were less than a block away from the house where she was stashed. What the hell should he do? If he called for reinforcements, Neil wouldn't be pleased.

If he tried to stop Harper and Chamberlain on his own, odds were fifty-fifty it could go sideways. He decided to err on the side of caution and take his chances with rousing Neil's ire.

Adams grabbed his cell phone from the Edge's center console. He dialed Neil's personal line and quickly got him up to speed.

"Keep the tail going," Flaherty said. "I will alert our men and secure additional resources. Do not lose them, Mike. Understood?"

"I've got it," he said, surprised at Neil's response.

"And, Mike..."

"Yeah?"

"Good work. You might have just saved this entire operation. John would be proud."

"Doing my job," Adams said. "Nothing more, nothing less."

"You'll be rewarded," Flaherty said.

Chapter 49

SATURDAY, SEPTEMBER 26

For the fourth straight day, Sophia and David Casey were brought hamburgers, fries and sodas to eat for lunch. The burgers were actually pretty good in a gut-grenade White Castle kind of way. But Sophia didn't have much of an appetite. Anxiety was gnawing away at her and a sense of helplessness washed over her like a tidal wave with a fatal undertow.

She ate anyway, not looking to give Joshua any reason for screaming at them. The dude was psycho. He'd go for hours staring at his phone without saying a word, just giving them an occasional death stare. Then, out of nowhere, he'd launch into a rant, getting more and more wound up as he went along. At some point during the tirades, which were often filled with conspiracy theories about how the US Army had done him wrong and how one day he'd pay them all back, Joshua would turn his rage on them.

He'd get to within inches of their faces, close enough for Sophia to smell his rank breath and get sprinkled with saliva like a violent summer shower. She was worthless, her father was a weakling incapable of protecting himself or his daughter. Why not end the suspense and just put bullets in their heads now? The fucking reporter wouldn't know the difference.

And so what if he did? Joshua would personally take him out, too. Sophia almost felt sorry for the other members of his crew, who rotated eight-hour shifts. She wondered if their purpose was to show overwhelming force as a deterrent for her and her father, or to keep Private Psycho from killing them prematurely.

Sophia finished her second small hamburger and nibbled at the fries. Her father insisted it was Saturday, but her sense of time was out of whack. It could have been Saturday, Tuesday or Friday.

A man named Deacon, or "Deak," as Joshua called him, cleared away her food containers and the Coke. Joshua's phone rang and Deak, a hulking Black man with legs as thick as tree trunks, walked to a trash can by the sink and dumped the garbage.

"Yes, sir," Joshua said. "Those are you orders, sir? Right away, yes, sir."

For all his raging, Private Psycho acted like a good little soldier, Sophia thought. She and her father were sitting on the couch with a rectangular, solid wood coffee table in front of them. It had long ago lost its luster and had numerous water stains from cold drinks, gouges made by who knows what and burns where cigarettes had likely been snuffed out.

Joshua walked to them. He removed the zip ties from their feet and then screamed for them to get up and start moving toward the door. He pulled a large black handgun and motioned with it for them to move.

"What's going on?" Sophia asked. "Where are we going?"

Joshua pushed her upper back with his free hand. "I said move and shut your fuckin' trap, or I'll do it for you."

David Casey rammed the younger man with his shoulder. Joshua was knocked backward but recovered quickly and kicked the older man's feet out from underneath him. Casey crashed hard to the floor, his glasses flying off.

"Knock that shit off, J," Deak yelled. He used his massive right arm to grasp David Casey's zip-tied hands and pull him up off the floor. "We don't have time for this."

Joshua got in the bigger man's face. "I'll say what we have time for and what we don't. I run the show here. Now get them into the hall closet and lock the door, Deak. Copy that?"

Deak invaded Joshua's space. "Copy. When this is over, you and me, we gonna figure this out. You feel me?"

Deak turned away, picked up David Casey's glasses and handed them to him. "Let's go. We gotta do what the man said. Come on now."

Joshua backed away as Deak led the Caseys up a flight of stairs. He turned to his left. A short hallway led to the front of the house. An old oak-stained door guarded what appeared to be a coat closet. After Sophia and her father stepped in, Deak closed the door and locked it.

"This door might look like it's a hundred years old," he said in a loud, firm voice, "but it's solid wood. Don't go bustin' up your shoulders tryin' to get out. It ain't gonna budge. If I hear y'all makin' a fuss, I will do somethin' about it. Ya hear?"

"Understood, Deacon," Sophia said, "and thank you for helping my pop."

She was disappointed when he didn't reply. Sophia had felt the tension between Joshua and the other crewmen before the incident with Deak. She tried to divide them further, but her efforts seemed to be fruitless at this point.

David Casey fumbled around in the dark, reaching toward the ceiling. His left hand touched a lightbulb and then a short pull cord. Despite the zip ties restricting his movements, he was able to yank the cord and the closet was illuminated. The light seemed to stun a tiny brown mouse near Sophia's feet. But it recovered quickly and scurried into an impossibly small crevasse in the wall and disappeared.

"Are you okay, Pop? You took a pretty hard fall back there."

"My ass feels like it's broken."

His matter-of-fact tone struck Sophia as funny and she started to giggle. She covered her mouth as the giggles turned into laughing.

"I'm sorry, Daddy, really," she said. "You're o—"

"I'm glad my discomfort could provide you with a little levity. Now, tell me, college girl, have you calculated a way out of this mess?"

Sophia took a couple of deep breaths before answering. "Sorry about that. Don't know why I'd be laughing at a time like this."

"Stress does funny things to people, pun intended."

She hugged her father tight. "I love you so much. You're the best man I've ever known, Pop."

"I love you, too, honey. Now let's put our thinking caps on."

David Casey looked about the closet, which was quite roomy given the home's early-twentieth-century construction. A wooden closet organizer was behind them. It was mostly open-faced, with several wire baskets, presumably for winter gloves, hats and scarfs. A single drawer was at the bottom of the organizer, running its full length.

Sophia bent down and put one knee to the floor. She tapped her father's calf for him to move so she could pull the drawer out. He took a step toward the door, and his back touched it as he turned to see what his daughter was doing.

Before she could pull it open, he heard feet running on the floor past the closet. It sounded like multiple men in a hurry to get out of the house. He lifted his finger to his mouth and let out a "Shh" to get Sophia to stop. A few seconds passed and David heard a loud thud against the closet door.

"I haven't forgotten you're in there!" Joshua screamed. "Your time on the planet is about up and so is your boyfriend's, bitch. My men are on the way to take care of him right now."

"Why don't you join them," David said. "It's not like we're going anywhere."

Joshua slammed the closed door again. "Nice try, old man. Not happening. You never served your country, did you, coward? If you did, you'd know prisoners are never left unguarded."

Sophia stood and her face flushed. She appeared ready to rip Joshua limb from limb with her bare hands. David gripped her by the shoulders and then motioned for her to calm herself with his right hand in an up-and-down motion.

"Turn that light out, now," Joshua screamed, "or I'll shoot it out. If I happen to hit one or both of you, oh fuckin' well."

Sophia yanked the cord and they fell back into darkness. She wondered if soon, both of them would be in a never-ending black void or whatever death really entailed.

Chapter 50

SATURDAY, SEPTEMBER 26

Growing up in the suburbs, Harper hadn't spent much time in the city, other than to go to ball games, a few restaurants and, every couple of years, the Detroit Institute of Arts. Now he was in a section of the city, Corktown, that he was almost entirely unfamiliar with, save a few scant childhood memories of old Tiger Stadium.

Chamberlain was a different story. He'd graduated from Detroit Southwestern High in the early 1980s and spent the first few years of his career in the city before migrating to Plymouth.

When Harper had started to type the Church Street address into his phone's map app, Chamberlain had bristled and told him to put it away. The duo had rolled east along Michigan Avenue before reaching Rosa Parks Boulevard.

"Hang a right just past that Firestone station on Eleventh Street," Chamberlain said. "That'll take us down to Church, where you're gonna make a left."

After turning on Eleventh, he found Church Street a moment later. The street was populated with well-maintained, large homes bunched close together. Most were either all brick or brick with aluminum siding. A few of the homes were adorned with elaborate landscaping, while most settled for neat. That homey feeling changed as soon as the Honda crossed Tenth Street.

Harper and Chamberlain reached their destination at Church and Tenth. Downtown Self Storage sat on the corner and was painted beige with a large horizontal dark brown stripe running from one end to the other. A drab yellow sign listed the business's name and advertised "business-household storage, 24-hour security."

A door painted to match the stripe sat underneath the sign, and a window to the left of the door held a black and red we're open sign. Harper led the way in. A small office space could be seen through security glass to Harper's left. He pressed an intercom button mounted on the wall.

"Hi, I need to get into unit four fifty-five," Harper said. His stomach was tight, and his pulse raced. He hoped his nerves didn't show as much as he felt them.

A woman appearing to be in her midforties, a dark-complected African-American with a thin build, swiveled her chair away from a desk covered with piles of paperwork and looked at him.

"Can I see some identification?"

Harper pulled his wallet from a back pocket, took his driver's license out and then slid it into a curved metal tray that sat below the security glass.

"One moment," the woman said. She took a computer mouse in her right hand and then typed. "I'm showing this unit is registered to a Mr. Nathan Glynn. Is this Mr. Glynn behind you?"

Chamberlain stepped forward and gave the woman a stern look. He then took a thin wallet from his back pocket, opened it and flashed it in front of the security glass. It was a silver-colored Plymouth Police badge. "We're here on official business, ma'am."

The woman, whose name tag read Monica, studied the badge carefully. She waited a beat and then responded.

"Very well. Step over to the door on your right, and I'll buzz you in."

Harper and Chamberlain walked into a hallway with corridors leading straight ahead and to their left. A set of wide metal stairs was to their right and led to a second floor of storage units, which were marked one hundred through three hundred. Units three hundred one through five hundred were apparently on the ground level. A sign pointed left to the four hundreds, and Harper led the way.

The units appeared to be Downtown Self Storage's larger offerings. The dark brown bay doors were roughly the same size as a two-car garage. It was impossible for Harper to gauge their depth. Unit 455 was in the middle of the corridor. A bay door large enough to drive a vehicle through was located on the facility's exterior wall across from the unit.

"You think a car is in there?" Chamberlain asked.

"Only one way to find out," Harper said as he pulled the keys from his front pocket.

He took the unit's padlock in his left hand and inserted a gold-colored key. The lock popped and he pulled it from a metal hinge. He nodded at Chamberlain to open the bay door and stepped back.

The storage unit was at least thirty feet deep. It was empty except for a car parked near the rear and covered with a gray tarp. Harper's heart continued to pound. He strode forward, grabbed the tarp with both hands and pulled it toward him. He tossed it to his right without taking his eyes off the car.

Harper's right hand came to his mouth as his eyes bulged. He tried hard to form words, but Chamberlain beat him to the punch.

"An old Ford Taurus," he said. "Looks like it's pretty banged up."

Chamberlain walked to the driver's side and reached to touch a rearview mirror that had been smashed and was dangling against the Taurus.

"That's evidence, don't touch it!" Harper yelled. "What's wrong with you?"

Chamberlain put his hands on his hips and shook his head as if to scold himself. "I guess I left my brains back in Plymouth."

"Can you step back, Dan? I want to snap some pictures of the Taurus."

Chamberlain did so and Harper took several steps backward to take a wide-angle shot with his iPhone. He then moved to with a few feet of the shattered mirror on the driver's side. A close-up revealed what looked like dried blood. Harper noted minor damage on the quarter panel around the driver's-side front tire. Max Bell must have been hit by the side of the car first and then struck by the mirror.

"Who can I trust in your department to send these pictures to?" Harper asked. "Is anyone up to speed?"

"Russell is on duty," Chamberlain said. "He's not up to speed but he's a straight shooter. He's not one of Flaherty or Adams's boys."

"Detective Russell, right? First name?"

"Bryan. Yeah, he's one of our best."

After taking the last of the pictures, Harper sent several of them to Russell. He then texted the address and a brief note about what he had found. As he hit send on the text, Chamberlain grabbed him by the arm and dragged him behind the Taurus.

"We're about to have company," Chamberlain said.

Harper had been so caught up in getting pictures of Rodgers's car, the world around him had melted away. "What's going on?"

Chamberlain pulled his service weapon from its holster and then reached to his ankle and handed Harper a black Glock 48 compact nine-millimeter. "Ever shoot a gun?"

Harper slid his phone in his back pocket. "It's been a while."

"Aim for center mass," Chamberlain said.

Seconds later, Harper heard a loud, familiar voice.

"Game's over," Adams said. "Come out and maybe the two of you get to live."

Chamberlain ducked down and looked underneath the Taurus to scan for the number of feet on the ground. "Can't tell how many he's got with him. They're behind him or off to the side. But I'd say more than three based on the sound I heard when they came running up on us."

"What do we do?" Harper asked.

Chamberlain pulled his phone from his pocket and dialed 911. In a hushed voice, he gave the dispatcher his badge number, name and location.

"Tell Russell to get his ass down here pronto," Chamberlain said.

Just then, a bullet shattered the front and rear windows of the Taurus. "Last chance!" Adams screamed. "Come out, hands up, or you're dead."

Chamberlain left the connection open and set the phone on the ground next to Harper. "Detective Adams. This is Captain Chamberlain. Surrender your weapon immediately. That is an order."

"Not happening, Dan," Adams said. "Let's not play games. You know the score. I'm not telling—"

"Screw this," Chamberlain said, looking at Harper. He rose from his crouched position behind the car and fired a shot in Adams's direction.

"Dan, stop! Get down!" Harper yelled.

But Chamberlain kept firing and advancing. When he reached the front of the Taurus, two of Adams's men dressed in riot gear did barrel rolls and came up firing. Chamberlain shot one in the face and the man dropped in a pool of blood.

A shot from the other attacker clipped Chamberlain in the left shoulder and sent him sprawling backward. Harper rose from the other side of the car and fired the Glock, striking a man in black fatigues in the right arm. His weapon dropped to the floor, and Harper fired a second shot that plinked off the man's black helmet. Harper then ducked back behind the Taurus.

All hell broke loose. A hail of gunfire peppered the silver sedan. Harper was hit in the right calf by a shot, and blood began pouring out of his leg, soaking his pants. He heard several shots come from Chamberlain's position and then nothing.

Harper was sure his life was about to end. Then he heard gunfire a little farther away.

"Detroit PD, drop your weapons!"

A few more shots went off, and then Harper looked around the side of the tattered Taurus. Adams was on the ground. He threw his weapon to his right and then moved toward the fallen Plymouth officer as quickly as he could with his mangled calf. He dropped to his knees and rolled Adams over on his back.

The big man had taken a pair of shots, one in the gut and the other in his chest. Harper could see the life running out of him. He grabbed him by his blood-soaked shirt and pulled his shoulders off the ground.

"Where is Sophia?"

A faint, crooked smile came over Adams's face. Blood trickled from his mouth. Harper leaned in closer and turned his ear to pick up what the man was trying to say.

"Fuck you, Raymond."

Chapter 51

SATURDAY, SEPTEMBER 26

"Before you head up to your room," Cindy Bell said, "I'd like you to bring the garbage cans into the garage. It should have been done yesterday, Sam."

"Sorry, Mom," the teenager said. "I'll do it right now. Thanks for making lunch."

"You're welcome. There's leftover tuna salad in the fridge if you get hungry this afternoon."

Sam nodded and then went to the front door. He slipped on a pair of Nike tennis shoes, opened the door and walked down several cement steps to the driveway. A blue recycling can on wheels lay in the grass next to a slightly larger green can. He stood them up, set them on the driveway apron and pushed them forward.

When he was about halfway to the garage, Mrs. Rodgers pulled into her driveway on his right in a black Ford Explorer. Sam stopped and waved. She returned the wave with a smile and then looked away.

As she turned her head, something clicked in Sam's mind. Mrs. Rodgers's hair was blond, and it was cut short. It was pretty, though, and didn't look like a man's haircut.

Sam pushed the cans a few feet and then stopped again. Mrs. Rodgers got out of the Explorer and walked up to her home holding a purse in her right hand. He watched her disappear and close the door behind her.

Mrs. Rodgers had hit and killed Max.

Tears came to his eyes and he bolted through the garage and into the house. His mother was at the kitchen sink.

"It was Mrs. Rodgers," Sam said, grabbing his mother's shoulders.

"What? What about Mrs. Rodgers?"

"She hit Max. She did it."

"That's not—"

"It was her, Ma, it was her. It was the side of her head I saw."

"Are you—"

"Yes, I'm sure. It was her. That's what I couldn't remember."

Cindy ran her hands through her hair and then held Sam for what seemed like an eternity. She tried to make sense of what her son had said but couldn't.

Sadie had been so supportive, so caring throughout the whole ordeal. How could she be the one who had caused it?

“Your mind blocked it out because you didn’t want to believe it could be Mrs. Rodgers,” Cindy said, looking into his eyes.

She finally let Sam go and reached for her phone on the counter. She dialed Jake, who was working at a home construction site in Birmingham.

“Hon,” Cindy said. She could hear the murmur of workers talking in the background along with the faint sound of hammering. “I need you to come home right now.”

“What’s going on?” Jake asked. “You sound panicky. Is everything okay? Is Sam all right?”

“I’ll explain when you get here. Please hurry.”

Chapter 52

SATURDAY, SEPTEMBER 26

A dozen Detroit police officers secured the scene. One ordered Harper away from Adams's body and cuffed him. Harper ears rang from dozens of rounds fired inside the storage unit as he looked at the carnage around him.

Dan Chamberlain lay in a pool of his own blood on his back. His eyes stared blankly to the ceiling as if peering into the abyss of forever. Besides Adams, three men dressed in black fatigues who Harper reasoned were hired operatives also lay dead. Two more were wounded and cuffed by Detroit officers.

Detective Russell arrived with a pair of other Plymouth cops and a female officer Harper recognized as an evidence technician. Russell huddled with several Detroit officers, who were in charge of the scene. One walked with Russell to Harper and uncuffed him.

"That leg looks bad," Russell said. "Ambulances are on the way."

Harper pushed himself up with his hands and then braced himself against the Taurus. He didn't respond to Russell, instead brushing past him, hobbling toward the two cuffed operatives. He got in the face of one of the men, who sported a blond crew cut and fierce blue eyes. Harper didn't care how tough the man looked or that he, too, was bleeding from a leg.

"Where is she?" Harper screamed.

Blond operative looked straight ahead, refusing to make eye contact. Harper used his remaining strength to jam his right index and middle fingers into the operative's wound. He twisted his fingers, trying to bore into the skin to inflict maximum pain.

"Where are the girl and her father?" Harper said in a more controlled tone.

Russell and a Detroit sergeant ordered Harper to stop, but he kept pressing into the man. The operative grimaced in pain, but he remained silent.

Harper then turned his attention to a large African-American man. The operative's massive pectoral muscles flexed with his enormous arms cuffed behind him. One of the man's ears was ripped and bleeding, and a second shot had grazed his left shoulder, tearing his black T-shirt and leaving a bloody gash.

"Your girl," the operative said, "she's a brave one. Her pop, too. Good people."

Harper dropped to his knees in front of him. They were both breathing heavily, perhaps from the trauma of what had just occurred, the loss of blood or both. "Please, tell me where they are."

The operative considered Harper's request. He looked up at the horde of officers in the storage unit, scanning to see if anyone was watching him. Sweat poured from his bald scalp and into his eyes, almost giving the appearance the enormous man was crying.

"Couple blocks from here," he said. "Corner of Wabash and Dalzelle in an old abandoned house. Been there since they were taken."

Harper put his hands on the man's shoulders and bowed his head. "Thank you. Was it you that took them?"

"No. Joshua and a couple guys took the old man."

"Sophia?"

"One of our older guys got her by himself."

He took his hands off of the operative. Everything made sense now.

Rodgers had hit and killed Max Bell. Neil Flaherty had engineered the murders of Doc Reston and Rob Snyder and the abduction of Sophia and David Casey. Harper wondered if Flaherty knew how sideways his entire operation had headed.

Harper looked at the operative again. "How many men are at the house with Sophia?"

"I already told you all I know," he said. "Now what are you gonna do for me?"

"Do for you?" Harper repeated. "I'm a reporter and that woman's boyfriend. I can't do shit for you. You made your own bed."

Harper felt hands on his shoulders. He was pulled away from the hulking operative.

"Joshua is there for sure," the man said with a bitter look on his face. He looked around the room and nodded toward his fallen colleagues. "Everybody else was here."

Harper turned to Russell and filled him in on Sophia's location. Russell went into another brief conference with the Detroit officers.

"You're going in that ambulance," Russell said. "We'll get your girl."

"Bullshit. I'm not getting into that ambulance," Harper fired back. "I have a right to refuse treatment, don't I?"

"You've lost a lot of blood," Russell said. "You need to go."

"Later. The only place I need to go right now is to get Sophia."

Russell waved a paramedic over. "Can you stop him from losing more blood?"

The paramedic, a heavyset white man with short dark hair and a day's growth of beard, cut away Harper's pants around the calf and then wiped away blood with sterile gauze.

"The bullet went through without hitting his femur," the paramedic said. "It's hard to tell for sure, but I don't think any major arteries were hit either. Blood appears to be coming from the pierced tissues and smaller feeding blood vessels. I wouldn't advise it, but I may be able to wrap it tight enough to staunch the blood flow."

"Do it," Russell said.

A Plymouth officer approached Russell.

"Sir, we ran the VIN on the vehicle," he said. "It's registered to Sadie Rodgers."

"Officer, I want you to go back to Plymouth. You are to arrest Mayor Rodgers. I want it done immediately. Do not call it in. You gather the officers you need and get it done."

"Sir?"

"Rodgers is to be charged with leaving the scene of an accident and conspiracy in covering it up. Am I clear?"

The officer nodded and ran toward his patrol vehicle.

Harper had hobbled over to Chamberlain as Russell spoke to the cop. His body hadn't yet been covered. He went down to one knee and his head dropped.

"I'm sorry, Dan," Harper said softly. "Why did you go charging at them, you dumbass? How am I supposed to thank you now?"

Chapter 53

SATURDAY, SEPTEMBER 26

Cindy and Sam met Jake in the driveway.

"I got here as fast as I could," Jake said. "What the heck is going on?"

Sam pointed at Sadie Rodgers's house. "She did it. Mrs. Rodgers is the one who hit Max."

Jake turned toward Cindy, his face a mask of confusion. His eyebrows shot up as if to ask for confirmation.

She nodded. "I believe our son. He saw her pull in the driveway, saw the side of her face and head and knew it was her."

Jake's expression turned from confusion to anger. His face flushed red and without another word, he turned and ran toward Sadie Rodgers's house.

Momentarily stunned, Cindy and then Sam followed, arriving at the door seconds later. Jake rang the doorbell repeatedly and then banged the door with his fist.

Tim Rodgers answered the door. "Jake? What the—"

"Where is she?" Jake demanded.

"What is this?"

"She hit my son. Now, where is she?"

"Sadie hit Sam?"

"Max. She hit my son and left him for dead."

Tim raised his hands in a stop gesture. "Hang on just a minute. Sadie might be a lot of things—"

Jake pushed the smaller man aside, slamming him into a foyer wall. Cindy grabbed Jake's polo shirt to restrain him, but he pulled away and tore up the steps leading to the second floor.

Tim recovered and gave chase along with Cindy and Sam. Five steps ahead, Jake glanced into the first bedroom on his left.

Sara Rodgers sat on her bed, her legs tucked tight to her chest and tears streaming out of her eyes. He took five more steps and looked into the next bedroom, the master suite.

Sadie was seated at a vanity calmly applying makeup. "Well, good afternoon, neighbor."

Jake's hands were curled into fists, his face still beet red. "You killed my son, didn't you?"

"I did no such thing. Why in the world—"

"Sam saw you in the car as you were hitting his brother. How could you? How could you comfort us in the hospital, talk about helping us find the driver, when it was you all along?"

"The dear boy is mistaken. Everyone knows the trauma he's been through, poor thing. I was nowhere near that intersection."

"Liar." Jake charged Sadie.

She pulled her gun from a vanity drawer and aimed it at his chest. "Not another step, Jake, or I will be forced to defend myself."

"Jake, stop!" Cindy screamed.

Tim sprinted toward him.

Jake launched himself at Sadie, twisting his body in midair. The gun went off and the bullet nicked the top of Jake's right shoulder. It didn't stop his momentum and he smashed Sadie's right hand with his left, dislodging the weapon before she could squeeze the trigger a second time.

Jake kicked the gun away and was then tackled by Tim. Sadie struggled to free herself from his grip but couldn't.

Jake bucked Tim off. The side of Tim's head hit the side of the vanity and started bleeding. Sadie dug her nails into Jake's face and scratched.

Undeterred, Jake straddled her chest, pinning her to the floor. He raised his right fist to strike her.

Guns drawn, three Plymouth police officers charged into the master bedroom and ordered Jake to get off of Sadie Rodgers.

"Dad," Sam screamed, "you've got to stop!"

Gasping for air, Jake looked at the officers, uncurled his fist and then raised both arms in a surrender gesture. He stood over Sadie and then took two steps away, went to the floor as instructed and put his hands behind his back.

Sadie got to her knees and then kicked Jake in the ribs. He didn't give any indication the blow hurt him.

"Ma'am, move away," an officer yelled. "Do it, now."

A second officer approached her with handcuffs. "Place your hands behind your back. Sadie Rodgers, you are under arrest."

"Excuse me? This man attacked me in my home and you're arresting me?"

"You are under arrest for leaving the scene of an accident and conspiracy."

She stood up and faced the officer. "You do understand that you've just ended your law enforcement career, right?"

He read Sadie her Miranda rights and put her in handcuffs.

"Hope you boys have new jobs lined up by Monday, because you're going to be fucking unemployed by then. Does Flaherty know you're here committing career suicide?"

"That's not your concern at this time," Officer Wade Stevens said. He tightened the cuffs and led Sadie out of the bedroom, down the stairs and out of the home. He pushed her head down while placing her in the backseat of a squad car.

Chapter 54

SATURDAY, SEPTEMBER 26

Neil Flaherty's metallic black BMW M5 sedan screamed across I-96, dodging in and out of traffic, at times topping one hundred miles per hour, on his way to Detroit. Despite his best efforts, events were spiraling out of control. He wasn't about to sit back and let a lifetime of work and the love of his life go down the drain.

Adams was on the way to intercept the reporter. Flaherty had underestimated Ray Harper, a mistake he was going to rectify if Adams and his private security forces didn't first bungle the job. He knew what Harper was after: the story and his girlfriend.

Flaherty exited the freeway onto Martin Luther King Junior Boulevard and dialed Adams on his cell.

"Report," he barked. "What's happening?"

"Me and my men are about to head into a self-storage facility at Church and Tenth Street," Adams said. "The subjects entered the facility five minutes ago."

Flaherty turned east on Michigan Avenue and a few moments later south on Fourteenth Street. He parked the BMW in a lot behind the Mercury Burger & Bar, got out and tossed the lot attendant a $20 bill.

"What are your orders?" Adams asked.

"I want to know what the hell is in that storage unit," Flaherty said. "Get in there, take Harper and Chamberlain out and report back to me when it's done."

He ended the call and then walked toward the abandoned home on Wabash Street where another of Adams's men held Sophia Casey and her father. He went to the rear of the two-story home, which featured white masonry work at its base and brick in various states of decay above. Flaherty pulled a key and let himself in through a steel door.

A private security team member spotted him and drew his gun. He lowered the weapon after recognizing who it was.

"The subjects are secured, sir."

"Very good..."

"Joshua, sir."

"Where exactly are they, Joshua?"

"Follow me, sir."

The younger man led Flaherty through what was left of the home's kitchen. There was no refrigerator, and the stove was vintage 1967. Pizza boxes were stacked on top of burners that likely hadn't functioned in years. Other fast-food wrappers were strewn about on beat-up countertops.

After walking through a short hallway, Joshua pointed to a hall closet. The rent-a-soldier banged on the door with his left fist.

Flaherty wasted no time pulling a long-barreled .44 Magnum, a Smith & Wesson modeled after the gun made famous by Clint Eastwood in the *Dirty Harry* movies of the 1970s, and aimed it at Joshua's head. The kid, no more than thirty years old, turned his head slightly, and his eyes bulged when he saw the silver barrel pointed between his eyes.

Joshua started to raise an arm, but Flaherty squeezed the trigger. Joshua's skull exploded like an overripe watermelon hitting the pavement after being dropped from a distance. Blood and brain matter sprayed everywhere.

Flaherty calmly pulled a white handkerchief from a jacket pocket and wiped the gore from his face and hands. He didn't bother dabbing at his suit jacket, instead peeling it off and tossing it to the floor.

Flaherty checked Joshua's body for a key to the closet door. He found it in a front pocket. Before dealing with the people inside, he walked back to the kitchen and dialed Adams.

The phone rang three times before Flaherty disconnected. Adams must have been engaged with Harper and Chamberlain.

Given his team's overwhelming firepower, he was sure the two of them were dead or soon would be. He didn't give a shit about casualties on his side.

Flaherty analyzed the value of taking one or both Caseys hostage. The great thing about him? He understood his own limitations. Despite his strength and good health, two people were too many to control. The old man would have to die. The girl held the highest value and could be dumped once he and Sadie were safely out of the country.

While he wasn't rich by any means, he had enough money stashed in Caribbean accounts for him and Sadie to live comfortably for years. Flaherty returned to the hall closet.

"I'm going to let the two of you out," he said evenly. "I am armed, so you'd be advised not to do anything in haste."

He held the Smith & Wesson in his right hand and used a black key that looked ancient to unlock the closet door and open it with his left. Flaherty then took three steps back, his foot brushing against Joshua's leg.

Stepping out of the closet, Sophia looked down at the body on the floor with panic in her eyes. The old man stepped in front of her and looked at Flaherty.

"I didn't want to believe the rumors about you," David Casey said. "I believed the image you projected, a pillar of the community. For god's sake, how many times did we break bread together over the years?"

Flaherty smiled. "You're just like all the rest of the naïve rubes in Plymouth. Oh, how you all want to believe you have some special little corner of the world. That your streets are lined with pixie dust or something.

"You don't want to see the cold truth: Plymouth is just another town and people are people. They have the same desires, the same lust for power and money, as anyone anyplace else."

"You're rotten," David Casey said, "like a shiny apple whose core is brown and infested with worms."

Flaherty cocked the .44 Magnum. "Whatever. It doesn't matter now, none of it."

He pointed the weapon and fired a round into David Casey's midsection. The shot sent Casey flying backward into the closet door. Blood poured from a quarter-sized hole just above his waist.

Sophia dropped to her knees and screamed like a wounded animal for her father. His eyes were bugging out. He'd be dead in minutes.

Flaherty waited a few beats, as if to give the girl a moment to grieve. He then pulled her up and shoved the weapon behind her left ear.

"I will blow your brains out right here, just like Joshua there on the floor, if you give me any problems," he said without an ounce of emotion.

Sophia smacked him across the face with her free hand.

"You murdered my father for no good reason, you bastard!" she screamed.

Chapter 55

SATURDAY, SEPTEMBER 26

Harper rode shotgun in Russell's Ford Explorer as Detroit police led the charge down Church Street. A caravan of six police vehicles made a U-turn on Rosa Parks and then a quick turn to the west on Dalzelle Street.

Russell was second in the pack that hit speeds of fifty miles per hour down the residential street. It took less than a minute to reach the corner of Wabash. Detroit Police cars peeled off on either side of Dalzelle and ten officers exited the vehicles with their guns drawn. Russell continued through the intersection and drove just past the abandoned house on Dalzelle.

While the officer's attention was on the house, Harper spotted a man moving quickly across a field toward Fourteenth Street. The man had his arm around the neck of someone who was resisting him, trying to pull away from his grasp.

Harper grabbed Russell's arm. "He's got Sophia," he said. "We've got to stop him."

Russell lurched the Explorer back into gear and gunned it down Dalzelle. He radioed the Detroit command officer saying the suspect was on foot and had the Casey woman as a hostage.

With Sophia in tow, Flaherty cut across the field and behind a vacant brick hotel. Russell ignored the one-way sign on Fourteenth Street and charged past the hotel. A moment later Flaherty and Sophia emerged from between two of the hotel's wings and stepped into a parking lot. Flaherty took aim and fired a large handgun at the Explorer, the round whistling through the rear driver's-side door and going out the passenger door as if cutting through tissue.

The Explorer kept rolling as Flaherty made his way to a black BMW. Russell pulled in behind the expensive sedan and blocked it from exiting the parking lot. Harper grabbed a shotgun stowed behind the seat and leapt out of the Explorer. Russell got out of the vehicle and drew his service weapon.

Moments later, three Detroit Police cars pulled behind the Explorer and four officers with guns drawn came from the same route Flaherty had just traveled. He was surrounded.

"It's over, you son of a bitch!" Harper screamed.

"Release the girl and drop your weapon," Russell commanded.

Flaherty held the barrel of his handgun against Sophia's temple. He cocked the hammer, and a crooked smile went across his face.

"If I die, she dies, too."

Harper wanted to squeeze the shotgun's trigger. But he knew if he did, the spray pattern would take Sophia down with Flaherty.

Before the thought left his mind, the right half of Flaherty's head hit the parking lot pavement. A sniper positioned behind the now-dead Plymouth police chief had taken the shot.

Flaherty's left arm was still wrapped around Sophia's neck when the bullet dislodged his brain from his skull. As he fell, he took her with him. With all the blood, Harper couldn't tell if Sophia had been hit, too.

He tossed the shotgun aside and hobbled to her as fast as his damaged leg would allow. He pushed Flaherty's body off her, and she immediately grabbed on to him with both arms.

"You're safe, I've got you," Harper whispered into Sophia's ear. "I've got you. He can't hurt you anymore, babe. I got you."

Chapter 56

SATURDAY, SEPTEMBER 26–Sunday, September 27

For the second time in less than forty-eight hours, Harper found himself in a hospital. Both he and Sophia had been rushed from the parking lot to Detroit Receiving Hospital. Harper went straight into surgery to repair his leg, and Sophia was resting in a private room after being heavily sedated. The sniper's shot hadn't touched her.

Three hours of surgery later, Harper found himself in a second-story private room. Despite the EMT's prognosis at the storage facility, his leg did have a hairline fracture to go along with the damage to his calf. His entire lower leg was in a cast and throbbed like a toothache despite the pain meds he had been given.

The room didn't have much of a view to the outside world, especially at ten p.m. Streetlights allowed Harper to see a portion of Wayne State University's Department of Neurology building and what looked like a medical office building. He knew Receiving was part of a larger medical campus, which included Harper Hospital and Children's Hospital of Michigan.

Harper's penchant for remembering such facts, like some kind of human Wikipedia, annoyed even him. It had certainly gotten on Sophia's nerves, even in the short time they had been together. Somehow, she didn't care to know the past uses of every building in downtown Plymouth.

She had taken to calling him Mr. Spock, and Harper played along with a raised right eyebrow and a "fascinating" in the best Leonard Nimoy voice he could muster. He smiled at the memory, which had been made over a picnic lunch in Kellogg Park. Harper wondered if he would get a chance to make new memories with Sophia.

Who could blame her if she ran the other way? If he hadn't ambled into her dad's party store searching for evidence of Max Bell's hit-and-run driver, David Casey would still be alive. There was no escaping that truth. Every time Sophia looked at him, she would think of being kidnapped by a madman and seeing her father murdered.

Lying in the hospital bed, Harper doubted his own motivations. From the moment he became a journalist, his credo had been to get the story, no excuses and no backing down. Period.

While getting to the truth in Max Bell's death and bringing those responsible to justice still felt right, it hardly felt like a win. How could it when so many lives had been lost or irrevocably altered, including his own?

Sure, his leg would heal in a few months. But could he ever approach reporting the same way? How much collateral damage was acceptable?

If he hadn't been on-scene at the hit-and-run, if Max Bell hadn't practically died in his arms, would he have pursued the story with the same ferocity? After all, it wasn't the first hit-and-run story he'd reported on over the years. He hadn't even bothered following up on several of them, at most writing small briefs to lead the weekly police blotter feature in the paper.

All the questions added up to a head full of doubts. Coupled with his aching body, it was a small miracle when sleep finally overtook him a few minutes before midnight.

"YOU GONNA SLEEP ALL DAY?" Detective Bryan Russell asked.

Harper opened an eye, exhaled and then stretched his arms out of the sheets and above his head. The pain from his leg reminded him why he was in the hospital. He looked at a digital clock on a nightstand by his bed.

"It's eight thirty on a Sunday morning, and I'm lying here with a gunshot wound," Harper said. "Why are you here?"

"Thought you might be needing this," Russell said. He handed Harper a computer bag. "You've got stories to write."

Harper shot him a sarcastic smile. "Well, this is a first. A cop telling a reporter to write a story? I must be hallucinating."

"You've already been scooped on the shootout," Russell said. "Are you gonna let everyone—"

Harper held his hand up, motioning for the detective to stop. "Jesus, you sound like Doc. What was I supposed to do, dictate the story while they operated on me and reset my leg?"

"Somebody is testy."

"Yeah, getting shot and seeing a man's head blown off has a tendency to do that to me. Sorry."

Russell stepped closer to the bed and grabbed a handrail. "Look, Ray, nobody is saying you haven't been through the grinder. But you've got an obligation to finish this, if not for you, then for Dan Chamberlain and your boss."

"It's not like I wasn't going to write the stories," Harper said. "Why are you pushing me?"

"Because Dan isn't here to do it. He was my friend, too, you know. It bothers the hell out of me, what happened to him. He was so close to retiring and getting on with his life. I want the facts out there and Sadie Rodgers to stay behind bars."

He pointed to the computer bag. "Your laptop is in there, and all the notebooks I could find from your work area, too. If there's something I missed, I'll go back and bring it to you."

The bag was so full, Harper struggled for a second to open it. He found his legal pads with notes from the Eldon Turner interview as well as others containing all the background information he'd gathered from his investigation.

He picked up his iPhone from the nightstand and checked the voice recorder app. All of the recordings were still there. Harper could write and publish the stories to the *Independent*'s website from his hospital bed. His annoyance with Russell faded.

"I appreciate it," Harper said. "Appreciate everything you've done. I tell you what, you and Chamberlain have kept my faith in cops alive."

Russell waved him off. "I know where you're going with that, and I don't want to hear it. All I've ever done is try to do my job the best way I know how. And that's what I'm asking you to do right now. Take everything you've learned, everything Henry Reston taught you, and write the living shit out of these stories, Ray."

Harper sat up in the bed. The doubts from the previous night were still with him. The thought that Sophia might not want anything to do with him made his heart ache worse than his leg. But Russell was right.

He did have an obligation. To Max Bell and his family, to Henry Reston, to Rob Snyder, to Lisa Ann Patton, to Dan Chamberlain and to David Casey. It was up to him to tell their stories, to fit all the pieces of the puzzle together for those to whom he had the biggest obligation: the people.

It was the unwritten and unspoken oath every journalist took, at least the ones who were worth a damn. Ray Harper meant to uphold it.

Chapter 57

WEDNESDAY, SEPTEMBER 30

The late September midday sun was high overhead and temperatures were pleasant despite a cool breeze that reminded Harper colder days weren't far off. He was joined by Victoria Reston-Coble as they sat waiting for their lunch at an outdoor dining space in front of Plymouth's Barrio Cocina y Tequileria.

"This is fine, fine work, Ray," Victoria said, reading the *Independent*'s front page.

The paper's final edition was thin but power packed. The multilayered cover-up of Sadie Rodgers's hit-and-run killing of Max Bell took the top half of the front page, and sidebar stories about the Detroit shootout and an exclusive interview with Jake and Cindy Bell the bottom portion.

The cover-up story had been updated from its web version published Sunday. Rodgers's arraignment details were near the top of the story, and Harper had snagged shots of the now-former mayor in handcuffs in front of Thirty-Fifth District Court judge Darwin L. Burke.

Rodgers had flipped Harper the bird after he took her picture. Burke had added contempt of court to the lengthy list of charges against her.

Harper and Victoria shared a byline on a history of the newspaper. A column by Victoria on an inside page about her father had left Harper in tears before he met up with her at the restaurant.

The world around him at Barrio didn't much care about the anxiety he was feeling. A pair of bleach-blond women in their late twenties sat to his left and were doing an excellent job of ignoring each other as they scanned their phones. A man of about the same age dressed in a blue and white long-sleeved plaid shirt and jeans was also engrossed in his phone to his right.

The contrast of him and Victoria reading a print newspaper while his contemporaries gulped digital content wasn't lost on Harper. He pushed the thoughts of trying to snag another job in the "dead-tree industry" aside and took a long drink of his ice-cold Corona with lime.

"Any bites so far on the loft?" Harper asked, setting the newspaper down.

"No, but I've had some informal discussions with the Irish pub's owner," Victoria said. "He's thinking of expanding the bar and creating a rooftop venue."

Harper rolled his eyes. "You're not actually considering it, right?"

"It's just a place, Ray. Like I said before, I'm looking to close this chapter of my life as soon as possible. It makes no difference to me what happens to the loft."

"I get it, I suppose," Harper said. He waited a beat and then raised his arms and made a circular motion with his hands. "It's just all of this gets on my nerves sometimes. Even though I didn't grow up here, I spent a lot of time in Plymouth as a kid.

"I get a little nostalgic for those days. The world didn't move quite as fast. I guess the loft represents those old days to me. Plymouth is still great, don't get me wrong, but I never envisioned it becoming a mini Ann Arbor or Royal Oak."

A waitress brought their food. Harper dove right into a fish taco after adding a little extra salsa verde. Victoria had gone with a plate of carne asada street tacos.

"Things change whether we want them to or not," she said. She bit into her first taco before finishing the thought. "The Plymouth you grew up with was a lot different than the one I grew up in."

"It was more of a blue-collar town then, right?"

"It was," she said. "There were no Barrios or multiple Italian restaurants back then. To me, normal was a grilled cheese sandwich from the lunch counter at Kresge's."

Harper had polished off two of his tacos before Victoria had one gone. The waitress came back and refilled their glasses with cold water and asked if she could get them anything else. Harper held up two fingers and pointed at his plate. Apparently three small street tacos weren't enough to satisfy his hunger.

"Speaking of leads," Victoria said after the waitress left, "any luck in your job hunt?"

"To be honest, I haven't really started yet."

"Are you going to be okay? I mean, financially?"

"For a little while," Harper said. "I've managed to save some money over the years. I'll probably wait a week or two and then start sending out résumés."

Victoria reached and took her handbag from one of the empty chairs surrounding their table. She pulled out a reporter's notebook and a pen. She wrote a name and number on a sheet of paper and then handed it to Harper.

He took it and read the name out loud. "Linda Morton. Isn't she—"

"Yes, metro editor at the *Detroit Times*," Victoria said. "She's a sorority sister of mine. She lives in Plymouth, so she already knows who you are and thinks highly of your reporting. But I tossed in my two cents, so any opportunity you may have had is probably out the window."

"Gee, thanks, Vic."

A broad smile stretched across her face. She finished her lunch and pushed the plate aside. "Anything from the loft you want to take?"

"Mementos?" Harper thought for a second. "No. That was your dad's sanctuary. Everything that meant something to me was lost in the fire."

The conversation went dry for a few moments. Victoria paid for their lunch when the waitress came back for the last time.

"So, I guess this is it," Harper said. They stood and embraced. "Thanks for everything. A lot of people would have just closed up shop right away. I'm thankful for the opportunity you and your dad gave me at the *Independent*."

Chapter 58

WEDNESDAY, SEPTEMBER 30

Harper's goodbye tour took him to several prominent advertisers in Plymouth after lunch. By midafternoon, he was at Plymouth city hall. He stopped by the clerk's office for a final talk with Don Easton.

Though he'd lost handily in the primary, Easton had been appointed as acting mayor with Sadie Rodgers in jail. He was likely to retain the seat even with the opposition party mounting a write-in campaign for the upcoming general election. Harper took a small measure of satisfaction from knowing Rodgers's biggest critic now had her job.

It wasn't the only interim situation. City commission had named Bryan Russell as the temporary police chief with Neil Flaherty lying in the Wayne County morgue. Harper spent an hour talking to Easton and then Russell. Both thanked him for his service to the community, with Easton promising a resolution on Harper's behalf at the next city commission meeting.

With his right leg out of action, Harper relied on Uber for transportation. A man in his early twenties, driving a new Honda Civic, picked him up in front of the police station.

Harper had listed his Old Village apartment as the destination in the app. Before heading in that direction, he asked the driver to take him to the Cap N Cork party store. As they sat at the intersection of Main Street and Ann Arbor Road, Harper took a long look around.

No trace of the trauma that had occurred at the location was evident. A split second had ended Max Bell's life and changed so many others'.

A minute later, the Uber driver pulled into the parking lot of the party store. Harper hadn't planned on getting out of the car, just wanted to be near a place that meant something to Sophia. It was an act of desperation, he knew.

When a Ford F-150 parked next to the Civic and a middle-aged white guy got out and walked into the shop, Harper's jaw went slack. He couldn't believe the party store was open.

David Casey's funeral was scheduled for Friday. Perhaps a relative had come in to run the shop while Sophia got her bearings and figured out what to do with it. Whatever the case, Harper had to find out for himself.

He grabbed his crutches and sent the Uber driver on his way. Harper still hadn't mastered walking with what he thought of as giant toothpicks under his arms. His steps were slow and deliberate. He'd already taken a couple of spills with the crutches and wasn't hoping for a third.

The driver of the F-150 held the door for Harper as he walked in. He maneuvered around an aisle of snack foods and then walked parallel to the counter. He looked around the shop and didn't see anyone. He expected an older man or woman, perhaps a sibling of David Casey's, to walk in from the back room at any moment.

When Sophia emerged, Harper stopped dead in his tracks. They stared at each other for an uncomfortable moment. Sophia looked away, turned to her right and set several cartons of cigarettes on the counter. She began stocking a bin standing above her head with Camels and Newports.

With his heart racing, Harper took a step toward the counter. "Need any help?"

"I'm managing just fine," Sophia said.

She was dressed in jeans, her hair pulled back with the ends tucked underneath a green Eastern Michigan University hoodie. Sophia finished her stocking chore and threw the cardboard boxes into a recycling bin tucked under the counter a few feet away.

Harper hadn't spoken to Sophia since Saturday. She had been released from the hospital on Monday and hadn't returned his calls or text messages.

"I don't blame you for what happened, Ray," she said, placing her hands on either side of the cash register. "You had no way of knowing what Neil Flaherty would do, or that deep down he was a psychopath."

"But—"

"My father is still gone. Part of me died when he died, and I'm not sure how I'm supposed to just go on. If you're here to ask me where that leaves us—"

Harper put his hands up as if to signal his surrender. "I'm not. Honestly, I didn't think the party store would even be open."

A customer walked up to the register with a six-pack of beer and a bag of Buffalo-wing-flavored chips. Harper stepped aside with some difficulty and Sophia collected the man's money without saying a word. A pair of young teenagers followed with cans of Red Bull and candy bars.

"Going for caffeine and sugar buzzes," Sophia said to the taller of the two, who sported a Plymouth Wildcats T-shirt cut off to show the beginnings of ripped abs. "Good luck."

The boys thanked her and ran out of the store. "Why did you open this place up?" Harper asked.

Sophia exhaled. "I needed something to do. I can't sit around and think about everything that's happened. I'll go crazy."

"What about school?"

Sophia came around the counter, turned to her left and grabbed a Coke from a cooler. She got a bottle of water for Harper and handed it to him.

"I'm taking the rest of the semester off. School is the furthest thing from my mind right now."

"Weren't you going to student-teach during winter semester?"

"I've already talked to my counselor," Sophia said. "There will be plenty of school districts to student-teach at in the fall. I think it will be better in some ways, being with the kids from the first day."

Harper took a drink of water, reached with his left hand and put it on top of her right. He was thankful when she didn't knock it away.

"I'm not going to push you. I just want you to know I'm here and I'm in your corner. If you need someone to talk to, or someone to work a shift at the Cap N Cork, I want to help any way I can. I care about—"

Sophia squeezed his hand. "I know you do, Ray. I care about you, too."

She set her Coke down and hugged him tightly. For once in his life, Harper didn't have any words. He just held her, putting weight on his right leg and not giving a damn for one second about the pain.

The hopelessness pervading his mood over the past few days lifted. His thoughts, filled with all the losses he'd suffered, drifted away.

Harper ended the embrace and kissed her tenderly. Sophia smiled and then handed the crutches to him. He pulled his phone from his back pocket and summoned yet another Uber driver.

Less than thirty minutes later, he was in his apartment. The quiet was deafening everywhere but in his head. After a final victory lap through the *Independent*'s online edition, he typed in the *Detroit Times*' URL and hit return.

He scanned through its front-page news items. Harper's mind cleared as he read the headlines and then clicked on a story about human trafficking on Detroit's east side. He read details of a significant bust by police, analyzed how the reporter wrote it and came up with several angles he believed needed to be followed up on.

Harper felt his pulse quicken and the journalistic fire in his chest ignite.

While writing *Justice For Max* was challenging, the novel wouldn't have been possible without the contribution of so many wonderful professionals.

To the editors that shared their vision, expertise and dedication, thank you. My team included Alyssa Matesic, Aja Pollock and Lee Snider.

Thank you to 100Covers.com who took my scattered ideas and designed a beautiful cover.

My fiction-writing journey has been helped along by many mentors. David Gaughran, James Scott Bell, Dave Chesson, Bridget Chicoine, D.K. Gaston, Scott Spielman, you all rock. Thank you to author Bryan Gruley for his encouragement. Do yourself a favor and check out his excellent *Starvation Lake* trilogy.

Finally, and most importantly, I want to thank my family, Cora, Matthew, Gabriel and Emily. Thanks so much for your patience and encouragement. You helped make my dream come true, in more ways than you will ever know.

Justice For Max is Scott Daniel's debut novel. He currently resides in Michigan with his family.

Prior to writing fiction, Daniel worked as a print journalist at several Detroit-area newspapers. He covered municipal beats, including city hall, police, courts, community events and sports. Daniel worked primarily as a reporter, but also spent time as a copy editor on the sports desk of the Ann Arbor News.

Prior to writing *Justice For Max*, Daniel wrote several short stories and a novella under the pen name PJ Lincoln.

If you'd like to connect with the author, he's available at: scott at authorscottdaniel dot com.

Author Scott Daniel

CPSIA information can be obtained
at www.ICGtesting.com
Printed in the USA
BVHW031818050921
616126BV00005B/253